A MIDNIGHT DREARY

The DeChance Chronicles Volume Five

By David Niall Wilson

Donovan frowned. He stared through the lights to where Amethyst still moved gracefully, winding and binding the strings of light and power. As they all watched, she reached out and jabbed something into the trunk of the old tree. Then she moved on and did it again, and again. The points where she made contact continued to glitter after her hands passed on, and after only a few moments, it was clear she was forming a large, uneven ring of light.

"That spell is strong," Donovan said. "It is dangerous to stand between such magic and its purpose. Time can be stilled, and for short periods reversed, for instance, but it will snap back into place given the slightest chance and take whatever is holding it back at that moment along for the ride. It's the nature of this trap, as well."

"Then we'd better be thinking about what, or who, that's going to be," Nettie said, "instead of worrying about stopping something that is almost complete."

There was a sudden shift in the patterns nearest to the tree. The colors, formerly gliding where they were guided by Amethyst's dance, picked up speed. They bent around the tree and circled like a whirlwind of color and sparks, but where the crystals had been pressed into the bark, the streaks of color bent. Cascades of blue and green and red light shot off like lasers to blast against the inside of the circle like a fireworks display gone mad. The spot on the tree darkened.

At first it was just a lack of color, a shadow against the brilliance, but as it spread and deepened, Cletus saw that it was more than that. As he watched, terrified and fascinated, a chasm opened in the bark, peeling back to all sides from the center. It was black and deep. Then things got really strange.

Author's Introduction

This is going to be a big, complicated story. It draws elements together from The DeChance Chronicles, the novels of the O.C.L.T., my novels about Cletus J. Diggs and the fictional town of Old Mill, N.C.—and even from an older work of mine, a vampire novel titled *Darkness Falling*. It also comes with a complication. What was originally going to be the beginning to this novel—a long flashback—got away from me. It became a novel unto itself—*Nevermore, a Novel of Love, Loss, and Edgar Allan Poe*. I love that novel, and yet, I hate it. I hate it because as hard as I've tried, there is no good way to begin this novel now without writing spoilers for that one.

But maybe there is a work-around.

I want you to read *Nevermore* before you read this book. There. I said it. I know—you already bought this one. In fairness, I warned you in the marketing text for this on whatever site you bought it on. I warned you on Facebook. I warned you in my blog. Now, I'm simply asking you. If you have already purchased this book, trust me when I say that not only will you enjoy *Nevermore*, but you will enjoy this book more if you read it first. I really want you to read *Nevermore*, and then I want you to dive straight into this one. That was the original intent.

If you don't want to wait, however, or you don't have the inclination to read the other book, I understand. I have created a second introduction to this book that follows this one. It explains all that happened in *Nevermore* and brings you up to the beginning of this book. It might not even be necessary, but it will certainly alleviate some confusion. If nothing else, the writing of this (and the subsequent spoiler-filled introduction) will serve to allow me to continue with the story.

So, like I started to say, this will be a big and complex story. It will send several groups off in different directions. It will draw multiple story lines into one single thread. It will resolve the tragedy inherent in the ending of *Nevermore*. Really—it will do all those things

And that's enough of this. I want to thank those of you following the DeChance Chronicles from the beginning, and those who have come to this because of an interest in the O.C.L.T. series, and those who are just here because they are fans of my work. I can't wait to hear what you think. You can always reach me at my website:

http://www.davidniallwilson.com

SPOILER INTRODUCTION

DO NOT READ IF YOU WANT TO READ NEVERMORE

Normally, if I write a prologue, it's just something I think might, or might not, be of importance or interest to those reading the book. I am a 50/50 reader of prologues, I'd guess. This time it's different. This time, I think, you'll want to read this because what was meant to be the beginning of this book, handled in a lengthy flashback, grew wings and became a book of its own. I think it's a rather good book—*Nevermore, A Novel of Love, Loss, & Edgar Allan Poe*, but the fact is—you need to know what is in that book to know where this one picks up.

Obviously, loving that book, I'd prefer that everyone rush off and read it before proceeding, but I realize that is neither polite nor practical for many. I can tell you that I believe it will enhance the experience of reading this book. I can tell you that the audio version of that novel, narrated by the talented Gigi Shane, is amazing. I can also tell you that the response to *Nevermore* has been nothing short of remarkably positive—but I digress.

Here, in a rather large nutshell, is what has taken place to lead Donovan, Amethyst, Geoffrey Bullfinch (of the O.C.L.T.) Cleo, and Asmodeus to the point where this story begins. It really started back in *Kali's Tale*, book IV of the series, and if you didn't read that one before reading this, shame on you. Still, I'll catch things up as best I can and get on with the telling of the tale. I tried to just go ahead and write this and leave the task of introducing it for later, but it itched at the back of my mind, and I knew it wasn't going to work. Things have an order.

At one point in *Kali's Tale*, Donovan is showing the others around the ruins of an old hotel. This was The Lake Drummond Hotel, which stood on the border of Virginia and North Carolina for about twelve years back in the days right after the Civil War. In passing, Donovan mentions that one Edgar Allan Poe was among the visitors to that establishment, and that he'd met the man—but leaves the story of that meeting for a later date.

Nevermore is that story. When you read the beginning of this book, you'll see how I originally intended on handling this story. Suffice it to say that when I began to write of Poe, his lost Lenore, the Great Dismal Swamp, and that long-gone hotel, the story took on a life of its own. It would not be denied, and after about three chapters worth of writing, I realized that by the time Donovan showed up at the end to hear the story, I'd have either a long novella or a short novel on my hands. I did the smart thing, I believe, and wrote that story first—ignoring Donovan for the most part—and giving it the attention it deserved.

On his way home to his ailing wife, Virginia, Edgar Allan Poe stopped at The Lake Drummond Hotel. In that hotel, he met a woman—Eleanor MacReady—with an astonishing gift. She saw faces in inanimate objects—the branches of trees, in water, stone, clouds—and when she saw then, she drew them. Then, by removing the faces and recreating the object behind them, she set their spirits free. These days, people write this gift (I call it a gift) off as *pareidolia*, a condition where one sees patterns in random data. Or trees. Or the tiles on the floor. I see those creatures, and people and things—and they fascinate me. Eleanor was special.

I should probably mention that the Poe of my novel is not the grumbly, pale-faced poet we know and love, but something of a mage himself, albeit by accident and without effort on his own part. He traveled in the company of a large crow he named Grimm, to whom he was bonded to by an odd mental link that led him into the pain and dreams of others. These became his stories.

On one of his journeys, Edgar found himself at the Lake

Drummond Hotel, where he was drawn into the spell of Lenore's art. The two shared in a vision of an incident that had taken place in the past—a duel—where one man was shot, and another lived. In the vision, it seemed certain that the better man—the "good" man—would be shot and killed. With an effort of will, Edgar twisted the story, caused the darker gunfighter to miss. By doing so his actions created the reality that already exists, meaning, that the events in the past depended on his going back and manipulating them. I know—I know—hard to follow. Read the book.

Beginning with this blending of their power and energy, Edgar and Lenore are drawn into a much bigger, more complex mystery. Lenore has come to the swamp because she is drawn by a vision of a woman trapped in a tree. Edgar is hoping to find something that might help him to cure his wife, Virginia, who had thus far refused all esoteric solutions to her illness, clinging to a faith that would eventually leave her to die slowly, rather than be party to "dark powers."

In the middle of all of this, Edgar tells a story. It is a story written by the brothers Grimm, but when he tells it—he changes it. He doesn't know why. The story—the original story—is "The Raven." (You might also want to read that before reading this book, but it's entirely up to you. You will lose nothing by NOT reading it, but you might gain some insight if you do.

Anyway, they learn that the story has come to Edgar because Grimm, his crow, has been harboring a "stowaway" for a very, very long time. In fact, once Lenore has drawn the young girl she finds inside the old crow to freedom, they learn that Grimm himself has changed—into a raven. The girl, who turns out to be very real, is spirited off into the swamp by an old woman named Nettie and her followers, leaving behind a man with an arrow in his shoulder and a lot of questions.

As *Nevermore* progresses, Edgar enters the Great Dismal swamp to seek out the swamp witch, Nettie, who faithful readers of the series will know from *Kali's Tale*, and fans of my work in general will also remember from the short novel *The Not Quite Right Reverend Cletus J. Diggs & The Currently Accepted Habits of Nature*. He hopes that she might have something that can help

Virginia with her illness, and he feels responsible for the girl that was taken into the swamp. Meanwhile, Lenore goes down a different path to Lake Drummond, in search of her woman trapped in a tree.

To make a short novel even shorter, the woman trapped in the tree is no less than the sorceress, Estrella, who trapped the princess in the raven Grimm years in the past and continents away, in a castle overlooking a German village by the name of Rathburg. Again—true fans will remember that Rathburg—and even that castle—featured prominently in my novel *Darkness Falling*. I have come to realize that my body of work is one great story—and I rather like it that way.

The ending of *Nevermore* is tragic. Lenore, in releasing the sorceress, becomes trapped in the tree herself. Estrella escapes, carrying away the rescued princess, and leaving behind only a single word: Rathburg.

Edgar returns to The Lake Drummond Hotel, where he pens an early draft of a poem. The title, of course, is "The Raven," and he gifts that early copy to Donovan DeChance in one of the later scenes. Edgar also makes another discovery near the end of *Nevermore*. He finds himself able to shift to another place—possibly another dimension—where there is a library. He finds the drawing there that Lenore made of herself, the one that trapped her in the tree, as well as a long, dark coat, and a worn traveling hat that are familiar—and yet not.

And that, I think, is enough so that those of you who do not want to be bothered with going to read *Nevermore* first will not be lost. Again, though, I urge you to get it. It's one of my favorites among the works I've penned. It has magic, tragedy, romance—and, of course, The Great Dismal Swamp—and in truth, it was meant to be part of this book.

Sometimes we have our way with words, and other times they show us the way. That is the magic of storytelling.

From near The Great Dismal Swamp
David Niall Wilson

Chapter One

The sun had dipped beyond the trees, and as the light faded, the world fell to shadow in stages. On the porch of the old plantation home, Donovan DeChance sat, his boots propped up on the wooden railing, and a glass of wine in his hand. His long, dark hair swept back over his shoulders, and where his eyes caught the last embers of sunlight, they glittered like violet gems.

Across a small table from him, leaning forward and staring into the night sky intently, sat Geoffrey Bullfinch. The older man's posture was expectant, as if he felt something in the bright, crisp North Carolina air that spoke to him of adventure, or ancient secrets. Bullfinch, as usual, looked as if he were dressed for some adventure in darkest Africa, or ready to join a caravan. His hair was slightly gray, and his beard grizzled. It was very difficult to place his age, but his eyes gave the impression of years, and wisdom

There was a rustle of cloth, a soft flutter, and Amethyst joined them, with Asmodeus, the ancient Egyptian raven who traveled in the form of a crow, perched lightly on her shoulder. Next came Cleo, an Egyptian Mau, a beautiful spotted cat about two sizes larger than her breed was known to grow, winding in and out around her feet.

Amethyst was a tall woman with bright red hair and eyes like blue chips of ice. Her hair was entwined with strands of crystal. Brooches and talismans dangled from chains and cords about her neck.

"It's strange," Bullfinch said.

"What could possibly be strange to you?" Donovan chuckled.

"And believe me when I say that I'm not at all certain I want to know the answer."

"Just this," Bullfinch said, waving his hand at the porch, the table, and the night. "Sitting here, drinking, and talking—with nothing trying to kill us. Despite having lived a staggering number of years, I can count moments like this on the fingers of one hand. It feels like taking a side-step through time."

"You have to take a moment now and then," Donovan said, "to remember why life is important, or you'll stop caring about it."

Amethyst stepped up behind him on the porch and laid her hands on his shoulders.

"If you ever start to feel detached," she said, "give me a call. I'll remind you what you have to live for."

They all fell silent a moment, and then, with a thump, Asmodeus dropped to the table. Donovan barely caught his tipping wine glass and Bullfinch pulled back, startled. As the bird regarded them with bleary eyes, they laughed.

The old crow turned in a slow circle and stopped, staring directly at Donovan. Just for a second, its features wavered. Donovan started to open his mouth to speak, but Asmodeus beat him to it.

It opened its beak and said a single word.

"Nevermore."

Then, without another glance at any of them, Asmodeus leaped up, flapped his wings mightily, and swooped out from under the porch roof and into the night sky. The snap of his wings sounded like a gunshot, and the wind of his passing seemed to suck the air from their lungs.

"Well," Amethyst said. "*That* just happened, but what exactly *was* that?"

"I'm not sure," Donovan said. "You know, Rebecca Yorke told me I would need to learn Egyptian. I'm sure Asmodeus would say more if I could understand him. I have an idea what he's on about though—"

"Spill it, man," Bullfinch said, leaning back, a bright twinkle in his eye. He glanced over at Asmodeus dubiously. "If need be, I could try and translate, but my Egyptian is a little sketchy."

Donovan shook his head. When Asmodeus had spoken, a bright flash of images had sparked between them. They were familiar images, memories from his past. Images the bird should not have shared or known. Not, at least, in the short time they'd been associated.

"I told you not long ago," he said, "that I'd tell you a story one day. A story about the halfway house, before it closed and crumbled. I believe I mentioned a name—"

"Poe," Bullfinch said promptly. "You said you would tell us a story about Edgar Allan Poe. But—"

"Exactly," Donovan said. "I have no idea how Asmodeus could have known, but just now, I'd swear—"

"That he knew?" Amethyst asked. She laughed. "That bird is older than all of us put together, Donovan. Did you really think you'd keep things from him, once you bonded? And seriously— this isn't just a memory, it's a memory about—a raven."

Donovan smiled ruefully. "I guess you're right. He continues to surprise us, eh Cleo?"

He turned and scratched the big cat between her eyes. She watched him, arching her back slightly so he could reach more easily.

"You have to tell it now," Bullfinch said. "You know that, yes? No way we experienced that without knowing why. I've always loved Poe."

"It was a very long time ago," Donovan said. "I had not yet put down roots. I wasn't traveling around in a wagon, selling card readings for ten dollars at that point, but neither was I ready to stay in any one place for long. The Carolinas of those days were very different. The War Between the States had ended. The dynamics of society were shifting.

"Here in North Carolina, many of the older ways outlasted the customs and laws of adjoining states like Virginia. It was legal to marry at a much younger age here, and though murder was illegal everywhere, dueling was still considered a 'gentleman's dispute'.

"It was common in those days for citizens of adjoining states to make their way here, openly, or more often in secret, to settle matters of hatred or the heart beyond the reach of families and Virginia law. It was that practice that caused The Lake Drummond Hotel to be built.

"The hotel rested half on one side of the border, and half on the other side. There were rooms on both sides, and there was a bar in the center that spanned the states. The front court was wide enough for the occasional duel to break out, and behind, as we saw in the ruins, it bordered the Intracoastal Waterway, so it was also accessible from the Dismal Swamp side."

"A place like that could be pretty rough," Bullfinch observed. "I'm surprised, legal or not, that the proprietors could remain in business.'

"There were plenty of payoffs to insure it stayed open," Donovan said. "The rooms were often filled with traveling dignitaries and performers. Not everyone who passed through was trouble, and there was enough trade in between to keep the hotel open. A lot of famous people stopped there, and as you have guessed by now, I was one."

"And another," Amethyst added, sipping her wine, "was Edgar Allan Poe?"

Donovan nodded. His features had shifted, and he seemed to be focusing on a spot in the center of a distant, moonlight-trimmed cloud.

"I wish I had seen it," Bullfinch said. "In those years, I was mostly traveling Europe, or Africa. I imagine a number of very interesting people must have passed through, with the swamp at their backs, and all of the folklore and legends surrounding the area."

"Did I not mention that?" Donovan asked. He turned to Bullfinch, and then winked at Amethyst. "You know Edgar was a talented writer. I wonder—did you know he was a mage?"

Bullfinch turned, placed his glass on the table, and stared at Donovan. Amethyst looked as if she was ready to protest.

"You don't have to take my word for it," Donovan said. "I could sit here and tell you this story, and probably even do it justice, but there are other ways."

"Like what we shared?" Amethyst asked.

Donovan had once shared a part of his childhood, and the story of how he came to do the things he did, and live the life he'd lived, with Amethyst. It had been a very intimate experience—a part of the bond that kept them close.

"Similar," Donovan said. "That was very intimate, and—no offense Geoffrey—but I doubt I'll ever share that again. What I have in mind is a little more complex. The sharing wouldn't work with three of us, but there is a way to channel the memory. It won't be the full story, but it will give you some of the flavor, and the background."

"So much for my quiet night," Bullfinch said, chuckling.

"I'm going to have to make some preparations," Donovan said. "Help me move this table out of the way."

They rose, and together they shifted the table off to one side of the porch.

"Normally, I'd say we'd stand for this," Donovan said, "but it might take longer than usual, and I need everyone to be relaxed and stable, so I'm going to modify the spell. We'll use our chairs—and we'll need a fourth."

"Who will sit in that chair?" Bullfinch asked, frowning. "Surely if they are to be compass points—"

Cleo glanced up at him and let out a soft, chastising yowl. Bullfinch laughed.

"Of course," he said.

"Cleo was there," Donovan said. "I expect she'll help to strengthen the vision, once I've forged it. If you need a drink, or a quick bite, now is the time. Once I set this in motion, it's like a roller coaster. We are in until the ride is over."

"In for a penny," Bullfinch said.

Amethyst glanced out into the darkness. "I'll set wards around the porch. I don't think there is anyone or anything out there, but—"

"I believe that I will finish this wine," Bullfinch said. He poured the last of the bottle into his glass and backed off out of the way, as Donovan knelt and drew a sliver of white chalk from his pocket.

Ignoring his companions, Donovan drew what looked like a tic-tac-toe framework on the porch floor. He placed each of the four chairs between two parallel lines, facing inward. In the very center of the squares, he drew a circle. Then, stepping back, he drew a larger circle that enclosed the entire design, and all four chairs. Outside this, he drew a third, and final circle. Working his way around the outer circle, starting in the eastern quadrant, he began carefully inscribing a sequence of symbols. Without looking up, he called to Bullfinch.

"Inside, in the right pocket of my jacket, there is a leather pouch. Would you bring it to me?"

Bullfinch nodded. As Donovan made his way around his circle, Amethyst took a wider pass, stepping into the yard beyond, and to the sides of the porch, before returning to stand just inside the door. She waited until Bullfinch had returned from the house, and then drew out a small bag of her own. She'd already placed crystals at each compass point, and this one she laid in the center of the doorway behind them. As she was about to speak the final closing ward, she was silenced by a great rush of air.

As quickly, and with as much drama as he'd departed, Asmodeus swooped in under the eaves. He executed an impressive figure eight beneath the porch ceiling, and then, lightly, dropped directly in the center of Donovan's inner circle.

There was a moment of silence. Donovan met the old crow's gaze evenly, trying to weigh the effect of another presence in the circle. Something in the bird's still, unwavering visage convinced him. Amethyst caught the gesture, and with a soft exhalation of breath, breathed the final sacred name and closed the wards around them tightly.

Donovan faced Amethyst. To his right, Bullfinch sat, and across from the older man, Cleo had perched quietly on the final chair. Asmodeus turned as Donovan moved through his final preparations, watching carefully. When Donovan took his seat, Asmodeus stood still. After a moment, as if listening to something only he could hear, or sensing the powers and wards, the old familiar dropped back and relaxed. He did not move from the center of the circle. His tail feathers did not brush the lines that had been drawn or break the barriers that had been set. He might as well have been a scruffy black shadow.

"I can't take us through time," Donovan said. "At least not in this way. I can show you things—show you what I saw—and bring it back to life. When I do, the lines that separate past and present are very thin. Once we are in, we must stay to the completion of the spell. We will not be able to influence events, and they will not be aware of us—though I should be fully connected to my mind in that past moment. I knew I would tell this story one day. I knew it because even then, though I had no real idea what it meant, I sensed the presence of the future. It would take most of the night to explain, so I'm not going to try."

He pulled out a very short candle from the leather pouch.

"I believe this will burn just about long enough," he said. "While the flame is lit, we will not be aware of this place, or this time. There is always a danger in this, so I want you both to be aware of the risks."

"As if anyone would say no at this point," Bullfinch snorted. "Get on with it, old man. I'm dying to see what you have for us."

"I trust you," Amethyst said, with a grin. "I've been into your past and made it back again. I'll take my chances."

Donovan nodded. He lit the candle and placed it on the floor before him.

"I was just in from Virginia," he said, "where I'd acquired a grimoire from a very, very old woman."

As he spoke shadows rose, shifting around the outer circle, coalescing and cutting them off from the world. The circle, and the symbols, and the square wavered, then faded, and Donovan's voice fell away. In its place, the clatter of pewter utensils, and the boisterous laughter of the halfway house rose, bringing the past to life.

Chapter Two

The shift was not subtle. One moment Donovan sat across from Cleo, with Amethyst and Bullfinch to either side, and the next, he was walking, climbing the steps to the long porch that fronted The Lake Drummond Hotel. Immediately in front of him, the door to the tavern waited, light and sound leaking out where it was slightly ajar. There was laughter, and the sound of clinking glass. The air tasted cleaner—fresher—than he remembered, and when he glanced back, he saw that Cleo paced at his heels.

He sensed the others, like a scent on the breeze, or a cool brush of—something—on his shoulder—but they were not visible, as he'd known they wouldn't be. He and Cleo had lived this moment before, and it had been odd then—now he knew why.

He pushed through the door and into the tavern. A few of the customers looked up to see who had entered, and then a few more. Donovan was a tall man, and his long hair, tied in back, was not a common style for the times. With his full-length dark coat and the cat, nearly the size of a bobcat, following behind, it was difficult not to attract attention.

He breathed a few soft words, and a mist floated out to join the cigar and pipe smoke. If any noticed, they gave no sign, and, after the smoky filament-like cloud had settled, one by one, the eyes of the other patrons slid to one side, or the other, ignoring him. Donovan walked straight through the center of it all toward the table in the back. It sat directly beneath a window, giving a view of the Intracoastal waterway, and the Great Dismal Swamp beyond.

A man sat at the table, thin, with dark hair. He was writing on the top sheet of a sheaf of papers. Donovan smiled. Edgar was just as he remembered, and he knew only too well what words would be found on the paper, because he had carried that page, carefully folded and tucked into a very old copy of Grimm's Fairy Tales, for most of his adult life. Except—at this moment, he had also yet to acquire it. The thought gave him just a moment's vertigo. He took a deep breath and stepped up to the table. Edgar Allan Poe glanced up, and Cleo leaped, planting herself firmly in the chair on the opposite side of the table from the author. She rolled into a ball and regarded the two men with mild interest.

Donovan smiled, and bowed with a flourish.

"Good evening," he said. My name is Donovan. Donovan DeChance. I'm afraid I don't know anyone here, and I don't know why, but you have an air of familiarity, as if I should know you."

"Edgar. Edgar Poe," the man replied. "I don't believe that we've met, but you are welcome to share my table. It can get busy here of an evening, and a little rough, depending on the crowd. Your cat seems already to have made herself at home."

"I'll confess that's another reason I felt I had to introduce myself. She isn't generally attracted to strangers."

"Have a seat Mr. DeChance," Edgar said. "Have some whiskey. It's my last night here, and I was feeling a little down. It's been an odd week, and I could use some company."

Donovan bowed again and sat across the table next to Cleo. He faced Edgar and smiled. It was an eerie sensation, the déjà vu hanging heavy in the air—so heavy he was sure the other man sensed it as well. And—did it have to be the same? Could he, knowing what he knew of what Edgar himself had done with his words, change the past?

He took the bottle on the table and poured them each a drink, then leaned back. He didn't have to remember what had been said, the words flowed naturally.

"I'm not sure why," he said, "but I have the strangest urge."

"What on earth could that be?" Edgar asked.

"There is something about you," Donovan said slowly, "that

gives me the notion you would tell a good story. Something with magic, and romance; something intriguing to erase the dust of the road."

Edgar stared at him. Beyond the man's shoulder, a dark, winged form shot past the window, circled back, and came to rest on the sill. Donovan glanced back, nodded, and returned his attention to Edgar.

"In the swamp," Edgar began, "there is a lake. They call it Lake Drummond, and I'm told it has deep, dark secrets to share."

"Told?" Donovan said.

"All stories," Edgar said with a smile, "begin with a grain of truth; even our dreams."

Donovan sat back and sipped his drink, and Edgar began to talk.

The story was as remarkable as Donovan remembered. It was about a crow named Grimm, and how he had actually been a raven, disguised as a crow, carrying the spirit of a stolen princess from someplace far away. It was a story straight out of a fairy tale penned by its own namesake; how Eleanor MacReady—Lenore to her friends—had been drawn to release the dark sorceress Estrella, from a tree on the banks of Lake Drummond, where she had been trapped by a swamp witch named Nettie.

Donovan knew Nettie well enough, having been saved by her himself in a future that suddenly seemed very distant, and now he knew why this story—so long ago—had such a familiar flavor. Finally, as the tale drew to its close, he heard once more how Lenore herself had been trapped, and the princess spirited away to some obscure place—with the only clue to its whereabouts the name "Rathburg." Edgar—seemingly walking through dimensions—had come to a library that he knew, and did not know, where he'd donned a coat and hat that he'd never owned. It was a story worthy of a master, and Donovan knew he sat across from such a man—such a storyteller—knew the tales and poems that would come, and how they would leave their mark on the world. He also knew how the body of one Edgar Allan Poe would be found, sitting alone on a park bench with absolutely no explanation for his death.

The moon had risen to her throne in the center of the night sky and begun to dip to the horizon by the time Poe finished. When he was done, he pulled a folded paper from the pocket of his shirt and handed it across the table to Donovan.

"That was remarkable," Donovan said. "What is this?"

"I'll ask you not to read it until I have gone," Edgar said. "It isn't a final copy; I still have work to do. Some truth requires concealment beneath several veils before being revealed to the world. Sometimes even the veils are insufficient."

Donovan did not question this. He tucked the paper into the inside pocket of his jacket, and he stood.

"I am glad to have met you, Edgar Poe," he said. "It was an amazing story, filled, I believe, with more grains of truth than most. It is tragic and shows a flair for the dramatic that is sorely lacking in most American literature. I suspect that I will see your name again."

"If you are ever near Philadelphia," Edgar said, "you must look me up. You owe me a drink, after all."

Donovan nodded, and bowed. Edgar, without realizing he had done so, mimicked the gesture.

Donovan stared at his companion thoughtfully. He spoke then, words that he had never spoken at their first meeting, words that might, or might not make a difference, but that he felt compelled to utter.

"Perhaps," he said, "I will seek you out in that library of yours. As you see, I have brought my own coat—"

Poe stared at him then, almost warily, as if trying to figure out if he was being mocked. Then he straightened, and his eyes cleared. "Have a good journey, Mr. DeChance," he said. "Perhaps when next we meet, you'll tell *me* a story. I believe you must have a bit of the magic about you as well, and I do love a good tale."

Without another word, Poe laid a handful of coins on the table, turned, and left the tavern. Donovan watched him go. He stood, then, knowing he must speak to the bartender and secure accommodations for the night. In that instant, the vision faded. He watched—just for a second—as that past version of himself walked away. Then it was suddenly dark

   He closed his eyes, spoke the words of a short incantation, and then, as if to blow the past away like dry leaves, he exhaled, and the world—the present—came to life around him.

Chapter Three

It was almost completely dark. A breeze that Donovan was nearly certain had not touched him moments before lifted his hair from his collar. He sat very still until the last of the images cleared from his mind, and then glanced at the others. Both Bullfinch and Amethyst stared straight ahead, still lost in that other time and place. Asmodeus watched him, eyes glittering, and Cleo, without much apparent concern, began to groom herself.

Donovan released the wards, one by one, careful not to move or break the circle until he was finished. Slowly, the others recovered and sorted their thoughts.

"That," Bullfinch said at last, "was remarkable."

"And tragic," Amethyst said. Her voice was very soft, and instead of turning to look at Donovan, she glanced instead out over the fields and the swamp beyond.

Donovan held his silence. His memory of that long-ago meeting had always been clear, but something had changed. While the first time around it had seemed a curiosity—this time it had taken on weight and substance. Rather than a very entertaining tale told over a drink in a long-crumbled hotel, Poe's words lingered. The images he'd spun hung like shadows just out of sight.

"She's out there, isn't she?" Amethyst said, finally turning to him. "My god, Donovan. Lenore—the lost Lenore I've heard of all my life. She's there in that swamp, trapped."

"I never thought about it," Donovan said. "When I met him, it seemed to be just another story. I sensed there was more to him than met the eye, and I saw the raven outside the window, but…"

"You weren't ready," Bullfinch said, standing and stretching, the movement breaking the spell of the moment, or at least diluting it. "There was nothing you could have done. If that woman, Nettie, you've told me so much about couldn't set her free, what could you have done?"

Donovan thought about it. He shook his head.

"I don't know what I can do about it now," he said.

"That's only part of it," Bullfinch said. "If she is out there, and I believe we will find that she is, what about the rest of it? The woman—Estrella—who trapped her; the princess who was stolen, all of it has the ring of truth. And what was that bit at the end, Donovan?"

"What do you mean?"

"About meeting Poe in his library. It felt—wrong. Almost like the words were forced. Where was it you meant we should meet him, the room he said he visited in his dreams? His home in Pennsylvania?"

"I'm not sure about that either," Donovan said. "I was thinking about what he told us about that gunfight. Remember, he said he was writing a story, and got drawn into it, into events that had already taken place, and he changed them. He rewrote the story, and a man's life was saved. I guess I thought that if I could force my past self to say words that I'd never uttered, I might do the same."

"And?" Bulfinch said.

"I suppose we'll have to test the theory," Donovan said.

"Where is Rathburg?" Amethyst asked. "It seems I've heard the name, but I can't place it."

"I have a hunch," Donovan said. "I remember it too, and the memory is vaguely associated with Johndrow and his council. Hold on."

He rose then, and the last wisps of the spell dissipated on the breeze. He retreated inside, and then returned, his cell phone in his hand, already dialing.

After a moment, he smiled.

"Johndrow," he said. "It's Donovan. Sorry if I interrupted anything, but I have an odd question I hope you can answer. Does the word Rathburg mean anything to you?"

Donovan listened for a moment, nodded a few times, and then turned to glance out over the swamp again, as if watching for something just out of sight.

"Thank you," he said. "It seems I will owe you again."

He hung up and turned to the others.

"I was right," he said. "There are two members of the council that I've never met. They are seldom in San Valencez—they spend a great deal of time in New Orleans. Their names are Copper and Alicia. It seems that their sire—their maker—died in a castle on a mountain. Beneath that castle is a small village."

"Rathburg." Bullfinch said.

"Exactly," Donovan said. "The place has had quite the history of dark events. There was something in the news a few years back as well. Something about a musician and his family."

"Von Kroft," Amethyst said. "It was Klaus Von Kroft, and that is why I remembered the name. He died on that mountain. The reports of his death were sketchy. He held a concert there, and soon after his band went their separate ways. There were rumors of a last album, but…"

"A fan?" Donovan said, smiling.

Amethyst smiled. "There are a lot of sides to me you haven't discovered, Magic Man. One day we'll take a stroll through my music archive. What now, though? Germany? New Orleans? The Great Dismal Swamp? Edgar Allan Poe's library?"

"This is starting to sound like a job for a larger team," Bullfinch said. "I don't see how we can be in all of those places at once, but I think I might be able to help."

"You know how I feel about joining teams," Donovan said, frowning.

"No strings," Bullfinch said. "I'm in either way, but I'm thinking we could split our forces and do more good. Someone should see about Rathburg—at least get the lay of the land and try to ascertain what has happened there, if anything. Someone should be checking on the woman, Lenore—to see what can be done for her."

"And," Donovan said, "I suppose that means Asmodeus and I must try to find our way to that library."

"I will find Lenore," Amethyst said. "I've met Nettie—I think she'll help."

"Take whiskey," Bullfinch said. "Never hurts to learn from the past."

"Take Cleo, as well," Donovan said. "If she is with you, we'll have a link, and she will be very useful in the swamp."

He turned to Bullfinch.

"Will your people have any problem interacting with the undead in a seemly fashion, Geoffrey?" Donovan asked. "As I remember, a few of them—Isabella in particular—would rather kill first and seek answers in the ashes. I believe whoever goes to Rathburg should at least speak with Copper and Alicia—to find out what they are getting into."

"Your show, your rules," Bullfinch said. "I'll keep Isabella out of it. I was thinking of another member of the team I've not spent enough time with. His name is Gunter Krieg. I'm not sure what his particular expertise will bring to the table—he's a theoretical physicist—but he was born in Berlin and having him along while visiting Rathburg might be a good idea."

"If Estrella is there," Donovan said, "you might be better off with Rebecca."

"Strictly surveillance," Bullfinch said. Then he winked. "I have no death wish. If things look to be out of hand in any way, I'll call in reinforcements. It's one of the advantages to the team."

"So you keep telling me," Donovan said. "Still, there are forces behind that team, and they cannot be trusted. You and I, Rebecca, some of the others, we've been friends longer than your team has existed, and I suspect that we will be friends when it all fades to dust."

"We've worked with other teams," Bullfinch said. "You haven't forgotten Alma, or her husband Lewis—Jerry—"

"I forget very little," Donovan said. "I'm not sure if that's a gift, or a curse."

"How will you find the library?" Amethyst asked.

Donovan glanced down to where Asmodeus sat and winked. "I believe I will have a guide, of sorts. We'll take the stairs at the ruins of The Halfway House and search among the doors in the tunnels. There's always a danger in such a search, but this has the feel of something *ordained,* so I have the sense it will work out."

"There's something else," Bullfinch said thoughtfully. "If Poe was right, and the story is entwined with the Brothers Grimm's tale *The Raven,* we may have to find a few things to rescue the girl."

Donovan and Amethyst turned to him.

"In the original story," Bullfinch said, "the hero had to find a cloak that made him invisible, a key that would open any door—I believe in the story it was a staff? Then there was the horse, a mount that could take him anywhere. He had to steal that."

"And of course," Donovan said, "everything was a little bit off. Still, you may be onto something. If there are clues in the fairy tale that can help to defeat Estrella, assuming she's still alive, and that she went to Rathburg, and stayed."

"I'll get Mack on it," Bullfinch said. "We might be able to tie some historical records to the Grimm brothers—or to Rathburg itself. It may be that we can find one or more of the things we need, and that this will lead to our goal. I love an adventure."

"You think the Brothers Grimm left a trail of clues—on the Internet?" Amethyst said. She shook her head and turned away to pet Cleo, who very clearly appreciated the attention.

"It's all one big pattern, isn't it?" Bullfinch said, winking. "If there is anything out there that might lead to stories hinting at the missing elements..."

"I know," Amethyst said. "It's just hard to get used to counting on such things. Mack doesn't have training, or power. He barely believes that any of us do."

"I disagree," Donovan said. "He has power and doesn't understand it. Think of what he can do. There are thousands of brilliant minds on the Internet. There are programmers, hackers, gamers—some of them live and breathe code and IP address sequencing. All of them are like children to him. It's an entirely new magic—a new world power that we don't fully comprehend. I have tapped into it myself. My archives are beyond the abilities of most others, but I believe that given the opportunity Mack could find a way to access them as well.

"What he does is like the tunnels, the catacombs that apparently lead to everywhere and anywhere you might want to travel, or any time. If you can choose the correct doorway. If you can find that perfect pattern. If your concentration never wavers. He has power. In the end, he may prove the most powerful of all."

They all fell silent for a minute, and then Bullfinch turned toward the house.

"I think we're going to need an early start," he said. "I'm calling it a night."

Donovan and Amethyst followed suit, with Cleo padding along behind. They entered the old home and closed the door behind them. As they did, a black shadow crossed the moon. Moments later, Asmodeus dropped back in under the eaves and landed on the table. He turned slowly, as if studying the remnants of the circle, and the symbols. Then, with a quick swoop of his wings, he rose to the rafters of the long porch and perched on one of the beams. He ruffled his feathers, fanning and stretching his wings, and then, as the night settled fully around him, he dropped back, blinking slowly, and drifted off to unknown places. Moments later, the last light inside went dark.

Chapter Four

Donovan woke suddenly to a loud, roaring sound. He rose quickly, then froze, listening carefully. Amethyst had heard it too, but she only sat up in the bed, frowning.

"What is that?" she asked.

Donovan walked to the window, pulled back the curtain and then let it go with a short laugh.

"I think Geoffrey's ride is here," he said.

They dressed quickly and walked out to the front porch to find Geoffrey already there. A sleek black helicopter with no markings had dropped onto the field outside. The rotors slowed, and moments later, two men dropped to the ground and made their way toward them.

"Sorry," Geoffrey said. "I called them last night; I didn't know they'd arrive so early."

"It's fine," Donovan said. "We should all get started."

"There's coffee," Geoffrey said.

Amethyst stepped up behind Donovan and wrapped her arms around him, laying her chin on his shoulder.

"That would have made me very happy," she said, "in about two hours."

Bullfinch laughed.

"Got to go," Geoffrey said. "Once I make contact in New Orleans, where can I reach you?"

"I'll call," Donovan said. "I'm guessing that where I'm heading, reception will be spotty."

"Right then," Geoffrey said. "Good luck." He turned his gaze to Amethyst.

"You will be careful?" he said. "I could send someone to assist…"

"You have got to get over the chivalry," Amethyst said, straightening and unwrapping herself from Donovan. "I am quite capable of taking care of myself, and I'm always careful. I'll be in good hands, assuming I can find Nettie, and if I can't, I'll call you."

"Fair enough," Bullfinch said. "In any case, I imagine Cleo can keep you out of trouble. She's kept this one safe for a very long time," he winked at Donovan.

Amethyst shook her head. She stepped forward and gave Bullfinch a quick hug, then turned away to look for the promised coffee. Donovan watched her go, grinned, and then held out his hand. Bullfinch shook it.

"It's always interesting," he said.

"That's what keeps us young, in a manner of speaking," Bullfinch said. "I'll see you soon."

Then he turned and was gone. A few moments later the chopper lifted off, turned, and whirled away into the clouds with a slowly diminishing roar. The silence that followed felt heavy and intense. Donovan closed the door. When he turned, Amethyst handed him a cup of strong, black coffee.

"You think he'll be okay in New Orleans?" she asked. "I know Geoffrey can mind his manners, but some of his buddies are going to be a hard sell with friendly vampires."

"He'll be fine," Donovan said. "I just hope they can find something useful. I know Copper and Alicia have been on that mountain, but I have only a vague idea what happened when they were there. They are an odd pair—council members, but seldom at *home* in San Valencez. I think they must be very different from Johndrow and his crew."

"That doesn't make me feel better," she said. "I'd be more comfortable knowing just what we sent them into."

"The quicker we finish our own tasks," Donovan said, "the quicker we can go to Geoffrey's aid."

"Or the vampires'."

"Point noted." Donovan said. "You can drop Asmodeus and me off on your way back into town. I called Cletus last night. He'll meet you in Old Mill and fill you in on the best way to find Nettie. I know you've already met her, but something tells me that, since this is different, you'll have to play by her rules. Don't forget the whiskey."

Amethyst snorted. "I'll be fine," she said. "I made a couple of calls myself last night. I should have the whiskey covered, and a few other things as well. You just make sure that wherever you're headed, you find your way back. I've been in those tunnels. I know you've been there more than I have, but they are so old, and so powerful."

Donovan stepped closer, wrapped her in a hug, and kissed her.

"I'll be careful. I have too much to come back to. I'm afraid Cleo would never forgive me if I left her up here with you and didn't make it back."

Cleo growled.

Amethyst laughed. "It won't just be Cleo, Magic Man. You get in there, find what you're looking for—Edgar Allan Poe? Find him and bring him back if you can. I have to see a lady about a tree, that's a lady."

"Everything we say, or seem," Donovan said. "I know you'll find her—Nettie has to know where she is. The question is, can you free her? Can anyone?"

"I have some thoughts on that," Amethyst said. "You aren't the only one who knows things," she said.

"We'd better get going," Donovan said. "I have a sense of impending change. I try not to ignore my intuition."

Amethyst leaned in, kissed him again, and then turned away to start packing.

Chapter Five

Bullfinch

Bullfinch climbed down the stairs from the rooftop of the Denver, Colorado headquarters of the O.C.L.T. and headed for the main control room. He passed no one on his way in, but that was not strange. There were not many permanent staff, and those who had access were usually occupied with one case or another or on the road.

The building, once the shell of a bankrupted Internet Startup company known as EnterWeb, had come together with remarkable swiftness. The huge, snaking snarls of cable and wire had been insulated and packed out of sight. The offices ringing the building were finished, about half of them empty. The lights in the conference room were dim.

The control room was a different thing altogether. As he opened the door and scanned the room, Bullfinch shook his head. Three of the four walls of the room were covered with video monitors, with banks of smaller screens topped by rows of huge, LCD panels. The walls beneath the monitors were an amalgam of desks, tables, wires, and more cables.

Nearly all the screens were lit, and images flashed across them, some so quickly it was difficult to focus on one before another took its place. In the center of the room, behind a semi-circular wooden desk, sat a tall blonde man. His eyes flicked from screen to screen, and his fingers flew over the keys of several keyboards, only pausing briefly to manipulate one of a sequence of track balls and mice.

When the door clicked shut behind Bullfinch, the man turned.

"Geoffrey!" he said. He disengaged from the control panels and keyboards and stood, turning.

"Mack," Bullfinch said. "It's good to see you. What are you tracking?"

"Everything," Mack said. Then he grinned. "As always."

Mack looked like anything but a computer expert. His blonde hair hung in curling waves over his shoulder, and he looked ready to run a marathon on a moment's notice. His smile was wide and genuine.

Bullfinch shook his head again. "I will never pretend to fully understand the scope of," he waved his hand to encompass the multitude of monitors, "all of this. I am glad, my young friend, that you are on our side."

"We all have our gifts," Mack said. "What can I do for you today?"

"I have a mission," Bullfinch said simply. "I am on my way to New Orleans, and I am in a bit of a hurry. I need to know who is available, and I need help tracking a pair of undead contacts."

"Friend or foe?" Mack asked.

"Friends—for now."

"The place is nearly empty, I'm afraid. The only one here right now, other than myself and some of the staff, is Gunter Krieg."

"Gunter?" Bullfinch said. Then he grinned. "I was hoping he would be here. I have the feeling that this is going to be an interesting trip. I'll see if I can find him. In the meantime, I'm looking for contact with a pair that I know only as Copper and Alicia—her last name is Contreaux, he doesn't seem to have one. They are members of the vampire council out in San Valencez, California, but they have been in New Orleans for an extended time. I am going to need to find them, and talk to them, and I may not have much time for searching."

"Leave that to me," Mack said. "I have my sources."

"I know you do, my boy. You do your magic. I'm going in search of Gunter. I must admit, I'm rather looking forward to this conversation. I am uncertain how he's going to react."

"That would be my thought on any conversation with Gunter," Mack said. "Sometimes I think he lives in an entirely different world."

"Don't we all?" Bullfinch said.

He turned and headed back to the door. Before he reached it, he heard the steady tapping of Mack's fingers on the keyboards resume. Somehow, the sound was reassuring.

Gunter Krieg sat alone in the cafeteria, staring into a cup of black coffee. On the table beside him was a small, jumbled stack of napkins, covered in scribbled diagrams, symbols, and equations. Bullfinch slipped into a chair across the table. After a moment, as if just noticing that something had changed, the old physicist glanced up.

He gazed at Geoffrey for a moment, refocusing, and then he smiled.

"Geoffrey!" he said, delighted. "It is so good to see you, old friend. You'll have to pardon me. I was lost in my thoughts."

"No apology necessary," Bullfinch said. "What are you working on?"

Gunter glanced down at the napkins as if he'd never seen them before and frowned.

"I am afraid that I have lost that train of thought," he said, shuffling the papers idly. "I'm sure it will come back to me. Was there something you needed?"

"A companion," Bullfinch said. "I have to make a trip to New Orleans, and it's not one I'd care to make alone—just in case."

"Not going to visit old comrades, then?" Krieg said, and grinned. "I am a man of science, Geoffrey. I am not sure how much help I would be in a pinch."

"You are sharper than most rooms full of academics," Bullfinch replied. "I think you'll do just fine, assuming you can break away?"

"From what?" Krieg looked puzzled. Then shook his head. "Oh—oh yes, of course. I would be delighted. I will have to pack, but I don't need much. How long do you think?"

"Probably not more than a few days."

"And who is it that we are going to see? Someone who makes you nervous; this is new to me."

Geoffrey sat in silence for a moment, and then, as if winning some inner debate, came out with it.

"I am going to New Orleans to meet with a pair of vampires," he said. "They have information that I need, and I may not have much time to retrieve it. I have never met these particular undead, and so, I would rather not do so alone, in case they are—reluctant—to part with what I need."

Krieg blinked.

"Undead, you say? Fascinating. Of course, the term is misleading. We do not know their state, yes? They are not dead, and they are certainly not alive—at least not in the sense that you and I are alive. When do we leave?"

"Would an hour be too soon?" Geoffrey asked.

"That will be fine," Gunter replied.

"Meet me out front, then," Geoffrey said. "I need to check with Mack to see what he's got for us. We'll have one of the drivers take us to the airport. The flight will only take an hour or two if we take the jet."

Gunter's eyes twinkled.

"I love to fly. It feels so—improbable."

Then, without another word, the man turned and left the cafeteria. Bullfinch sat, waiting until his friend was out of sight, then rose and headed back toward the control room. He needed time to get his own equipment together as well. He hoped Mack had been successful. Then he thought about that and laughed softly. Of all the things he had to doubt, Mack's information-retrieval skills were not one of them. If there was information on Copper and Alicia, Mack would have it.

Chapter Six

Mack's report was surprisingly short. There was a single sheet with an address, that of a small tavern on the outskirts of New Orleans, on the edge of the swamp.

"Not hard to find at all," Mack said. "They don't appear to be making any attempt to hide."

"Curious," Geoffrey said. He took the paper and tucked it into the breast pocket of his jacket. "Makes our journey a bit simpler, I suppose."

"Wish I could go along," Mack said. "I haven't actually *met* any undead so far, though I have the sense that I've conversed with them several times on certain social networks."

Bullfinch eyed the younger man for a moment, and then shook his head. "I don't know whether it bothers me more that I have little idea what a social network might be—or that *they* do."

"It's another medium for communication," Mack said.

"I have always preferred more direct methods," Bullfinch said.

Mack smiled. "Job security, I suppose," he said. "I took the liberty of alerting Dodd. He'll be waiting on the runway. I told him the destination, and flight plans have been filed. He'll be ready to go when you arrive."

"Thank you," Geoffrey said."

"No problem," Mack said. "I'd ask you to take pictures, but I don't know how that works."

Bullfinch laughed. "They photograph, these days. In my day, when the cameras were manual and required mirrors, it was a different story. It's the mirrors that seem to be vexed, and that might be a question for Gunter, now that I think of it. I already saw the spark in his eye. I suspect I'll be subjected to a lengthy lecture on his theory of how—and why—undead can exist. He didn't even seem to question that they do, just leaped right on to their 'state of existence' without a flinch."

"Not the professor's first rodeo," Mack said. "Your report is one I'll be looking forward to."

Geoffrey gave a short, mock bow.

"Conceded. I will have that report to you as soon as I can, but I suspect that the bigger picture—the overall mission—is going to prove a lot more interesting. If you hear from Rebecca, or Isabella, I'm going to want a conference call."

"You've got it," Mack said.

Then, as if he had turned off the conversation and mentally logged in to some other world, Mack turned away and returned to his central workstation, eyes flickering from screen to screen.

Just for a moment, the blinking lights, screens, flickering data, all of it, merged with the image of the tall young man—a single pattern. Then Geoffrey blinked to clear his mind and left the room. He thought back to what Donovan had said about the Internet and the computers being an entirely new aspect of magic, and he thought—just possibly—it was time that he began to pay attention.

He'd left his bags outside the control room door, strapped to a rolling luggage cart. Most of it was books. He had a small satchel of items he thought might come in handy, but he wasn't anticipating violence. On the top of the piled luggage was a very old copy of *Kinder- und Hausmärchen—Children's and Household Tales* in the original German. Commonly titled—Grimm's Fairy Tales. He also had a translation. His own German was rusty, and the text in the older book was dense and archaic.

He expected the comparison of the two versions to provide light reading on the flight. He smiled as he thought of sharing that reading with Gunter. He didn't need the older man for translation, but for his interpretation and knowledge set; he would provide an invaluable perspective.

"An interesting journey, indeed," Geoffrey said softly.

Gunter was waiting for him out front next to a sleek black limousine. A driver stood by the trunk, ready to load their luggage and whisk them off to the airport. The old German had brought a worn duffle bag, which sat on the ground at his feet. He carried a polished leather valise in his left hand and clutched a bundle of papers and notebooks in his right. He looked ruffled and unkempt, but his eyes shone brightly, and his expression was one of delight.

Gunter Krieg had come to O.C.L.T. in the first wave. He'd been irritating, baffling and fascinating the greatest minds in the worlds of theoretical and experimental physics since he was a boy. He stood just under six feet, three inches; he was thin, and had hair that was as happy standing out at odd angles as it was lying flat, and prone to one or the other—or both—at any particular moment.

Geoffrey knew that when not working on various projects for O.C.L.T., the man taught at Evergreen University, though that hardly narrowed it down. Several institutes of higher learning claimed the name Evergreen, but Gunter was either unwilling to reveal his academic associations or unable to recall it when someone inquired.

"All ready?" Geoffrey asked.

"Indeed," Gunter said. "I have gathered some research material for the flight. I believe this will prove most interesting. But really, Geoffrey, you must give me some context. I assume there is a bigger picture? A puzzle?"

Geoffrey chuckled, patted Gunter on the back, and hefted the older man's duffle bag from the sidewalk. The driver had opened the trunk and loaded the rest of their luggage. Geoffrey tossed the last bag inside and opened the rear passenger side door. Gunter slipped in behind the driver, and moments later, they were on their way.

Gunter turned to him and laid a hand on his arm.

"I have a theory," he said. "About your vampires. I wonder— do you think they will discuss it with me?"

"I have no idea," Geoffrey said, "but I daresay that if they do not, they will be missing out."

Gunter looked as if he might respond, and then his eyes glazed slightly, and he tilted his head. Something had distracted him—some thought—and he was off again, following wherever it led. Geoffrey leaned back and closed his eyes. The car pulled away from the curb and turned toward the airport.

There was a jet fueled and waiting for them when they arrived. The powers funding O.C.L.T. had resources that could be mind boggling at times. There was a small sigil on the tail-wing of the sleek, private aircraft. Beneath that, in a semi-circle, the words "Colorado Star." The pilot, a tall man with dark hair that was just beginning to gray at his temples, greeted them as they climbed aboard.

"Lewis!" Geoffrey said. "I didn't expect you to be available."

"Just in from the Amazon. We had a long flight back, but I've had a day's rest, and you know me. When Mr. Dodd's call came in, I was first out of the gate."

"Just like your father," Geoffrey chuckled. "With a bit of your grandmother thrown in for good measure."

"I will take that as it is intended," Lewis said. "As a compliment. Perhaps, once we are in the air, I can join you for a bit. You have stories that even I haven't heard."

Geoffrey nodded, and smiled, then climbed on board. Gunter followed, and within moments they were seated, their luggage stowed, and the jet began rolling slowly across the tarmac, turning down a runway in preparation for takeoff.

"This isn't one of our regular aircraft," Gunter observed.

"Everyone is out," Geoffrey said. "Colorado Star—and, Lewis and his parents—are old companions of mine. We tried to recruit them for O.C.L.T. but they have a lodge—an old group— and they keep mostly to themselves. His grandmother, Stasi, was one of the most gifted Seers I've ever encountered. I'll tell you one day about how they met Nikola Tesla—I believe that story would be right up your alley."

Gunter eyed him for a moment with an assessing expression that Geoffrey had come to expect from the old physicist.

"Sometimes," Gunter said, "The things we surround ourselves with—the people—distract me so much I can't think. For instance, you speak of Nikola Tesla almost as if he were a contemporary."

Geoffrey smiled.

"When time permits," he said, "I'll tell you some stories. You can judge for yourself how much you believe, and how much you credit to the wandering imagination of an aging mind. In any case, Lewis is one of the best pilots in the world, and this craft—much as I love our own—is likely protected in ways we'll never understand."

As the jet reached airspeed and lifted off the ground, Gunter leaned back, and stared out the window as they nosed up toward the clouds. He sat very still, and very quiet, until they leveled off, and then he turned back to Geoffrey. When he did, his eyes twinkled, and his face was a mask of wonder.

"I feel like a bird," he said. "A very lazy bird. Did I tell you? I have developed a theory about your vampires. I have studied what is available in the library and questioned several of the others—Isabella and Rebecca, even Mack, who found a bit more than I was able to with his wires and computers."

"A theory?" Geoffrey said. "About their existence?"

"Indeed. There is little in the world that does not have an explanation, but there is much for which those explanations have yet to be discovered. How can a man die and still live? How can drinking blood, something that would not sustain a living man, and which can certainly not rebuild a respiratory or circulatory system, be the key?"

Geoffrey remained silent. He knew of no scientific answer that could do justice to the question.

"Exactly," Gunter said, responding to the silence. "It defies logic, but that is often the way with things we do not understand. It's not nature that is flawed, but the logic. So, let me propose that one of the pet theories of quantum physics is true. There are many dimensions—this is only one. Possibly every decision we make, every word we speak, splinters off and becomes a form of the original. If this is true, your vampires would be—in some dimensions—alive and well, and in others quite dead."

"That makes sense," Geoffrey admitted. "The vampires here, however, seem to be neither."

"And that is the key," Gunter beamed. "They *seem* to be neither. What I believe is that they have somehow managed to forge a bond with another version of themselves. A living version, living a life without any awareness of the connection. As our vampire lives, and moves through the world, it saps energy from its 'host' in that other dimension. Very likely, at times, it is near to causing a second death. And then? It feeds. The ingestion of blood, while of no use to the vampire itself, feeds the life force of the victim across the dimensions to replenish the strength of the 'host'."

Geoffrey stared. He opened his mouth to say that he believed it was totally preposterous, but even as his lips parted, he realized—it was not. In some way, it made perfect sense.

"What of the longevity?" he asked. "If the connection is to a single other self, and that other self lives a normal life, why does the vampire not perish when that other's life ends?"

Gunter grinned.

"There are infinite possible selves, and I believe the longer such a bond exists, the more versions become connected. For all we know there are dimensions where death doesn't exist at all, where the idea of such an ending would be as foreign as the idea of immorality is to you—or to me. Is it not true that the longer such a creature exists, the more powerful it becomes?"

Geoffrey nodded.

Then Gunter's grin widened. "It is only a theory. Feh, perhaps they are supernatural creatures of the night who are magically regenerated by the blood of the living. What do I know?"

Geoffrey laughed, and Gunter joined him.

"I think," he said, "that this will prove a most interesting adventure."

Chapter Seven

Donovan

Donovan watched until Amethyst and Cleo had driven out of sight, then began walking back to site of the Lake Drummond Hotel. Asmodeus took to the air and followed him.

He was a little bit worried about them. Nettie wasn't anyone to take lightly, and Amethyst wasn't always particularly subtle. He thought Cleo would help, and he remembered the stag that accompanied Nettie—how it had carried him out of the swamp after they'd defeated the vampire and alchemist George Starkey. When he reached the ruins of the hotel—no more than a bit of foundation and a set of stairs leading down into rubble—he gathered his thoughts and cleared his mind. Asmodeus landed on the ground nearby.

He knew he had to let go of his concern for the others and concentrate on what was ahead of him. He'd spent a lot of time in the labyrinth of tunnels he was about to enter, but each time he had pushed the boundaries, seeking something he'd never found before, it had chilled his heart. The doors along those tunnels could open to almost anywhere—to any time—and if he chose poorly, he had no way to know if he could divine the charm that would bring him back.

He wished he'd had a chance to visit his home before attempting this and thought, not for the first time, of using the tunnels to make his way back to San Valencez first. Unfortunately, there was very little time. There were so many things he might have brought along had he known he'd be making this journey.

But he did have the two things he thought he'd need the

most. He still had the paper that Poe had given him so long ago. He' read it many times, of course. It was a hand-written copy of a poem; a work in progress. It had been originally titled "Grimm," but then, as if in anticipation of the future that would swallow him so completely, Poe had struck the title with a single bold line and written, "The Raven" beneath it. Though it was a very early draft, it was still very close to the poem that would eventually lead to Poe's fame and notoriety.

With that paper folded in his pocket, and the pendulum he carried, he thought that—even through time and space and the dark passageways of the labyrinth—he could find the room he sought. He knew there had to be a doorway leading to it because Poe himself, without even bothering to use the stairs, or a charm of any sort, had found his way there—or perhaps he had been led.

He thought, and not for the first time, that the most likely reality was that the labyrinth of tunnels and doorways was there for him, and for those closest to him, because it was a way of conceptualizing something that was otherwise too complex to understand. He knew the rituals. He trusted the steps, sigils, and signs, and the doors were there for him. For Poe, it had simply been a matter of closing his eyes and stepping into another world. For Amethyst it might be a matrix of crystals, and for Gunter Krieg, the physicist, it might be a formula.

Donovan glanced down to where Asmodeus sat on the ground, preening his wing feathers. Donovan had already seen how Cleo could traverse the hidden trails. He didn't understand it, but there were times when understanding was overrated. It was very likely that Grimm had led Edgar in, and then out of the labyrinth, and if they'd made it in once, it seemed probable that they could have done so again. Donovan was counting on it.

"You ready, old friend?" he said.

Asmodeus glanced up, tilted his head so that one bright eye fixed on Donovan. The old bird let out a soft caw and hopped into the air. He landed with a thump on Donovan's shoulder.

Without a word, Donovan rose to his feet and started down the stairs. He counted steps as he did, climbing back up, moving down again, the motions almost a dance, creating the pattern and rhythm that would gain him access. He finally reached the bottom and pressed his hand into the open air, he felt solid resistance. He murmured a single word under his breath, pressed forward, and stepped through into cooler, damper air.

The world shifted. It felt as if it flowed back and around him, almost liquid. When his vision settled, he turned slowly, taking in his surroundings. Usually when he entered these hidden paths, he found himself in a stone corridor. But here the doors to either side were spaced evenly, and hewn from thick, solid planks. It was the same, and also very different.

He stood in a wide, spacious hallway that stretched into darkness in either direction. Each doorway—spaced just as he had expected—was flanked by ornate sconces that held flickering gas lamps. Sometimes, these were torches, and other times the entire passage was illuminated by some undefined glow. He had never given it much thought, but now he believed that he understood another piece of the puzzle.

This was someone else's vision of the labyrinth. What he normally saw was a manifestation of his own impressions. What he walked through now was something entirely different, a version of the same passageway, but viewed through the lens of another mind. He smiled, then, because he thought he knew whose.

The question remained, which door? Which direction?

Asmodeus seemed to understand his dilemma. With a quick push, the bird launched into lazy, gliding flight. He swooped low, then glided up one wall, and back. Donovan followed. He had to move quickly—even in slow flight the old raven was much faster. He tried to count the doors, or to make some sense of their progress, but it was not long before the lights and bricks and doorways faded to a blur.

Suddenly, with a flourish, Asmodeus whirled up, dropped to the floor of the passageway, and stood facing a heavy wooden door. There was no knob, but instead an arched brass handle with a push-button mechanism. Beneath this was a keyhole, large and dark. A skeleton key would be necessary to release it.

Again, Donovan smiled. Of course Edgar's library would have a lock with a skeleton key.

He took a deep breath and reached out. When he pressed on the door's latch, it opened smoothly. Donovan didn't hesitate. He pushed inward and followed the door through its arc. Asmodeus swooped in before him, circled the room inside, and lit on the littered surface of an old wooden desk.

The room was all deep, dark wood, with polished floors, mahogany shelves lining every wall. The desk was clear except for a decanter of some liquor, a stained glass, a scattered pile of paper, a capped ink bottle and a quill lying beside it. Just inside the door to one side an empty hat tree stood silent sentinel. There was the faint scent of tobacco in the air. Donovan didn't know why, but the room had the feel of a place recently vacated.

Asmodeus lifted off from the desk, did a slow circle of the room, and lit again. This time he settled onto a large perch in the far corner. Donovan had missed it in his first cursory glance around the room. He smiled.

"Can you sense Grimm, then?" he asked the old bird. "I believe we have found our destination, but not our man."

He stepped over to the desk and glanced down. The pages littering the surface were covered in even lines of script. Donovan picked them up, shuffled and straightened them. He read the first few lines, and realized it was a story. He thought he recognized it, but something was different. Like the doors and the passageway he'd entered from, it was not quite what he remembered. There was a title—*The Masquerade*. It had been deleted with a single slash of the pen through the center, but nothing replaced it.

Donovan seated himself behind the desk, glanced at the bottle, smiled. A quick search of the drawers revealed a second tumbler, and he dashed two fingers of what appeared to be bourbon into it before settling back.

It was not lost on him that he might be the first, or possibly *only* reader of this particular tale by Edgar Allan Poe, and though he'd met the man, and followed his career, it still brought a shiver of anticipation. He took a sip of the surprisingly smooth whiskey and began to read.

Chapter Eight

The Masquerade

By Edgar Allan Poe

Each time I wander out from the strange, book-lined study I entered so long ago there is the sensation of fingers tracing spider-silk lines down my spine. Each time that door—solid oak and thick as a man's arm—slides softly closed and the latch falls into place, I wonder if it's the last time that I'll hear it, if I'll find my way back, or if the universe will finally, reluctantly pen the words denied me for so long, and write "The End."

And I wonder where—and when—I will go.

I have tried every notion, every trick of literary magic and intellectual gymnastics I can imagine, to find my way back to Lake Drummond at an early enough point in time to make a difference, but the quest eludes me. At times, I am certain the worlds I enter, while following similar lines of time to my own, are in some way divergent. Indeed, more than once I have met a semblance of myself, though subtlety, or wholly changed. Introspection is a dark enough practice without a living, breathing mirror casting long shadows on your soul.

I was not two steps into that cool, empty passage when I sensed the movement of air at my shoulder and felt the comfortable, familiar thump of Grimm's landing. As usual, while transiting those dark ways, the bird was silent. I wondered if he was leaving all mistakes and ill-chosen pathways to me to avoid blame.

It didn't matter. I concentrated. Somehow, I knew that the

key to finding the doorway I sought would be found in the whirling morass of my imagination and not by some ritualistic trickery. I needed to focus on my goal, visualize the outcome, and act. In all my journeys, the only time my destination has been certain was in the return. The study, the desk, the books— in some way they remained static while the world, as I once knew it, disintegrated into a shifting pattern of possibilities.

I erased the passageway from my mind's eye and pictured the lake, that tortured, twisted tree that had captured her so completely. I imagined the old woman and the stag, the drawings. As I had a hundred times before, I spoke her name— Lenore. I felt a gentle tug on my mind and turned. As I always had before, I faced a door. There was no knob, just a heavy latch, like the one that opened my study.

I stopped for a moment, thinking about that. I had come to think of that room as mine, but I had no idea where it had come from, how it could possibly exist, and why it was filled with the things that mattered to me, some of them things I hadn't realized mattered before I ever stepped foot inside. I wore the long coat that I'd found there, and it fit as though tailored for me in the finest clothier. The books that lined the shelves ranged from the familiar to those I might have sought in the far-reaches of the globe, had I the time or wherewithal to make such travels. Some had marginalia. I'd studied them, and though I sifted and searched my memories for anything that might explain the notations; I do not remember writing them. Still, they are clearly written by my hand, and though the words are not familiar, the moment I read them they feel a part of me, and something itches in the dark recesses of my mind.

The only constant is Grimm. I have still not completely adjusted to his new form. When we met, he was a crow—old, tamed by some hand I could not fathom—and bonded to me by loneliness and wanderlust. And dreams.

At Lake Drummond, I learned the truth. He is no crow, but a raven. He holds keys to things I may never understand and shares them with me. I have heard the word *familiar* used in reference to our bond, and, in every real sense, it fits. As the years have passed, we have shared many adventures—as well as many nightmares. I do not know how he copes, but for me, the only answer is to write them down. In my accounts these events are changed, of course, twisted and warped, but with their essences left intact. The works have become my legacy in a world where I no longer feel welcome.

The door beckoned, and before the melancholy of the past could draw me back, I gripped the latch and pushed the door inward, stepping through into a dimly lighted hall.

Grimm rode easily on my shoulder, his sharp gaze sweeping ahead and to the sides. We were not alone. A team of carpenters labored near a great door, placing timbers across it, and pounding them firmly in place. Other workers waited to brace these timbers with angled posts to prevent them being knocked loose from the outside. I stood still in the shadows, watching.

One turned and caught sight of me. He frowned into the shadows, and then, just as I was afraid I'd have to try and find my way back through the portal, his features softened, and to my consternation, he executed a short bow.

"Sorry, Lord," he said. "I did not know you were there, and I did not recognize your attire."

I held my silence, nodding to acknowledge him. I knew that anything I said might bring my identity into question. It seemed, as had been the case so many times before, that mine was not an unfamiliar face to those around me. Something about my presence or my appearance bothered him. He stared at me long and hard, but I met that gaze, and a moment later he turned back to his work.

I didn't hesitate. I was interested in the work they were doing, the sealing of the doors, but aware that they would expect me to understand. I would have to seek my answers in other places and by other ways. I walked slowly down the hall and into the interior of the large, grand building, following the scent of incense and candles, the strains of music, and peels of high-pitched laughter.

From the hallway, I stepped into a large and grand foyer. At the far end, staircases swept up to the right and left, disappearing into shadows. There were doors on all sides of me. More doors opened from the second story, where a balconied walkway branched from the twin staircases. Light washed out from each to stain the railing above, and each of those lights was of a different hue, giving the room the aspect of a circular rainbow, a kaleidoscopic effect.

There was no way to isolate sounds. Voices, music, the clatter of heels on hard flooring, the clatter of silverware. I felt Grimm shift on my shoulder and glanced at him. I'd nearly forgotten he was there, and almost laughed as I realized that it might not have been me the man by the entrance had stared at but the bird.

"What next, old friend?" I asked.

Receiving no answer, I walked slowly to the stairs, choosing the one on the right, and wound my way upward. There were rooms on the lower floor, but from the sounds I heard whatever was happening seemed to be limited to the upper story.

As I stepped onto the upper walk, I saw that there was an alcove just out of sight against the wall. In that shadowed place a woman sat, facing an easel. There was dim light from a flickering candle. I had to step much closer to make out what she was painting. As I approached, I saw she worked on a large canvas, and was depicting a street scene littered with bodies. The corpses tumbled and sprawled as though tossed aside like garbage. Deep red lines swam from the corners of their eyes, drained from their nostrils and washed in rivulets of drool from their lips. The faces were incomplete, their features symbolic of forgotten numbers, all individuality lost in the pain.

Several of the bodies lay before a great door, and in a strange juxtaposition, I realized it must be the far side of the portal I'd just seen sealed. The woman wore a long, diaphanous gown. As I approached, I saw that it was fashioned of a deep red fabric. From a distance it had seemed black. She heard my footsteps and turned, slowly, her brush pausing in its dance on the canvas.

The gaze that met mine was that of a strange harlequin, created in shades of pink and red and lined in deepest black. The images she had created on canvas were mirrors to near perfection of her own aspect; strokes of rich red slid from the corners of the eyes, as from her eyes, from her downturned lips. Those deep-set orbs were circled in dark haunting rings that drained any color to pits of gray. She didn't speak but cocked her head to one side, and I felt her gaze wash over me, studying and picking at the edges of my features and form. That gaze lingered long on Grimm, and he returned it with gravity. It was the artist who looked away, and though I felt his talons grip more tightly at the shoulder of my coat, my companion did not move.

As she turned away, the spell was broken, and I shifted my attention to the door on my left. Shadows shifted beyond that dark portal, all lit in flickering blue light. I stepped through and drew a heavy breath smelling of lavender from an array of candles to my right. There was a central room, topped by a glittering crystal chandelier. Lamps with globes of blown blue glass circled a cleared central space. From one corner, the voice of a lone singer rose. The notes shifted subtly around the room, caught in some geometric progression of acoustic resonance. The tune was haunting; the lyrics, if indeed they were lyrics, were too low and indistinct to comprehend.

Couples glided through the center of the chamber, wrapped tightly in one another's arms, their dance languid and devoid of emotion. They seemed unaware of their surroundings. I spotted a window and began walking toward, it, making my way through the center of the crowd. Regardless of what they wore, the color of their hair, or their eyes, they were blue people in that odd light. They wore the hue in various shades and gradients. It glittered in their eyes and melted downward to a royal blue so dark it deepened to purple near the floor. As I passed, they turned their gaze upon me and backed away. I watched them but held my silence.

At first it was a slight ripple, a shift in their rhythm, but after a few moments I realized that, though they did not move swiftly, they opened before me, pulling back and away, shifting from my path. When I swept my gaze around the room, they avoided it. I've witnessed similar motion in schools of fish, avoiding encroaching shadows, trying to avoid the attention of predators.

I reached the window, and pulled back the long, heavy drapes, but if I'd hoped to see something beyond the walls, something beyond the blue, I was denied. Long planks sealed that portal, nailed to the framework and painted the same dark shade as the curtains. I spun on my heels, crossed back to the door I had entered through, and stepped out into the hall. Behind me, I heard the shuffling and shifting of silks and the scrape of shoe leather spreading out to cover my track.

The painter did not look up from her work, and I did not linger. I moved on, seeing another room ahead, marked by a bright ruby-red light shimmering across the polished floor beyond its door.

The antithesis of the blue chamber, this one sparkled. Laughter peeled like the tintinnabulation of bells. Glasses clinked. Along one wall a long table ran, centered by a huge punchbowl. In the glare of crimson-tinted light it was impossible to tell if the glass, or the liquid within, was clear, or blood red. There was no music. Men and women gathered in groups, laughing and chattering. As in the previous room, there was a tall, curtained window, but I ignored it. Instead, I stared directly across the chamber's center to the table.

A tall man stood beside it. He held a glass in one hand, and a ladle in the other. He had not yet noticed my presence, and so I watched, keenly aware of his every motion. The tilt of his head, the way he stood casually, one knee slightly bent. When at last his glass was full, and he turned, I studied what I could make out of his features.

He stood very still and returned my gaze.

No one passed between us. In fact, those who noticed his presence, or mine, or both, shied away. He gleamed red, but I realized at once he wore bright white, and the red hue was shaded by the lights. I knew, without knowing how, that whatever room he passed through he would match, when he passed between two of them in the hallway, he would take on the aspect of a rainbow.

My clothing, as always, was dark. The long jacket swept the floor. Grimm still rested on my shoulder, head cocked. I knew that if I stood a moment longer, my twin would cross the floor to me and confrontation would be inevitable. There was a stir of laughter by a second door, leading into a chamber that leaked orange light, fading to brilliant yellow and deep gold beyond. I turned and made for it. He did not follow. Not immediately. A way was cleared for me, and I passed into the next room without a backward glance.

There was a rustle of activity at my heels, and not wanting to be drawn back into it, I turned again, this time to the left, and skirted along the wall. The golden room was awash with the music of stringed instruments and vocal harmony—like hymns, but not any songs of worship I was familiar with. The effect was seductive rather than uplifting. It was languid sounding, as if created from some too-sweet syrup or honey. I caught the eye of a woman in passing, and she slid her gaze up and down my body, hesitated at the sight of Grimm, then gave me a quick, intrigued smile. She took a step in my direction, but I didn't slow or pause. I turned left once more, back toward the hallway, and stepped out, this time glancing to my right.

The last room off the hall glowed a deep green. There was a loamy, earthy scent in the air, moist and sweet with an underpinning of rotted vegetation. I stopped in the hall and glanced back. No one followed, but the rainboesque ambiance of the place was shattered by a cry, followed by a high-pitched scream, and then another. Voices rose, and all pretense at music was swallowed in the din.

The green room beckoned, and I slipped inside.

Ferns cascaded over the lips of pottery lining the walls, held in place by a maze of wrought iron stands, shelves, and finery. The air was thick with the perfume of too many flowers, some dead and dying, others blooming, still others soaking in stagnant water that kept stems and roots from drying up and dropping away, while bringing slow death by rot.

There were not so many revelers here, and those there were matched their aspect to that of the room. They leaned on walls, sat on benches, propped only by their neighbors. No voices rose. No attempt at music disturbed the heavy air. I followed the wall to the left and came to a stone-rimmed fountain footed by a fetid pool. There was movement in the water. It rippled as something slid beneath the surface. Koi? Something else?

A man and woman sat, backs to that short wall of stone. Her

head rested on his shoulder, and he held her hand to his breast. I approached and bent to speak. The blood that leaked from their eyes, and ran from the corners of their lips, seemed so dark as to be black. The pale dead whites of their eyes shone luminous and green, as though weeping some sort of suppurating poison.

I stepped back. I had no idea how long it might take for me to be infected, or if it was even possible—if perhaps I were in some way immune, being from another world. Grimm was, as always, my guide in the face of danger, and he did not flinch from those morbid, corpse-faces. I turned and left the room.

In the hall, I saw the man in white a few yards away. He stood beside the artist and, knowing that my time in this realm was growing short, I crossed that short distance to stand at his side. At first, he did not look up. His white clothing glowed with the many colors of the room. All around us, sobs, cries, screams of pain and terror filled the air.

The girl lay on the floor, her brush forgotten. Paint was spilled around her, splattering her stool and the base of her easel. Her final line, blood red, trailed off down the canvas and on toward the floor, lost in space as she had fallen away. Her face matched those in her painting, blood blending with spoiled paint to create a single work of something more than art.

The man in white faced me then, and our gazes locked. He studied me, as if memorizing my features—or trying to pierce them.

"I do not want—that." He said, pointing to the girl. "It cannot end thus—can it? Are you, then, my death, come to claim me? Am I already gone?"

Despite the danger, I reached a hand out and laid it on his shoulder.

"I am not death, but neither can I prevent it," I said. "I simply am—and sometimes that is more than any man should be forced to bear."

The other nodded. The speech was not necessary. I felt his futility and pain. I felt the emptiness of dying with no mark to leave—no final message to the world. Forgotten. Wasted.

It was Grimm, at last, who moved. He walked in his careful, side-to-side gait, down my arm toward this man who must—and must not be—me, and stopped at my wrist. He cocked his head, and my impossible companion turned his gaze from mine to that of the bird. Something in Grimm's deep, pitch black eyes drew him. I saw his features, already pale, drain of all color. Those eyes, those wide, curious, pain-wracked eyes widened. His shoulder stiffened under my fingers, and I thought, just for a second, that he would pull away—that he would flee. He did not.

Grimm spoke. I have no idea what was said, as he was turned from me and his tone was far too soft and lost in the screams and the wails of those around us. The man's mouth opened, as if to reply. No sound emerged. He stared, transfixed by something I could not see, something he found in the old raven's eyes, or beyond them.

My twin turned to me, just for a second, and said: "We must leave this place. We must go, before we become a part of this macabre landscape for eternity."

Then he fell to the floor, and in that instant, was dead.

I knelt at his side, turned his face up to study his features. There was no sign of the disease. There was no blood. His eyes were still wide, as if terrified, and I gently lowered the lids to shade them—for my own peace of mind.

I rose and made to leave, but Grimm, who had made his way back to my shoulder, gripped me and tugged at my jacket with his beak. I frowned. At first, I could not imagine what he wanted of me—what he might expect. I thought of the man—of this place, the death that surrounded me—the death that waited on the streets beyond. I thought about my own death, how many times I'd been near to it—felt that cold horseman's breath on my collar. I thought of my wife, long gone; of my love, Lenore, taken from me. I thought of a world where I lived only in words, and then—in an epiphany that nearly dropped me to my knees—I understood.

His wish—his dying wish—was not to be part of this. Not to be forgotten. Not to have wasted his life—our life? I knelt, gripped him beneath his arms, and lifted him. It was not easy, but I managed to get a good grip, and paying no attention to those around me, I began to drag him away from that painting and to the stairs.

I will not detail that journey. I am not an athletic man, though my military time was not without its merit. Finding my way past that sealed main entrance and into the tunnels beyond, all the while dragging a lifeless corpse, was nearly more than I could manage. I drew some strength from Grimm, but it was my task—my burden.

I have no real memory of the trek through the tunnels, or how I came, at last, to open yet another door, which I knew was the only one that led back to my own world. I stepped into a dark, foggy night. A few short steps upward led to an alley, and then to the street. Behind me, the door I had just passed through, looked as if it only led to a basement.

I knew the place, and from the familiar scents and sounds, knew the time. I have visited there many times over the years, both before and after the odd circumstances of my trip to The Lake Drummond Hotel in North Carolina that had so changed my existence.

It felt oddly like a homecoming, though having arrived, I was uncertain what to do with my burden.

It was as I contemplated this that I noticed two singularly odd things. The first was that the other man—the other aspect of myself—was no longer dressed in white. He wore an unkempt suit, not unlike one of my own, but he wore it improperly, as if he had neither the sense nor energy to dress himself.

The second oddity was more profound. The man's hand moved. His leg kicked once, and then again, and with a shiver that wracked his frame, he turned to one side, coughed up some viscous fluid, and raised his head.

I could have helped him up. I could have seen him to a hospital, but I did not. Clearly, though he—by some miracle, or curse, lived—it was but a transient state. His gaze, when he turned it upon me, was dull and vacant. There was no sign of the man I'd faced in that faraway place—no hint of any real intelligence.

Grimm tugged at my collar again, and I stepped back and away. Then, without a backward glance, I left the streets of Baltimore behind me once again, and followed that stairway back down, closing my eyes and willing the door to open, as I knew it must, on those ancient labyrinthian tunnels. I did not know where they would lead me that night, but I knew it must be away.

My desk and pen awaited, and I knew I would have to write this tale or allow it to devour me slowly from within—tormented by the image of my own features in death, the blood draining from the artist's eyes.

I have titled this piece *Masquerade*, but before I take it—on some future journey—back to a time when it might actually see print, and become part of my legacy, I may give it a new title, and cut from it certain aspects that would only confuse readers, and undo what I had wrought. I think perhaps that title will involve masks, and death, but that story is for another place and time. This one will remain here, in this strange study between worlds.

I feel a great weight has been lifted. The world I knew—the world that knew me—has been exorcised. I don't know why I am so certain, but I feel the man I left behind is dead. I doubt he was able to provide details of what befell him, but if he did, he will be deemed a madman, and will take that to his grave—my grave—just another riddle in a long, unfortunate, yet incredibly interesting life.

I will return to my efforts at finding the proper door, the portal that will lead me to a place and time where there is a way to reunite with Lenore. Perhaps I will find allies along the way, perhaps I will die a second death. All a man can do is to put one foot before the other and trust to the fates. I am more fortunate than most. I also have Grimm, and though I cannot see the path laid out for me, in some way, I believe that he does.

I do not know if—in that forgotten past—my death was mourned, but I swear by whatever spirit guides me, my rebirth will have meaning.

E. A. Poe

Chapter Nine

Donovan replaced the manuscript on the desk. He stared at it for a while, then shook his head, and tried to bring the ends of several strings of thought together and weave them into something coherent. The ink bottle and the quill on the desk beckoned to him. It had been many years since he'd used such writing utensils, but he was very familiar with their use. He unstopped the ink, dipped the tip of the quill in, waited until the channel was full, and then, his hand holding the paper firmly in place, he penned: "The Masque of the Red Death" beside the lined-out title "Masquerade."

Asmodeus fluttered over to the desk and cocked his head, staring up into Donovan's eyes.

"I know, old friend," Donovan said. "We have to go. I could likely lose a year in here, just reading and sipping whiskey, but we have to find him. It seems that 'where' is not the only question we have to ask ourselves now, but also when. After we find our friend, we'll have to make sure that he *is* our friend, and not some doppelganger from the pages of a story that was originally very different from those I've read and enjoyed over the years.

Asmodeus gave no answer but ruffled his wings and hopped from the desk to Donovan's shoulder.

"Off with us, then," Donovan said. "Let's hope we don't have to travel through too many of these tales to find him, and that once we do either Edgar, myself—or you—or even Grimm—can find our way back in time to help the others.

The passageway stretched off into the distance. Donovan had to center himself and breathe carefully for a few moments. He had traveled these hidden ways more than once, but always with a well-formed goal in mind—short journeys that led from one door to another and back into the world beyond. This was a horse of a different color. He had always wondered if there were limits, boundaries he could pass where a return to the world he knew would become more difficult or even impossible.

Apparently, Edgar had been plagued by no such concerns. Asmodeus launched from Donovan's shoulder the second they were out of the office, veering left and gliding easily down the old passage, which was so much more like a hallway here in Edgar's world. Most of Donovan's trips through these portals had led to stone passageways and heavy wooden doors. This was a long stretch of wood paneled walls, gaslights, and ornate doorways leading—possibly—to the same worlds as his own personal image of the labyrinth, and possibly to a unique set of existences only accessible through the imagination of Edgar Allan Poe.

Just as the journey was beginning to stretch beyond Donovan's comfort zone, Asmodeus slowed and circled back in a graceful arc. The bird did eerily graceful figure eights until Donovan reached him. With Asmodeus once again settled on his shoulder, Donovan studied the door to his left. It looked identical to every other he'd passed. There was no lock, just a heavy brass grip. With a deep breath to steel himself for whatever was to come, he lifted the handle and pushed through.

As the door closed behind him with a soft click, he took in his surroundings. He stood in the courtyard of a large brick building. There was something both stately and grim about the place. The gardens surrounding it were simple green hedges edged with stone. The heavy, thick windows were shuttered and dark, staring into the courtyard like pale, dead eyes, dimming any joy that might have risen from the flowered gardens. The stone walkways were overgrown and shoddy. The general impression was one of dilapidation and neglect, disguised by a very thin and patchy veneer of normalcy. Donovan raised the collar of his jacket against a sudden chill and started forward. It was hard to believe that anyone resided within those walls, but he knew better than to distrust the raven.

As if reading his thoughts, Asmodeus lifted off, floating over the front grounds of the imposing structure and rose to perch above the arched doorway. Donovan nodded to the bird. It was always best to assess the situation first before appearing with an avian companion, and it was equally prudent to keep the old bird free in case he was needed. Enough of Edgar's stories ended in murder and madness to suggest caution.

Donovan climbed the stone stairs and, with some trepidation, raised the brass knocker on the massive wooden door and gave it a sharp rap. It echoed hollowly, and he stood, wondering if Asmodeus had made some mistake. The structure did not so much feel uninhabited to him as it did malicious, as if it might be better if no one were inside. Then he heard footsteps, and he stepped back a bit to put space between himself and whoever might open the door.

He was a bit taken aback when it swung wide to find himself face to face with a heavy-set man, well-dressed, if a bit unkempt. The man had dark hair, eyes sparkling with something bordering delight, and a wide smile.

"May I help you?" the man asked. He spoke French, and Donovan was inwardly glad he'd not spoken first.'

"I am sorry," he replied, aware that his French, long unused and much more modern than that of his host, was likely to sound odd. "I am looking for a friend and was told he might be found here. His name is Edgar, Edgar Poe."

Some emotion flickered across the man's face, but it was difficult to tell if it was from the reference to Edgar or Donovan's no-doubt strange accent. The expression passed very quickly— so quickly that if he hadn't been paying close attention, Donovan would have missed it entirely.

"But of course," the man said. "It is not often we get visitors here, much less two on the same day. I am Monsieur Maillard, caretaker of this facility. Please, come in."

Donovan did as he was bid but glanced sidelong at the man holding the door. "Facility? Then it is not your home?"

"It is both," Maillard replied with an odd grin. "I am both doctor and caretaker, owner and jailer. Welcome, Monsieur."

"Donovan. Donovan DeChance."

"Welcome to my *Maison de Santé*. I assumed you know the nature of this place. Why else would one travel so far into the middle of nowhere?"

"I assure you," Donovan said, turning slowly to take in the vast entrance hall, "I had no idea. I was led to believe my friend had made his way to your door, but that was the extent of it. I will admit, I am not surprised by the news, because Edgar is a writer. I believe most involved with the arts are at least a little mad."

Maillard nodded.

"Your timing is fortuitous. I have invited Mr. Poe to dine with me this evening, and there is more than enough for another. We will all be celebrating, you see. I believe you will find the experience—illuminating."

"It would be my honor, then," Donovan said. As he spoke, he mentally inventoried the voluminous pockets in his long jacket. He was going to have to find a credible excuse not to allow someone to take it and hang it out of sight. There was something off about the man, and the building, but until he'd actually caught sight of Edgar and gotten the lay of the place, he felt it best to remain as low key as possible. If Edgar had walked into another of his tales, Donovan's best hope to be of assistance was likely to simply blend in and become a member of the supporting cast.

Another thought came to him, and he almost voiced it. Then he thought better. It concerned Grimm, Edgar's raven. The two were inseparable, but he didn't want to mention the bird because he did not know if Maillard was aware of him. Something was itching at the back of Donovan's mind that he really wanted to remember—a story? Something about Edgar and France?

"I'll show you to a room where you can freshen up," Maillard said. "When you are ready, you can join us in the dining hall. It's going to be quite the splendid feast."

"What of your patients?" Donovan asked, uncertain if "patient" was the correct word for the time period. "Will they be in attendance?"

"Oh, no," Maillard said. "Truth be told, there was a time,

not long ago, when they might have. Our methods here were—shall I say—experimental. We gave them more freedom than we should have, watched them with less diligence. In any case, now they are confined, both for our safety and their own."

The itch in the back of Donovan's brain grew more insistent.

"Your previous method?" he said, tilting his head quizzically. "What was it called?"

"The Soothing Method," Maillard said. "We treated them as if their psychoses were normal. In fact, we insisted on carrying each to its limit. They dressed as they pleased, interacted as if they were as normal as any other group of men and women. We grew lax. It was a mistake. As is the case with wild animals that the rich attempt to keep as pets, we forgot the inherent danger. It did not end well.

"But this is talk for later. You must clean up and join us. There are plenty on my staff, as well as my family, who will be happy to speak to you of what has been, and what is now. Your friend will be waiting for you, and I am certain he will be happy to know of your arrival."

With that, the man turned, and Donovan followed him up a winding stair to a balcony on the second floor. From the landing at the top, hallways ran in three directions, left, right, and straight ahead. Donovan heard strange sounds emanating from the passage on the left. The passage directly ahead was well-lit, but silent. Maillard led him to the right. Dim gas-lit sconces illuminated the hall, which was lined with heavy wooden doors. They passed the first two doors, then Maillard paused and pushed open a door to his right. He stepped aside, and Donovan, seeing no other option, entered.

The room was dark, but Maillard pulled matches from a jacket pocket and lit an oil lamp on the dresser just inside the door. The flame licked upward, and the shadows melted away slowly.

The room was oddly decorated. There was a large bed, its frame of dark wood, and the mattress was fitted with a garish, bright yellow sheet. There was an immense pile of pillows at one end. There were books stacked high on a dresser to one side of the bed, but they were stacked in such a way their titles could not be browsed, or read. It looked more like a scene from a haunted house movie. The volumes were balanced symmetrically so even standing near to them felt dangerous, as if the wrong brush of air could send it toppling—possibly onto the head of the observer.

In surreal contrast, a washbasin stood on its stand. Steam rose from the surface of the water, and there was a cloth beside it, and soap.

Keeping his features as empty of emotion as possible, Donovan nodded to his host.

"I will send for you in—say—twenty minutes?" Maillard said.

"I am looking forward to it," Donovan said.

Without another word, Maillard turned and stepped into the hall, closing the door behind him. Donovan cranked up the wick on the old lamp. The stacked books fascinated him. It did not seem possible they could balance as they were. He studied them more closely, checking the titles on the spines.

They were, as he'd expected, French volumes. Some were poetry, others discourse on religious and philosophical topics. He was about to turn away from them when the book dead center in the pile caught his eye, and he froze. This one was not French.

Children's and Household Tales—by the Grimm Brothers, Jacob and Wilhelm. Donovan had not seen the first English edition in many years. The chances of that book existing in this remote place, in France, were almost non-existent. Donovan knew one man who owned a copy—a copy he was never without.

Very carefully, starting at the top, barely willing to breathe lest he topple the literary tower and alert anyone who might be lingering in the hall, he began to free the volumes one by one. Despite how it had looked when he first noticed them, there was a pattern, a very intricate, almost beautiful pattern. There was an unfamiliar aura of power clinging to the books—a spell? A curse?

He willed himself to move slowly, stopping as he removed each volume to study what remained, and to get a sense of the stability. He reached for the book resting directly over the

Grimm brothers' volume, but before he could grip it there came a sound from outside the room. A footfall? Something being dropped?

He pulled back with a soft curse and quickly drew an old watch out of a pocket of his jacket. There were several stems jutting from its sides. He turned one very carefully backward. There were five soft clicks. He pressed on the end of that stem and returned the watch to his pocket. He crossed swiftly to the door and opened it.

In the hall, he saw a man in a dark suit leaning close by his door. On the floor, a tray lay in a puddle of red wine. A metal goblet rested in the center of it. The man was frozen in time, caught halfway through the motion of retrieving the glass, one hand on the wall.

Donovan only spared the man a glance, then closed the door and returned to the books. He closed his eyes, regained his focus, and removed the book directly atop the one he sought. He was about to reach out and grab it when a screech rose from the rafters above. A dark shape shot down at his hand like an arrow, and he pulled it back.

Donovan staggered away, raising his arm to protect his face. As he did so, a dark black shape slammed into the books. It was a bird. At first, he thought Asmodeus had somehow made his way into the building, but the bird was smaller. It somehow gripped the toppling volume of fairy tales in talons that should not have had the strength and lifted it from the pile.

Donovan cried out, reaching for the books, though he knew he was too far from them to stop them from falling. There was a flash and a crack like contained thunder. The remaining books simply disappeared. The bird dropped the book on the bed with a soft thump, circled the room once, and dropped to the headboard, glaring at him.

"Grimm?" Donovan said.

He pulled the watch from his pocket. Its two minute hands slowly ticked closer to one another. He dropped it back into his pocket. Working quickly, he gathered the books he had managed to remove from the pile and stacked them on the nightstand. He didn't try to balance them as they had been, though he left one or two at slight angles, so they would give the appearance of having been browsed. He grabbed the book off the bed and tucked it into a pocket in his jacket. The garment was custom made, and he'd added a few arcane touches of his own. He was able to carry a great number of oddities when he traveled, and more than once the long dark coat had saved his life.

There was another sound at the door, and without speaking, Donovan gestured toward the ceiling with his chin. Grimm glared at him a moment longer, as if chastising him for carelessness, then launched back to the rafters and out of sight. Donovan crossed to the door once more and opened it. The man stood in the hall, the tray back on his arm, the goblet standing atop it.

"Very sorry sir," the man said, his eyes shifting from side to side, as if he saw shadows dancing away. "I—I will fetch another glass. I was told to bring…"

"That's fine," Donovan said, forcing his rusty French to do his bidding, and doing his best to mimic the accent of his host. "I will be ready in a few moments, and I can get refreshments when I reach—do you know where I am to go?"

The man stepped further into the doorway, as if to glance into the room. Donovan matched the movement and held out a hand.

"Please," he said. "Directions?"

The man frowned, just for a second, and then something else—an expression as if the man saw some other place, or straight through him, the walls, and time, to something fascinating— passed over his features. It was so fleeting that, as with Maillard, had Donovan not been watching carefully, he would have missed it. Then the man smiled and gave a slight bow.

"Down the stairs, monsieur, and to the left. You will see the lights. You will hear the music. They are waiting for you."

Donovan returned the smile. As the man left, Donovan closed the door firmly, leaning forward to rest his head on it. He didn't know why he had worried that the man would see the disturbed stack of books or catch a glimpse of Grimm, but his heart pounded. Something was very, very wrong. He concentrated, trying to remember exactly what he'd seen in the other man's eyes, but he couldn't bring it into focus.

He took a quick mental inventory of the charms and talismans he'd managed to stuff into his pockets. Without knowing what he might face, there was no way to know if he had enough, too much, or even the right combination. It was a gamble, the sort he was very familiar with.

He tucked the ancient volume of Grimm's Fairy Tales into a pocket, straightened the collar of his jacket, and turned to the door. There was nothing to be gained by further delay—whatever awaited below.

Despite his successes, including the home and luxury he'd attained over more years than most men are granted, Donovan could not help but be impressed by the casual, decadent luxury of the place. It was in disrepair, neglected and in need of a good cleaning, but the lines and "bones" of the place were elegant. Smooth wood panels lined the lower half of the walls, and above the paneling, at eye level, he found a number of portraits—a family, he was certain, though none of them in any way resembled his host, though there was a familiarity to them. Just before he reached the top of the stairs, one of the paintings caught his eye.

Someone had altered it. There were recent brush strokes. They angled the pupils of the eyes in a skewed manner that gave the subject, a dark-haired man in a woolen cloak, a crazed, deranged expression. There were poorly wrought tears on his cheeks, and his lips had been reddened comically—like the makeup of a clown. There were more modifications, but Donovan didn't pause to check details. Despite the alternations, it was clearly a portrait of Edgar, or someone so similar they could be twins. Something was off about the place, and he did not want whoever might be watching him to know that he had noticed.

He heard music rising from the floor below and followed the sound. Behind him, very softly, the flutter of wings shivered through his senses, and then passed. He didn't look up to see where Grimm would hide himself, but he sent the old bird a thought, concentrating and hoping their brief acquaintance would provide a link.

Asmodeus is beyond the walls. Find him. Bring him.

For an instant, he felt the world falling away. His vision

grew sharp. He gazed into rafters approaching far too swiftly as the bird took flight—and then he was alone once more. He shook his head, gripped the bannister and made his way slowly down to the lower level. He followed the main hall back until a second wing opened on his left. There were lights, and he heard music and laughter.

He stepped into a ballroom, lit by lamps and candles that provided pools of brilliant illumination amid pools of shadow. Figures moved about, some dancing, others gathered in conversation. There was a piano, but at that moment no one played. The far end of the room was lined with tables that bore bread and plates of food. A tall, slender man in a black silk hat poured wine into a long row of crystal goblets lined up on a counter while at the same time laughing and carrying on animated conversations with a steady parade of others.

Something pulsed beyond the light. Donovan could not quite place it. On one level, the room resembled many parties he'd attended, if a trifle archaic and overblown. On a deeper level, power hummed. It was difficult to pinpoint. There was no focus, no particular pattern. A spell would have had symmetry, but what he felt—what he sensed—felt almost untapped, as if it existed without purpose.

A hand fell on his shoulder, and he turned, slightly startled.

"Welcome!" Maillard said. The man's rounded face had taken on a rosy blush, and from the twin goblets he held, Donovan guessed it was more due to the wine than the celebration, whatever it might be.

"Thank you again for your hospitality," Donovan replied. "I admit, this is a bit more than I expected. Is there a special occasion?"

"Life," Maillard replied, waving one of the goblets vaguely in the air. The wine almost, but not quite, sloshed over its edge, and he brought it to his lips in an oddly graceful motion. Nothing spilled, and though he gave the impression of being slightly drunk, there was something false in the impression.

Donovan smiled. "A worthy subject," he said. "These are all your colleagues? It is a large staff for such a secluded facility."

Maillard started slightly, glanced at Donovan sidelong,

and then continued, smoothly. "No, of course not," he said. "My family resides with me, my sister, her husband, and my two brothers with their families. They assist where they can, of course, but our staff is very small. As I said, we have contained the inmates carefully. Their schedule is extremely structured. We find the less interaction they have with others, even the staff, the easier it is to keep them calm and healthy."

"So, you have given up on their treatment entirely?" Donovan asked. He couldn't help being intrigued. "It seems such an extreme turnaround from the process you described. The 'Soothing Method,' wasn't it?"

"I believe you will find more information of the sort you seek mingling with the others," Maillard said. "Each of them has had their own direct experience, and I fear that any explanation I might offer would be filtered through my own academic prejudices."

Donovan nodded. "And my friend? What of Edgar?"

"He will arrive shortly," Maillard said. "Never fear. He has been informed of your arrival and seemed quite pleased."

Without a further word, Maillard turned away and Donovan was left to make his way across the room toward the man dispensing wine. He scanned the others, catching the eye of a woman who was dressed in what would have been an elegant gown, had it fit properly, and not been torn near the hem. There was a circle of men, all dressed in evening attire, though a bit oddly colored and matched. They were deep in conversation over a book, which one of them was waving about to make some point.

As he reached the counter and the wine, the man in the silk hat winked at him and gave a slight bow.

"I am Ferdinand," he said. "My claim to fame is that my great grandfather was a fool in the court of the Emperor Napoleon. My mother, less presumptuously, sang bawdy songs in a café for tips. The answer to such a life?"

He handed over a glass of dark red wine and winked again.

Donovan could not help smiling. He took the offered drink, tipped it slightly in Ferdinand's direction, and sipped.

The wine was dry and very fine. His smile widened slightly,

though his guard never wavered.

"I am Donovan," he said. "I'm here to find my friend, Edgar, but I must admit—now that I've spoken with Dr. Maillard I find myself very intrigued."

"Life is a single intrigue, start to finish," Ferdinand said. "My mother, the painter, sketched things as she found them, transferred them to canvas and saved them. Do you know why?"

Donovan wanted to ask if the man's mother was a singer, or an artist, or both, but instead he shrugged and listened.

"They tell you that your memories are the first thing to go when you age. She wanted to keep hers, but, with so many memories, and only so much time to record them, she painted faster and faster, drew everything, carried napkins and papers, drew on her skin, until it drove her quite mad."

"How did your father react to that?" Donovan asked, uncertain what to say.

"He was a lawyer," Ferdinand replied. "He went to the courts and spoke on her behalf. He was eloquent. He told the stories of her drawings and her paintings. The court was mesmerized, and they let her go. When he was done, they could not remember why she had been arrested, and each had grabbed paper and pen, unwilling to forget what they had seen and heard, and feeling the press of age."

Donovan took another sip of the wine, and nodded, keeping his expression as controlled as possible.

A woman walked up to them and stood very still, staring straight into Donovan's curious gaze.

"She is a mirror," Ferdinand said. "What you see is your reflection. Always. My mother, the dancer, would have looked like a statue, toes pointed, arms to the sky, and my father—how he would have played for her. He was a pianist, a virtuoso—"

Donovan turned away and wandered slowly through the crowd. He did not want to hear more of Ferdinand's fabulously morphing parents, and was not interested in his reflection in the woman's eyes.

He caught Maillard's eye, on the far side of the room, and cut straight through the crowd. The threads of normality were unraveling rapidly. He saw a woman barking like a dog, and she shivered and backed away as he passed. He saw a man playing percussive beats on another man's head, and though it was not possible, heard the sharp snare-beat rhythms ringing out. A woman whirled like a top on one toe, so rapidly she seemed to glide across the floor. He stepped aside as she passed, stepped up beside Maillard, and tapped the man on the shoulder.

"My friend," he said. "I believe you said he would be in attendance?"

Maillard grinned. There was little of sanity in his expression, and yet it was cunning and cruel.

"And so he shall be," the man replied. "I really am quite happy to have you here, because, you see, we have something of a conundrum to be solved. A mystery. Do you like a good mystery, Monsieur DeChance?"

Donovan met Maillard's gaze but opted for silence. He sipped his drink.

"It seems," Maillard continued, "that our experimental treatment methods have brought about some rather unique results. I'm sure you recall?"

"Allowing delusions to run their course freely? Encouraging them?"

He managed not to glance at the bartender, who he heard in the periphery explaining to another guest the story of his mother, the author, and his father, who had stood by her side, replacing each sheet of paper as she completed the last and carefully stacking them for presentation to the Queen.

"Exactly," Maillard beamed. "Exactly. And what would you say if we allowed this encouragement to one man, a very unsettled man, who believed he was—two men—and then? Well, let me show you."

Donovan turned slowly. Curtains had been drawn across one exit from the room. They began rolling slowly to the sides, pulled by men in incredibly ill-fitting suits. Their motions were clumsy and erratic. He ignored them and concentrated.

A small group of men walked through the now open archway as the suited men stood solemnly, holding the curtains aside. As they approached, Donovan saw they held two men between them. One was long-haired, wild-eyed and glared about himself crazily. The other, slightly more well-groomed, watched the proceedings with a curious, but detached expression. Donovan knew that face—those eyes—they were haunted and dark—but they belonged to Edgar Allan Poe.

The second man, despite his crazed aspect, was a dead ringer for his fellow captive. His dress was more appropriate to the period, but there was no mistaking the features, the carriage—or the eyes. Had Donovan been confronted with this man alone, he might have been fooled.

Donovan turned from the spectacle to his host. He eased his grip on the glass in his hand, fearing the whitening of his knuckles would give him away. Fearing to ask the wrong thing, he raised an eyebrow.

"You see?" Maillard said, waving an arm at the two captives, who by this time had been brought to stand directly before them. "A conundrum! An impossibility! The man who claimed that he was actually two men has made good on his promise."

Donovan turned first to the crazed man, and then to Edgar, but he did not speak. Instead, he sipped his drink and contemplated the situation. It was, as his host had said, a conundrum. What he had walked into was a story, or, rather it would be a story eventually. He had come uninvited, and yet, if he judged wrong—and his presence was intentional—he was uncertain what danger he might put his friend—and himself—in the way of.

"There is certainly a deep resemblance," he said at last. "Though one seems to have been here longer, and their dress is dissimilar."

"Yes, yes indeed," Maillard said. The man rose up on his toes as he said this, then dropped back down, like an excited child.

The bartender stepped up beside Donovan, staring past him to the prisoners. He took Donovan's glass and replaced with a full one, then leaned in close.

"My mother studied the new art of photography," he whispered. "She would have captured this and called it 'mirror'." My father was a chemist and he could have developed the film—a new art form, you know? A moment in time."

Donovan ignored the bartender, and spoke to Maillard. "You say this was his delusion, then?" He said, sipping his drink. "I mean to say—before there were—two—he spoke often of this division, and then he walked arm in arm with his doppelganger through the grounds?"

Maillard's face darkened for an instant, then it passed.

"Not so much that he spoke of it," he said. "Nor do I recall conversations with empty air, and yet, you see the result?"

Donovan nodded, feeling his way carefully through the intricate conversation. "I do," he said. "I am just uncertain the result of what. Magic? Perhaps a creature has walked from another dimension? A shapeshifter?"

Maillard cocked an eye and turned to stare.

"I am a man of science, sir, and of medicine. Surely you don't countenance such thoughts."

"Priests recognize the supernatural," Donovan said. "Healers and shysters have walked the roads for all the days of civilized men. Science accepts what is new, when it is proven, yes?"

"Two very similar men, in one place, is—I grant you— remarkable," Maillard said, "but hardly proof of magic."

"Agreed," Donovan said. "And yet, what if I were able to offer you a sign?"

It was the moment of truth. The entire room had fallen silent, whether by some quietly spread command, or by the arrival of the two men, it was impossible to tell. Even the bartender, who hovered nearby, eager to spread the details of his mother, and father's endless lives, held his tongue, eyes bright with anticipation. Either Donovan had over-stepped, and was about to fight for his life, and Edgar's, or a very strange evening was about to twist to the truly bizarre.

"An experiment, then?" Maillard said. The words broke the almost total silence and hung there. Like bait.

"If you say so," Donovan replied. "An experiment is a thing, that—once performed—must be tested a second time, yes? You find your result, but then you perform your test a second time to be certain you have not achieved a false result?"

"Exactly as you say!" Maillard said, clapping. He performed a small, wholly ridiculous dance step then, before composing himself. "What do you propose?"

"One of these men," Donovan said, "is your patient. One of them, as you have no doubt gathered, is my friend. I could merely point and tell you the answer, but you do not know me, and who knows? I might be as crazy as the rest."

"That thought had already occurred," Maillard said. "You must admit, it is an oddity, your friend finding his way to my door and the circumstances to follow. And then, on his heels—there is you."

"Of course," Donovan replied. "But then, I am equally taken aback by your patient, who appears to be little more than a captive—and his resemblance to my friend. I came only hoping to reunite with a comrade, but it seems I have found—"

Donovan was interrupted by the presence of a woman. Her makeup was light, with hints of blue and purple on one side of her face, but gold and highlighted in yellow on the other, so that if you looked at her in profile, and then she turned, you might think her a different person. She leaned in.

"It's a conundrum," she pronounced, her voice and gaze very serious.

Donovan nodded and tipped his glass in her direction. "Exactly so."

"Then let us solve this," Maillard said. His eyes twinkled, and he could barely contain some emotion—glee? Rage? "Let us see your sign, and then, we shall see if it repeats itself, and gives us scientific proof of magic."

Donovan had little time to plan. There were any number of signs he could have provided, and given a truly dangerous situation, he was certain he could get himself, and Edgar, free of this place, but what he really wanted was a simple, effective, and non-violent solution. He was fingering the objects in his pocket with his free hand when he heard a soft flutter, and the answer flickered to life in his mind.

He reached out with his thoughts, praying for the familiar connection. What he found was close, but not exact. It took only a second to realize it was Grimm. He tried again, stretching the limits of his mind, seeking the touch of Asmodeus' quick, sharp thoughts. He felt something, the slightest itch, but then Maillard was speaking, and he dropped back into the present.

"Your sign, Mr. DeChance?" Maillard said. "We do have a dinner to get on with."

Donovan took a deep breath, sent a single thought with all the strength he possessed, and then nodded to Maillard.

"Of course," he said. "I will offer a sign, and that sign will show you the truth of which of these," he gestured to Edgar, who stood watching him coolly—eyes bright—and to the other man, whose crazed features were twisted in a pleading, desperate expression. The man made no sound, and Donovan surmised that there would be a swift and violent punishment if that silence was broken.

Raising his eyes to the vaulted ceilings, and then his hands, careful not to spill his drink, Donovan lowered his voice to a deep, theatrical tone and said—simply—"Behold!"

For just a second, nothing happened. Maillard looked at him, a smile beginning to curl the corners of his mouth. Then, as if from thin air, a dark form dropped from above with loud cry. With a solid *thunk*, Grimm landed on Edgar's shoulder, gripped the now ragged material of his coat, and stood, glaring around at those gathered in open disdain.

Maillard took a step back, eyes wide. His drink sloshed onto the end of his sleeve, and he glared down at it accusingly, then he turned to Donovan.

"That is a good trick," he said. "I have seen this bird flitting around the rafters, but I have no idea how you tamed it."

"I did nothing," Donovan said. "You stood beside me the entire time. I said that I would give you a sign, and, as you can see, one has been provided."

There was a light ripple of voices, and a very subdued wave of applause, which was stifled by Maillard's scrutiny. However free this group appeared, any direction Maillard turned, the silence could be sliced with a blade.

"So it would seem," Maillard said at last. "It is truly unfortunate for you, however, that there is a second part to your scientific proof of magic. You have provided what might be a sign, and also might be a very clever ruse. As I say, I know that the bird was already here. Now we shall put this to the test; it is time for a second sign."

Donovan was barely paying attention. Every tendril of thought and will at his command was stretched out, calling and listening. At first, there was nothing, and he feared he was going to have to shift his plan to a more active method of escape. Then, very suddenly, Asmodeus linked with him.

It was sudden, powerful, and in that instant, Donovan lost himself, and his thoughts, entirely. He felt fatigue, a great exertion. He saw a pane of glass nearing at blinding speed. A release, and—

Far above, the silence of the moment was shattered. A window imploded, shattering and spilling shards of glass down over the food and drink in the rear of the chamber. A dark shape plummeted from that height, and Donovan, snapping to his senses in time not to fall to his knees, thought it must be Asmodeus. He cried out and reached, but he fell short of the object, which—dropping at great speed—struck Maillard's outstretched hand.

The stone shattered the man's glass. Red wine splashed into Maillard's face, over his shirt and jacket. Shards of glass shot up, and he raised his arms for protection. As he stumbled back, Asmodeus dove with a cry, and, after circling Donovan in a tight loop, landed on Edgar's free shoulder.

The room fell silent. Maillard, after taking a few steps backward, stared wild-eyed at the birds, who glared back, unblinking.

Edgar did not wait for Donovan to figure out his next step. Shaking free of the two confused attendants who had been holding him, he turned, and addressed the crowd.

"I am, indeed, two men," he said. "And one of those men you are all familiar with. I believe that it is time for this experiment to end."

He reached out, grabbed the arm of his disheveled doppelganger, and pulled him free as well. Maillard drew himself up and tried to push past the two to stand before the crowd. Donovan stepped over, took him by the arm, and held him, ready in case he needed to act. Edgar ignored the man and continued.

"The 'Soothing Method' has not brought about the desired result. Dr. Maillard has shown great patience, but it is time to resume treatment. It is time for this party to come to an end."

"Nonsense," Maillard bellowed. "We—"

Edgar spun on the man.

"That will be enough from you," he said. "You least of all have benefited from this charade. I have consulted with Dr. Maillard," he gestured to his twin, who had finally begun to gather his wits, "and we agree that there is another method we may try, a way to steer you back toward health. It is rarer still than the Soothing Method, but much simpler in its application."

"What—what do you mean," the man stammered.

Donovan watched now with interest. The man he had known as Maillard, who had been so confident and boisterous, deflated before his eyes to a state of conflicted emotion. The guise he'd worn flickered in short bursts across his features, but could not gain a solid hold, giving way to confusion and even fear.

"It is a method developed by some former colleagues of mine—you may have heard of them. Dr. Tarr and Professor Fether. It is a jarring experience, I am told, to undergo their treatment, but its efficacy cannot be doubted. I know that you truly want to heal, so I will leave that to the real Dr. Maillard."

Edgar turned then, and found the bartender standing beside him with a tray. On the tray were three goblets of wine. Edgar took one, handed it to Maillard, and took the second for himself. The bartender stepped over to Donovan and offered the third. Donovan set his now empty goblet on the tray, took a full one, and smiled.

"My mother raised chickens," the bartender said. "She would sprinkle feed for them every morning and afternoon and gather their eggs. My father patched roofs. He would follow her around, gathering each and every fallen feather, saving them to create a mattress and pillows so that she might sleep comfortably. One day, while she carried a bundle of down toward storage, a bucket of his tar spilled from the roof, striking her—and her burden. The tar was very hot, and she died as they tried removing the feathers from her skin."

The true Maillard shook his head, as if waking from a long, dark dream. He called out to two of the men who had served as attendants. It was not clear whether they were patients, or worked for him, but they listened. Moments later, their host of a few moments before was being escorted off to a locked room. The "guests" milled about, unable to regain the momentum of either gaiety or laughter. The music had ceased altogether.

"You will be able to contain them?" Edgar asked, turning to Maillard.

The man nodded. He looked as if he had not bathed, or slept, in days, but his expression was serious.

"There are enough of my staff mixed in here, and enough patients who believe they are staff, for the moment, to get things back under control. I have no idea who you are," he said to Donovan. "or you—" he turned to Edgar, "but I thank you both. Without your assistance, I am not certain how all of this might have ended."

"I suspect that the world is not yet ready for something as advanced as 'The Soothing Method'," Donovan said. "I am not certain that it ever *will* be ready."

Maillard nodded distractedly, already glancing around the room, searching out those who would be most helpful.

"You will excuse us if we do not tarry?" Edgar cut in. "I trust that you have things under control, and still, I will feel better once beyond the doors and on the road."

Maillard held out his hand, and Edgar shook it. Donovan's eyes unfocused, just for a moment, when the two touched. It was as if they shifted in and out of phase with the light, their hands sinking into one another's flesh, then withdrawing.

"Of course," Maillard said. "I trust you can find your way to the door? I do not know how you will call for a carriage."

"We'll be fine," Edgar said.

As if to emphasize this, Asmodeus hopped off Edgar's shoulder and landed with a plop on Donovan's. The bird cawed softly.

"Yes, yes," Donovan said.

With a final glance at the room and its odd occupants, now

suddenly confused and disjointed, Donovan turned away, and Edgar followed. They made their way through the hall, the sounds from the ballroom fading as they made their exit in silence. The silence held until they were well down the path where the door opened back into the passageway and its ornate, wooden doorways. Finally, Donovan spoke.

"It has been a long time, Edgar," he said.

"Indeed," Poe said, taking in his companion wearily. Incarceration had taken its toll on him, but his stride was strong and steady. "What in the world brought you here, at this moment?"

"I wish it were a pleasure visit," Donovan said. "And I suppose, in a way, that it is, but we need your help. We are going to try and free Lenore, and we are going to rescue the princess."

"We?" Edgar said. "You and the bird?"

"And others," Donovan said. "It's a rather long story, and you look as if you could use some rest. What do you say we stop by your study, that you gather what you may need, and get back to my time and to a hotel?"

"The Lake Drummond?" Edgar asked.

Donovan shook his head. "Long destroyed and nearly forgotten," he said. "But there are others. As I said, it is a very long story."

Chapter Ten

Amethyst rolled into Old Mill slowly. There was a bridge across the Perquiman's river, a very old one, and then you swung around slowly to get a view of the one main "downtown" street. There were a number of antique shops, a barber shop with an honest-to-god whirling peppermint-stick sign out front, and even a drugstore with a soda fountain. If you found yourself there without any context, you might start believing in time travel. Driving in, after recent events, it felt oddly comforting to hit such a wall of apparent normality.

She knew it was a façade, for the most part. Too many strange things had happened in Old Mill in recent years, most of them involving the man she was coming to meet, Cletus J. Diggs, for anyone to believe the lie. Everything from elder gods, to vampires, to living breathing dinosaurs had turned up in or around the sleepy little town, and she remembered hearing Donovan say once that Mack, the Internet scanning computer genius behind the O.C.L.T. data network, claimed the Great Dismal Swamp, and this town in particular, came up on his oddball searches more often than almost any other spot on the globe. Bullfinch said it was a massive crossing point for the Earth's ley lines.

Whatever it was, she felt the energy of the place. It tingled through the soft hairs on her arms and warmed the many crystals she wore. She felt like a battery, and the world was recharging her. She wondered where Donovan was, and what he was doing, but shook it off. Cleo, seated in the passenger seat, caught her thought and let loose a soft meow of commiseration. It was never easy for a bonded familiar to be away from their companion. Thankfully, the bond that Amethyst and Donovan shared had gone beyond emotion, so she was a suitable surrogate. She was also happy for the companionship.

There was a small coffee shop on the right, The Daily Grind. Amethyst pulled over and parked behind a beat-up old Ford Bronco. She was early, and she took a moment to get a better look at her surroundings. Down the street, standing on the corner, a tall black man in camouflage pants and shirt stood, a ball cap tilted down over one eye.

"You'd better wait here, for now," Amethyst said to Cleo. "Not sure what they'd think of someone walking in with you, and I'm likely to stand out enough here without any help."

Cleo returned her gaze. She couldn't tell if the cat was miffed, or just accepting. But without complaint, the cat dropped to the floor, out of sight from the street, and curled into a small, furry ball.

Amethyst climbed out of the dark, nondescript SUV, closed the door behind her, and clicked the door lock button on the key fob. The left window on the passenger side was cracked only slightly. She wasn't worried so much about anyone breaking in as she was about what Cleo might do to them if they were stupid enough to try.

Inside, four men and one old woman with gray hair and a cowboy hat tilted back on her head sat at the counter. They were all nursing coffee and nibbling at an assortment of donuts, bagels, and toast. The air was thick with the scents of fried bacon and stale tobacco. Either modern no-smoking laws had not quite taken hold in Old Mill or the walls, floor, and ceiling were so permeated with the stench that it could not be excised by any combination of elbow grease and cleaning compounds.

In a booth along the left wall, beneath a string of black and white photos depicting a variety of vintage scenes, baseball teams, local businesses, autographed shots of visiting celebrities and framed, yellowed and faded newspaper headlines, a man sat reading a newspaper and sipping black coffee.

As Amethyst came through the door, he glanced up, smiled, folded his paper and stood, offering his hand.

"You must be Amethyst," he said. "I'm Cletus Diggs."

She smiled and took his hand.

"Am I that obvious? What gave me away?"

"Well, I've haven't seen so many crystals in one place since the last flea market," he said. "But to be honest, everyone in Old Mill knows everyone else, and most of their relatives. If you go as far as Hertford, Winfall, or Elizabeth City you might find someone not related, or who is the center of some sort of local gossip, but nothing like you. Besides," he added, "Donovan talked about you. A lot."

"He'd better," Amethyst said.

She slid into the booth across from where he'd been sitting, and Cletus waved at the tall, thin woman behind the counter, who grabbed another cup and a pot of coffee and hurried over. Apparently, Cletus wasn't the only person who'd noticed something interesting.

"That's Iris," Cletus said, returning to his seat. "If we let her get started, she's going to ask you a thousand questions. Let me handle this."

Amethyst nodded and grinned. After the adventures of the past week or so, she was ready for something a little calmer. This was beginning to feel like it fit the bill. She leaned back and watched as Cletus rose once more, cutting the waitress off about two feet short of the booth. He took the coffee pot from her hand before she knew it was happening.

"Thank you darlin'," he said with a bright smile. "I was going to call you for a refill, but you beat me to it."

Iris tried to sidestep him and make for the table, but Cletus shifted casually, making the motion seem almost accidental. She bumped into him and glanced up in irritation.

"It's a personal thing," he said, leaning close. "She an old family friend, and there are problems. *Man* problems."

Iris' eyes widened.

"He's gone off and left her alone—it's work, but there are issues. You would not believe. Let me get some coffee into her and see what I can do? I *promise* I will come back and tell you everything when it's just you and me. I know I can trust you to keep secrets, but them?" he nodded toward the counter, and the other patrons, all of whom had turned slightly but were pretending not to be watching the confrontation.

Iris' expression shifted instantly. She nodded, gave Amethyst a sympathetic glance, and patted Cletus on the shoulder. She handed him the empty cup, and he leaned in, giving her a quick hug, while somehow managing not to spill the pot of coffee. Iris made her way slowly back toward the counter, and Cletus slid back into the booth, poured Amethyst a cup of coffee, and topped off his own, setting the pot aside.

"We won't stay long," he said. "Something tells me privacy is going to be an issue."

"I'll have to get to the bed and breakfast before long," Amethyst said. "I have a package coming in. I'm hoping it will be here in time. I didn't really plan on this extra side-trip when we left San Valencez, and there are a few things I might need. Also, since I have a little insight on your friend, Nettie, I ordered in something special."

"I hope it's not some weird, California small batch or something," Cletus said. "Her tastes are a little simpler."

"Never fear," Amethyst said. "The bottle I will have is small, and it's filled—mostly—with Old Crow. I had it shipped from an old friend, a man—I suppose he's still a man—named Johndrow. He had a lot in common with some others you know—Kali and Vein?"

Cletus raised an eyebrow.

"Johndrow has a wine cellar you would not believe, every vintage known to history, I think, in some variation or other. He also has several fine liquors, some cognacs, and a variety of other things picked up over the years and tucked away for the odd occasion. This small bottle is one. Johndrow owed me a favor."

"I've heard Donovan talk about that," Cletus said. "I don't think Nettie would appreciate blood-infused whiskey very much, no matter whose it was."

Amethyst laughed.

"Nothing like that," she said. "Did you know that the whiskey that became Old Crow was brewed first in Kentucky in the 1830s? When James C. Crow died, they continued to distill bourbon using his recipe, but the process? That died with the creator. There was a great deal of that whiskey left at the time—1848—but over the years, it became scarce. It's now one of the holy grails of bourbon, created using that lost recipe and distilled near the earth, by hand."

"Are you telling me you have some of that coming?"

"I am. Enough for three glasses, if you'd care to join me? I don't really need an introduction, but something tells me you should be part of this. Intuition, I suppose. I have flashes of it, and they are very seldom wrong. There is something that has to be played out in that swamp, and in some way, we are both tied to it."

"I know the tree," Cletus said. "Been there many times. Used to fish there, before they put in the State Park and fenced it off. That's likely to be a bit of a problem, getting in."

"I doubt if there is anywhere in the swamp Nettie can't get us to," Amethyst said. "Also, Donovan may have told you that I am not exactly helpless."

"He might have mentioned that," Cletus said. "What do you say we finish this coffee and get out of here then. We won't want to go out to that shack much before sunset, but it will give you a chance to unpack and settle in."

"I hope they aren't going to mind Cleo, Donovan's cat," Amethyst said. "I don't know if Donovan mentioned it when he booked the room, but she's with me. He took Asmodeus."

"That crow?" Cletus said.

"He's actually a raven, and quite a bit older than either of us. Probably even older than Donovan, and let me tell you, that's a rabbit hole you don't want to go down without a stiff drink."

"I'll take your word on that, though it might make an interesting bet if he's in the same league with Nettie."

"He's not," Amethyst said, draining her coffee and standing. "I have heard the story. He could have bought that Old Crow from James C. Crow himself, but Nettie? How old is your swamp, Cletus?"

Cletus took that in, shook his head, and dropped a five-dollar bill on the table next to the coffee pot.

"You know," he said, "things like this happen to me way too often. Most times, it seems as if the universe is just desperate to keep me from going fishing. I know I'm going to regret it, but I'm in. I've been drinking Old Crow for years, but something tells me I've never seen anything like what you're talking about."

"Probably never will again," Amethyst said. "But that's what makes it special."

Cletus laughed. "You follow me in to the bed and breakfast. I'm gonna have to sweet talk Lila to get that cat into your room."

"I wouldn't call Cleo 'that cat' where she can hear," Amethyst said.

"Duly noted, and no offense intended," Cletus said. "I've had my ass saved by a double-D-Goddamned Cockatiel, run afoul of a freaking dinosaur, communed with some sort of holy deer—and you haven't even met Dog. In my life, the borders between humans and animals? They barely exist. Remind me to tell you about the albino twins who tried to transplant a deer's head on a man's body and resurrect the "Great Horned God."

"Now *that* sounds like a story."

Waving at Iris, they turned toward the door and the street beyond.

It took very little convincing for Lila to agree to let Cleo stay in the room. Cleo, her own best ambassador, leaped out of Amethyst's arms and onto the counter, butting her head into Lila's arm with a loud purr. Things went very smoothly from that point on. The expected package was waiting behind the counter.

"Never seen that delivery man before," Lila told them. "Strangest thing. The truck was the same as always, and he was so nice, but then, an hour later, the regular guy, Earl, from over to Edenton? He pulled into the driveway and brought in three more packages. When I asked him about the first driver, he just stared at me like I was crazy."

"Probably breaking in a new guy," Cletus said. "Maybe ol' Earl's worried about the competition."

"He ought to be," Lila sniffed. "That new guy was handsome! Blonde hair and looked like he could have run all the way from Edenton carrying that package. And do you know what he did?"

She waited, and with a chuckle, Cletus shrugged. "What?" he asked.

"Why, he fixed my dang printer!" she said. "Took one look at the lights on the front, tapped some stuff into my terminal, and away it went. It had been giving me heck for three days!"

Amethyst glanced at Cletus, who shrugged again.

"I'd say that's going above and beyond," he said. "Wish he'd deliver something to my trailer. My fax machine has been on the fritz for weeks."

After a few more moments, and with a printout of her receipt in hand, she and Cletus headed upstairs to her room. Cleo had hopped up onto her shoulder and curled around her neck like some sort of living stole, content and purring. When they were out of Lila's earshot, Amethyst let out a short laugh.

"I sent my request for supplies through Bullfinch," she said. "I didn't think he'd have Mack deliver the package in person."

"That one is unpredictable," Cletus said. "Guy has his face buried in a computer more than anyone I've ever known, but damned if he couldn't run here from Edenton, and keep going. Wonder why he didn't stay?"

"He's tracking Geoffrey and the others," she said. "He is always connected, but to really keep track of things, he needs to be in Denver. He's probably halfway back there by now. They have some seriously buffed-up private jets."

Cletus shook his head again. "Bought my laptop at Walmart about five years ago. That guy scares me. I'll tell you though, you spend much time around those folks, you begin to see the serious advantage of a team."

"Yeah, but I'm not really much of a team player. Donovan feels the same. He has been around a long time and has serious issues with organized leadership."

"Can't fault him for that," Cletus said. "You could spend a week of Sundays looking for an honest local politician in Old Mill. Closest you'd come is ol' Bob, the Sheriff, but he has to get riled up to show it. So, what else you got in that box?"

"A girl has to have her secrets," Amethyst said. "I expect you'll know before we're done with this. Come on, you can watch TV or something while I get cleaned up and ready for this evening. Just in case we end up stomping through the swamp, I'd better get dressed for the occasion."

"Tell you what," Cletus said. "You go ahead and get ready. I'm going to run into town and pick up a couple of things myself. I can be back here in, say, two hours? That puts us about half an hour before sunset. We don't want to arrive too soon, or too late. The Great Dismal—sometimes it's just a swamp. Other times? Best not to think about that. I'll feel better if Nettie is there, but at the same time—that lady gives me the willies."

"I know you have a history," Amethyst said. "I hope before I leave, I'll have time to get some of those stories. Especially the one with the albino twins."

"It's a deal," Cletus said. "You can tell me what it's like living with that Magic Man out in California. He dragged double-D goddamned vampires here—but you know that. If I hadn't seen all the things I've seen…"

"I know the drill," Amethyst said. "I have other stories too. I haven't always lived in California, and I haven't always known Donovan. I learned what I know from my mother, who dragged me on some adventures that would curl every hair on your body. I had to learn young and fast how to take care of myself, and there was more to worry about than teenaged boys and a drunken father. In my world, the Boogey men were all-too real."

"Well, see if you can keep them out of your room," Cletus said. "And, if you don't mind, keep them as far away from me as you can. I'm on the kind of serious run of good luck with things like that that only ends in snake eyes and all your money going to the house, if you keep betting on it."

Amethyst laughed.

"Get back as soon as you can, I'll tell you one of those stories while you drive us out to that shack."

Cletus tipped the brim of his ball cap and turned back toward the parking lot. He wanted to pick up his gun, not that it ever did him any good, and to make sure Dog had plenty of food. His life had taken a lot of odd turns. If he could ever get enough time and courage together, he thought Willow over at the Cotton Gin might agree to the beginnings of a relationship. He had a dog—another long story involving decapitated animals and crazy people—and now? Now he was fixing to wander back out into that damned swamp again with not one, but *two* confirmed witches, or whatever they were—and likely a third he had failed to mention to Amethyst.

Cletus' first encounter with Nettie had led down a very strange, surreal trail that had ended with some very intimate memories that might, or might not, have happened with a younger woman who might, or might not, have been Nettie. (At the time, Cletus had been channeling parts of his own father.) Ever since that night, when he got close enough to meet with the old woman, a younger girl was there as well. She was young, but still seemed too old to be in any way connected to that dark night, but then, nothing in the swamp, or Old Mill, for that matter, was ever exactly what it seemed to be.

He pulled back out onto Hwy 17 and headed toward home. The One-Stop in Hertford was open, and he figured he could stop by there for beer and some kind of snacks. Nettie might show up right away, or she might take her time. He might get that story he'd been promised, and he thought, just once, hearing about someone else's weird-ass life might be just the ticket.

Chapter Eleven

Amethyst glanced over at Cletus and raised an eyebrow when he popped the top on a beer and offered it to her. They were bouncing slowly down a shadowed back road toward the swamp. He winked, and she took it.

"Things work a little different out here," he said. "Normally, my truck is a no-drink zone, but this is going to be one of those nights, and I thought it might be easier to get that story out of you if I gave you a little liquid incentive."

"Trying to get me drunk?" she said. "Donovan is not going to like that."

"Not at all. I have heard a few stories about you already, you know. You and the Magic Man are well-suited for one another. Believe it or not, I actually go out of my way to avoid the weird. Still, kind of glad his cat didn't come with us. Something about the way it watches me—it's like the Magic Man was standing there behind it."

"Her," Amethyst said. "Cleo has a mind of her own, but yes, the two are linked. I thought she might come along, but when we stepped outside, she turned, and she was gone."

"Is that safe?" Cletus asked. "There are a lot of animals around here, some of them not too friendly, and kids…"

Amethyst laughed.

"Cleo can take care of herself—has been doing so for longer than I'd care to imagine. If she thought there was any danger to me—or to you—she'd be with us."

"Guess that makes me feel better then," Cletus said. "But what about you? I'd be lying if I didn't admit I was curious."

"Fair enough. My story is definitely -different. Donovan is

the only other person I've ever told this, and I'm not sure why I feel the urge to talk tonight. Maybe it's just being so far away from anyone that I really know, and a little bit worried about Donovan, and Edgar."

"I've been involved in several nights like this," Cletus said. "I have found that what I might have thought, or wanted, going in has very seldom had much impact on what I did or said. Probably best to go with your gut, for lack of a fancier term."

Amethyst nodded.

"The first time I knew I was different—weird—I was five years old. My father was off drinking—something he did when my mom was doing her "crazy witch crap," and mom had set me up to watch a movie in the family room and headed down to the basement where she had her altar, books, and other things. Daddy never went down there, and I was only ever allowed to come to the head of the stairs, and only then when she was not working. At the time, it just made me more curious, but now I know she was trying to protect me."

"From your father?" Cletus asked.

"No, from what she was doing. Most of the work she did, unlike most of what I can do, was performed within the protection of a magical circle—sort of a fence against evil. Donovan uses them when he interacts with anything truly powerful. She worked in the center of a circle that protected her, and beyond that was a concentric circle intended to keep whatever she might summon from escaping into the house—or the world."

"Huh," Cletus said. "In the movies they usually put the demon or whatever inside the circle."

"There are a lot of different methods. Few of them are even close to what you'll see coming out of Hollywood, though occasionally a writer with a bit of knowledge lets some actual ritual slip through the veil. There are things you want to contain, and things you want to keep out. Anyway, she didn't want me involved in her world—at least not then. Things took a different turn that day, though. I guess I'm lucky to be here talking to you about it.

"The movie had just started. I was alone on the couch,

settling in, and I felt something like fingers running through the hairs on the back of my neck. I think my hair actually lifted a little, like it would if there was a big field of static electricity, but that memory isn't clear enough for me to be certain. I just knew something was happening, and that I wanted to know what it was.

"I opened that basement door and started down the stairs. The TV was on pretty loud, but for some reason the slight rise in volume when the door opened didn't alert my mother. She was probably already engaged in the spell, chanting, and reaching out for her power. Whatever the reason, she didn't notice, and I crept down those stairs as quietly as possible, feeling the air around me get stranger and sort of—thicker—as I went.

"I knew the voice I heard was my mothers, and that probably gave me some courage. I had never been hurt by anything, other than the constant fights between my mother and father over her magic—and his drinking. Even those were sort of background noise, because they were both kind to me, and I believe, deep down, they were very much in love. Worlds colliding, and all that.

"But even though I wasn't really scared, I knew something other-than-normal was happening in the basement. When I'd been down there before, the lights burned steadily—not bright, but—you know—normal. That day they were flickering, and a light shade of blue.

"I remember reaching out and running my fingers through that air—it seemed as if whatever was there, whatever was glowing, I could touch it. I felt it tickling my skin as I continued down the stairs.

"I wanted to call out, to let her know I was coming, but I knew mother would be angry if I disturbed her, and I didn't want that. I just wanted to peek around the corner at the bottom of the stairs and see what she was doing—

—this is where the story gets a little weird."

Cletus laughed.

"Well, I'm glad you told me that, because I was starting to think nothing interesting was going to happen at all."

"I warned you," she said.

"By the time I reached the bottom of the stairs, my mother's voice was very loud. I had heard her yelling before, but this was different. She seemed to be speaking normally. There was no rise in her tone, or screech, but the volume increased like you'd turned up some cosmic volume knob.

"I was only going to stick my head around that corner, but on the last step I tripped. I tried to catch myself on the railing or the wall, but it was too late. I stumbled forward. For some reason, I didn't fall. I had the sense that the air—that glowing, blue air—held me up and gave me back my balance.

"What I saw brought me up short. My mother knelt on the stone floor of the basement in her circle. I'd seen that before. Her arms were raised over her head, fingers twisting and turning through the air. Her eyes were closed, and tendrils of the blue light, much brighter than the air, almost like flickers of lightning, extended form her fingertips to some border that rose from the floor upward. I sensed it went far beyond the ceiling and into some other place...

"She didn't notice me at first, and even though I was fascinated by what she was doing, my attention was caught by something just beyond her force wall—something dark and wispy like smoke with flames flickering inside. The memory is very clear—probably because of the intensity of the moment and what came next.

"I didn't know what that force was, that dark shadow, but I saw my mother, and I saw it whirling around her, like she was in the middle of a circular fishbowl of some sort, and it was swimming between glass walls. I felt its hatred, and its fear. I know now that it was the source of that, but at the time I associated those sensations with my mother.

"I didn't think. I ran at that wall from the outside, where the second circle surrounded the thing. I put my hands against the surface of a wall of force—a wall that should not have been there. I closed my eyes, and I screamed. Not just a sound, or a screech. I screamed a single word: No!

"Things happened very quickly then. I felt an incredible surge of—something. The blue light sort of engulfed me. It flowed out from my mother into the inner ring of that wall and—somehow—I connected with it from beyond the outer ring. The thing in the center swirled faster, so fast that the flames I'd seen dancing in its depths became tiny flickering sparks, like glitter caught in a tornado. It just got faster and faster. I looked at my mother, and she caught my gaze. She was scared, but, at the same time, I saw something else—surprise?

"Then, that thing that separated us vanished. It didn't go quietly. It slammed out of existence with a roar of sound and a flash of light. The inner and outer circles compressed until they met, and a second later I was tumbling forward, straight into my mother's arms. My mind blanked then, and all the lights went out."

"Was it really gone?" Cletus asked. "I mean, I know a little bit about that kind of thing, and appearances can be deceiving."

"It was. I didn't know it then, but when I woke, I was in my bed. There was a terrible pain in my chest, like something burning. My mother was there, and my father, but as soon as my eyes opened, and she brushed her hands through my hair, he left.

"I wanted to ask what had happened. I mean, I knew what I'd seen, but I didn't understand it. I had no memory of anything hurting me, just that flash of light, but I had never experienced pain like that. At five years old, it was terrifying.

"My mother pulled my nightshirt off my shoulder and gently rolled it down. Long before, against my father's wishes, she'd given me a small pendant—a garnet set in the center of a circle of agate. I thought it was pretty. My father wouldn't even look at it, but I have a vague memory of her explaining to him that her beliefs—and her work—required that I be protected."

"Why agate? And garnet?"

"I know now," she said. "I'm sure she told me then, but I was a little girl, and I was in a lot of pain. At the time, all I got was that she was very sorry, but that the pendant had protected me— only, there was more. That amulet alone wouldn't have even slowed that thing down. The thing she was excited about—the thing she was trying to explain to me—was that what happened was mostly due to me.

"She showed me the skin where that pendant had rested. It

was burned. She had bandages and salve by the bed, but she'd waited for me to wake up, so she could show me and explain. There was a dark circle on my chest, and though the garnet had been set on the front, as well as the symbols carved into the agate, their patterns had somehow been driven through the stone. It was imprinted on my skin—like a brand.

"And to answer your question, agate is a very powerful protection against evil spirits, and the garnet enhances a person's protective energy—focuses the will. She had thought if some tendril of power escaped when she was working—some unforeseen wisp of danger—the stone would deflect it from me and keep me safe."

"That's not what happened," Cletus said.

"No, not even close. When I saw my mother in what appeared to be danger, something broke free inside of me. My gift, as it turns out, is of the earth. Stones, crystals, geomancy— and my fear, and anger, combined with that talisman, literally blew that demon back to wherever she'd summoned it from. My mother could never have done that with any spell or ritual she possessed. Donovan could, but he uses a variety of spells, talismans, incantations, and wards. I've never met anyone with the sheer breadth of knowledge he's amassed.

"But that? I'm not certain I could do it again if I had to. I've learned to channel and control my power—that was an open blast of power, absolutely reckless. It could have killed me. It could have destroyed my mother, as well, but somehow it didn't, and from that moment on I was in training—for my own sake, and for that of those around me."

"I'm going to take a wild guess that didn't go over well with your father," Cletus said.

The road ahead had darkened. Trees leaned in from either side, draped with lichen and moss. The air was thick with the scents of lush vegetation and rotting leaves. The sun had dropped beyond the tops of the trees, and the headlights of the old Bronco sliced through the shadows, whipping up and back, and side to side as they navigated the rough country road.

Amethyst didn't answer at first. The memories flooding back had hit her harder than she had believed possible. It had been too long since she'd told this story, and parts of it had been hers alone as long as they had existed.

"He left." She said at last. "Not right away, but soon after that. At first, it was going to be a separation—a chance to sort out their differences so that we could move forward—but even then, I had enough of the sight to know it wasn't true. He came to see me on my birthday for a few years, sent cards and money at Christmas—but never presents. He didn't know what to get and didn't want to know. Then he was just gone. Mom and I were alone together for a very long time, though alone is probably a poor word for it. She had friends, associates, others I learned from. I had a very magical childhood, but I've always wondered…"

"What it would have been like to be a normal girl?" Cletus said softly. "I know the feeling only too well. I have never fit any of the molds of this place. I read too many books, I can spell, don't listen exclusively to Hot Country 105.9 or spend every weekend watching grown men drive too fast in circles—though I *do* spend *some* time with it. I have a few good friends, and there are few other things we have in common. Then there was the first time I met Nettie, and everything that happened after that. You know what I think?"

"What's that?"

"I think I would have been miserable any other way."

Amethyst smiled. "I believe you would, and so would I. As much as it sometimes seems difficult to be different, the things I know, the things I've seen and done? I wouldn't trade them for anything."

They broke free of the trees then. The drive leading up to the old shack was not long. There was no electricity or lighting, but the moon was bright. Cletus slowed and finally brought the truck to a halt. He killed the engine and the lights, and then sat there for a long moment, staring.

"Memories?" Amethyst asked

"Too many," he said. "A lot of water has gone by under this particular bridge. I'll tell you one day—seems only fair. Tonight, though, we have business. Kind of wish you had enough of that whiskey for more than three glasses."

"I brought this too." Amethyst pulled the bag from between her feet on the floorboard and dragged out an amber bottle. Old Grand-Dad. Cletus grinned.

"I'm starting to understand what Donovan sees in you."

Chapter Twelve

The moon had risen, and the level in the whiskey bottle had set when things began to go a little hazy. The two had mounted the steps to the old porch and taken seats facing one another across a worn, rough-hewn table. Cletus had been telling the story of Foreman James and the long, sordid history of a particular peanut factory fire. Amethyst had been sipping and listening, letting the fresh air—so different from San Valencez with the smog and exhaust—slide through her lungs. There was no noise near the swamp—though there was sound. It felt natural—it blended with the scents and soft glow of the moon. It was the natural voice of the planet, and Cletus's soft drawl matched it perfectly. There was a rustle in the brush off to the right of the shack. They both turned and saw a majestic buck step free of the trees. It stood, returned their stare for a long moment, then tossed its head with a snort, almost as if laughing at them, spun, and bolted back through the trees.

Cletus knew what he'd see even before he turned back to the table. The air had shifted. There was the scent of flowers and grass, mud and deep, cold water where a moment before he'd smelled musty planks, cheap whiskey, and the light touch of whatever perfume Amethyst wore.

Nettie grinned at him. She was now seated in the empty chair between the two of them, her back to the fence rail. Cletus didn't blink. He'd been down this road before and was just waiting to see what tree she'd jump out from behind. He noted with interest that Amethyst also showed no surprise or nervousness at the sudden change in circumstances.

"Howdy, Nettie," Cletus said. "It's been a while."

"Longer for you," she said. "I watch."

Cletus felt something uncomfortable drift down his spine but managed not to react outwardly.

"Reckon you do."

Amethyst pushed aside the Old Grand-Dad bottle and reached into her bag. She pulled out the smaller bottle, the one she'd spoken of earlier, but had yet to show him. It was a clear decanter, small, and possibly made of crystal—if not, then very fine cut glass. The stopper was sealed with wax and a symbol that was meaningless to Cletus, but it gave him the same sensation a chance encounter with a black widow spider did. He would not have touched it for all the catfish in the swamp.

The whiskey itself was darker than he was used to. It caught glimmers of light refracted through the design of the decanter and shifted colors hypnotically.

'What'd you bring old Nettie," the old woman said softly. "That bottle is damned fancy, but the whiskey—it smells of old wood and age. Not old to me, mind you, but so few things are."

"Old Crow," Amethyst said. "Not what they sell at the local ABC store, but what John Crow distilled in Kentucky before the world started shifting faster. The decanter is sealed, both against the elements and time itself. I believe that the occasion on which I seek your help demands a proper toast. If there is power in age, and in spirits, both liquid and elemental, what could serve better?"

"I knew this day would come," Nettie said. "She has lived in my swamp for many years, but she is not *of* the swamp. She sacrificed herself and saved something very precious to me. Though it has not been long when measured against my life, it has been far too long measured against her own. Nothing that I have tried has freed her. The spell that holds her is not of this place. I cannot break the binding."

"I have some thoughts on that," Amethyst said. "First things first, though. I'm not a huge fan of bourbon—it's more Donovan's thing—but I have to admit I've been curious about this ever since I learned that it existed. I've only read a few of the stories, but very famous people did very crazy things to own some of this before it became so scarce. Even then it was legendary. Having grown a lifetime in ways and places of power, I have something of a sense for when a thing is more than it seems. What do you say, shall we drink to old Jim Crow?"

"The whiskey aged in wood, soaked in kegs provided by the oak," Nettie said. "now lives in crystal, and I feel it reaching to me, and the trees, and at the same time seeking one to draw it from stone."

"What about me?" Cletus asked.

Amethyst broke the seal on the old bottle with her thumbnail, scraping away the symbol that had bothered him while breathing a single word over the top. There was the tiniest wisp of something—smoke—mist? With a quick twist she unstopped the flask and handed it to him.

"You have been the focus of many stories," she said, "but for now? You pour."

Cletus took the proffered bottle carefully. His hand shook—just for a second—but he steadied it. It would be easy to make more of this than it was, but if there was anything he'd learned in all his meetings with Nettie, if they were meant to drink they would drink, and even if he tried to spill the whiskey, it was likely he'd wake up a few minutes later with an empty glass and the last vestiges of dreams he vaguely recalled that would not seem like dreams at all.

Best to keep his senses and see if he couldn't ride it out. He tipped the small decanter, which was considerably heavier than it looked, and poured what turned out to be a nearly perfect two fingers into each of three tumblers. He thought he heard both of his companions speaking, very low, under their breath. He also thought he heard something, or someone, moving in the trees. He was certain that the wind had filled his ears with cryptic, jumbled sound. The scent of the nearly ancient whiskey cut through the odors of the swamp. His thoughts blurred, but again he steadied himself. Something told him he did not want to miss what was about to happen—that he would be needed, and not just to pour, but it took all his will power to set the bottle down carefully and slide one of the three glasses over in front of himself.

"Shall we?" Amethyst said, lifting her glass and tilting it toward the center of the table.

Nettie lifted hers as well, sliding it beneath her nose and closing her eyes before holding it out as well. Cletus tapped the edge of his tumbler against the other two with a soft clink.

"To broken seals," Amethyst said.

"And deep roots," Nettie whispered.

Without knowing why, and only vaguely remembering where the words had come from, Cletus added, "To everything we see, or seem." He tipped the glass and took a slow sip of Jim Crow's finest.

Cletus didn't see the tendrils of green and blue light that slipped from Nettie and Amethyst's drinks to wrap around one another's wrists. He didn't hear their soft gasps or sense the sudden wash of energy that pulsed around them. As he sipped his whisky, he turned, and he saw something else entirely.

First, the great buck strode out of the trees for the second time. Behind and slightly to one side, the girl followed. She had one hand on the deer's flank, and her gaze was locked on Cletus the second she moved out of the shadows.

Cletus had seen those eyes a million times, watched them reflected back at him as he shaved and winked with them at Willow over at the Cotton Gin. The girl was short, about Nettie's height, athletic and muscled. Her hair was long and golden, drifting over her shoulders and down her back.

He'd seen her several times. Every one of those times, the meeting had left him feeling uncomfortable, empty in some way he knew he could define, but was unwilling to acknowledge.

The first time Cletus had met Nettie, before the Harvest festival, he'd experienced a vision that he knew in his heart had been so much more than that. He'd seen his father. He'd *become* his father. He'd been part of a ritual so ancient that it was attended by powers that were no more than whispers by firelight, and he'd experienced the most intimate, exciting, and incredible moment of his life, but that moment had not been his. Not exactly. It had been his father's, and his grandfather's—no telling how many generations back. And he knew, in his heart, that the woman his father had lain with that impossible night, the woman he'd lain with in the shadows cast by a horned totem and the light of a burning bonfire, had been Nettie, and not Nettie, some version of her—some incarnation.

The girl—his sister? Daughter? It didn't matter. They were connected. She watched him through his own eyes and drew closer. A bow hung over her shoulder, with a soft leather quiver slung beside it.

She came within a foot of him and stopped. Then, very gently, she reached out and ran the palm of her hand against his grizzled cheek.

"One day," she said, "you will understand. You will have a child, as will I. The swamp is in your blood. Not like it is with Nettie, but strong and true. You will have a son. I look forward to meeting him."

"I've barely met you myself."

She smiled, and it was a brilliant, beautiful smile. In some way it conveyed more than a week of long conversation could have. Cletus' heart melted.

"A son?" he said.

She smiled again. She turned and returned to the buck's side. She waved gently.

"Tell Willow not to name him Jasper."

And then, she was gone. Cletus tried to turn then, to see if the others had seen, or heard, but his head was fuzzy.

Christ on a stick, he thought, *how strong is that whiskey?*

Amethyst sipped the whiskey and watched Nettie. Nettie returned that gaze with an enigmatic grin of her own. There was nothing coy about it, nothing false. When the old woman glanced over at Cletus, Amethyst did the same. He had leaned back in his chair, his eyes glazed, and was staring in the direction of the trees. Amethyst saw nothing, but there was a blurred, out-of-focus patch in the tree line, and she sensed it was a block—a veil of some sort, separating his experience from her own.

"He's fine," Nettie said. "He is talking to an old acquaintance; one he should know better than he does. Your friend—he is more a part of this swamp—of this world—than he has any notion of. The things he has seen, and the things he, and his father, and his father's father before him have sacrificed and endured, would have killed most men. It only makes him stronger."

"That doesn't surprise me," Amethyst said. "He was telling me some of what's happened on the ride out here. But we didn't come to talk about Cletus. There is another that needs our help. I believe I can free her, but I would not come into your place without your approval and would likely not succeed without your help."

Nettie took a long drink of the whiskey, then stared down into what was left.

"That dark one who came here," she said, "she was black to the core. She could not stand up to me in my home, but she still hurt me. What she did to that girl, what she did to my own, my friend—she glanced toward the woods, and there was a rustle of great antlers on leaves—is unforgiveable. For all that, I have failed. It was my magic that bound the sorceress, but she twisted it. I have tried a thousand times to free her captive, tried through the swamp, through the mists, called to her through doors that only I have seen, and I have heard her answer—but she remains trapped."

"The earth, your swamp included, is a part of me," Amethyst said. "The stones, the crystals, they speak to me and I work with them."

"She is not trapped in stone," Nettie said, frowning. "It is wood, growing, living wood, and its roots extend beyond my control, not in this world, I think, but in another. I can't break them free, and they will not bend to my will. Even if I managed to loosen those roots long enough for her to escape, the tree would take another. It's a trap. That is how she ended up in the tree."

"I know," Amethyst said. "And that is why I didn't share my plan with Donovan, or with Cletus, before coming here. I intend to let that trap take me."

Nettie's gaze didn't waver, but those old eyes narrowed. "You'll pardon my saying that sounds like a very bad plan," she said. "I don't believe I'd like to face that Magic Man of yours if he knew I let something like that happen."

"He doesn't make my decisions," Amethyst said, "but don't worry. I'm not suicidal, and I'm not planning on sacrificing myself. I had more sent out from California than just that bottle of whiskey."

"Don't underestimate this, child," Nettie said. "I know you believe you can do this—I sense it—and you may be right. You may also end up trapped in that damnable tree for the next thousand years."

"I can't leave her in there. I can't walk away. My mother taught me that every spell has a heart, that there is a central focus that binds the power. You won't find that focus on the bark of that tree, or in its leaves. But I believe I can find it and break it."

Nettie's eyes glittered.

"Broken spells are unpredictable," she said. "And dangerous."

"You know how I'm like a cocky young guy going to his first school dance?" Amethyst said, leaning forward.

Nettie frowned.

"I have protection." Amethyst said.

Nettie broke into a grin.

"Breaking that spell might be the easy part," she said. "First you have to break *in*. Lenore, she did it with her art. She had that gift, the ability to free trapped things. It was powerful magic, but it's not among my own talents."

"I have a thought about that, too," Amethyst said. "There are many ways to represent one's essence. A drawing can be a powerful link to its subject, but there are others, like a photograph taken just so, a poem written from the heart."

"Edgar!" Nettie said.

Amethyst smiled. "I have access to things. You would not believe the treasures that Donovan has locked away, the things he has collected, the gifts he's received. Among those, there was a poem. When I heard it, it was very familiar—very close to what I studied in school—and yet it was different. More powerful. I know you have read or heard, 'The Raven'."

Nettie nodded.

"You have not heard the original. Donovan is old. You will understand that better than I do. I suspect that I am destined to be long-lived. There was a drink I shared with him—a gift from a vampire—but Donovan has been old since I met him. When he met Edgar, and when he met you, he was not truly young even then."

"I am both old and young," Nettie said. "My life and my existence are cyclical, not the same as your Magic Man, but I have always been here. As long as there has been a swamp, I have been a part of it. This form is not as old, but my spirit is a part of something primal. For reasons I don't fully understand, during the ages of man I have become more and more human."

"We are better for it," Amethyst said. "And I believe that before we are done with this, your connection to the swamp, and to everything in it, will be very important to all of us. I need to see the tree. I need to study it and be near it. I need to know that Donovan is near—returning—before I complete my plan. I also need to do it before he is actually *here* because he would never allow it if he could prevent me."

"He is a wise man," Nettie said. "I do not like the thought of watching over you for the next hundred years—or more, if you fail—and are trapped."

"My power is more akin to yours than Donovan's," Amethyst said. "My connection is with the earth and the stones. Even if my initial plan is not successful, I do not believe the magic of that tree will hold me."

"I have often wondered the same," Nettie said. "If I were to break that spell and take her place."

"No doubt you would be free, and one with your swamp, as you have always been," Amethyst said. She reached out and placed a hand over the older woman's smaller, thinner fingers. "And should I need you, I know you will be there."

"Do you?" Nettie asked, her expression honestly curious.

"I do," Amethyst said.

"I believe you. As soon as you can get that man up and out of his bed, have him come get you and bring you to the tree. He knows the way. I will be there. You may not see me, but I will be watching. Take your time with her, reach out to her. When you are ready, I will know."

Amethyst nodded and squeezed Nettie's hand."

And then she was holding nothing but air.

Cletus shook his head slowly. Amethyst met his gaze. They were alone. The moon was high, and bright enough that they could see the shadows beneath the trees that surrounded them, as well as Cletus's truck. The glasses and the bottle sat on the table, empty.

"Did you see her?" Cletus asked. His words came out broken, as if they were being forced across dry sand.

"Nettie?" Amethyst asked.

"No—I—never mind," Cletus said, "I suspect you saw what you were meant to see, and it was the same for me. This place is never what you expect it to be, and still, it has always been what I needed it to be, if that makes any kind of sense."

"It does," Amethyst said. "We have to get back. I have preparations to make, and we both need sleep. Tomorrow, I'm going to want you to take me to that lake, and that tree, and I think it would be good if we were both fully awake and alert."

Cletus nodded.

"I'll be ready," he said. "Still, after what I just saw, and what I just heard, I believe I'm going to have to make a stop on the way home. "I have a message to deliver, and I'm not sure how many shots it will take before I'm ready. Hell, I don't know if there is enough whiskey in Kentucky."

"Promise me you will be good to go in the morning," Amethyst said. "This is important, maybe the most important thing I've ever done. I am going to need you."

"I'll be ready," Cletus said. "I'm always talking a good game about drinking, but the truth is, most nights I'm the guy drinking coffee before ten so he can drive home safely. The Magic Man asked me to look out for you, and I owe him a lot. I'll be ready."

Amethyst nodded and stood. She packed away the bottle, the glasses, then turned again to stare at the trees.

"I would like to know how she does that," she said softly.

"You and me both," Cletus said. "Then again, some things I'm probably a happier man not knowing. Let's get out of here."

They walked slowly back to his truck, and Cletus steered it carefully back onto the dirt road, pointing toward Highway 17 and reality. As he pulled away, a slender figure stepped from among the trees. She stood and watched as the old truck rolled into the shadows and away.

Just out of sight, a pair of bright green feline eyes stared after them, and then disappeared into the trees.

Chapter Thirteen

Donovan followed Edgar through the tunnels, trusting the other man's sure steps to guide them. Out in front, Asmodeus and Grimm flew intricate figure eights around one another, avoiding the ceiling and stone walls with ease. It was hard to tell, but even though they were both ancient creatures, Donovan thought the two might actually be playing. It made him smile. He was no spring chicken, and any reminder that age need not be a fetter was encouraging.

"I must admit," Edgar was saying," I did not expect to see you. "I believe I would have found my way out of there, eventually, but the way it turned out was certainly interesting."

"I am nothing, if not entertaining," Donovan said.

"There must be something very important to bring you so far," Edgar said. "I have walked these hidden ways alone for a very long time with only Grimm for company. My awareness of the passage of time is, at the very least, compromised, but surely it has been—"

"More than a century," Donovan said. "It has been a very long time, Edgar, and I am truly sorry that I did not seek you out sooner. It's about Eleanor. I need you to return with me to the swamp."

Edgar stopped and stood very still. The temperature seemed to drop, and the lights to dim. Donovan felt the sudden desire to slide his hand into one of the deep pockets of his long coat, just in case he needed something for protection, but he resisted the urge, and the moment passed.

"I have returned there many times," Edgar said. "I have brought artifacts and spells. I have brought charms, and I have sat on the bank of that lonely shoreline and recited my poems, told my tales, and felt nothing but the feathery touch of her presence. I have considered cutting it down with axe, or saw to free her—have even toyed with the notion of searching out a demon to purchase her freedom with what mortality remains to my soul, but I have failed. She is trapped in that tree, trapped in a story I should have understood more completely and which I should have saved her from."

"We will set her free," Donovan said. "You are not alone, and there are others waiting—others with power. The connection we need is with you. When the time comes to draw her out, you will be the anchor."

Edgar started walking again.

"We must hurry, then," he said. "I will need to stop by my study and gather some things."

"Of course," Donovan said. "Whatever is necessary."

They continued in silence, and when they reached the heavy wooden door to the study, Edgar barely hesitated. He pushed it open and stepped inside. Donovan held the door as the two birds dove gracefully through and started to follow. A few feet away, approaching quickly, came two bright green eyes fixed on him, and he stopped. Before he could say a word, or react, Cleo slipped through the door and into the room beyond. Heart hammering, Donovan followed.

Once inside, Cleo jumped immediately up onto Edgar's desk, and Asmodeus dropped beside her, glaring at her balefully. Grimm chose his own perch, on the coat rack where Edgar had hung his jacket.

"The cat," he said. "I remember her. She was there—so long ago."

"Cleo has been in this world, or some world, longer than the two of us can imagine," Donovan said. "One day I will share her story, but she should not be here. I left her with someone I love. For protection."

Donovan leaned down to stroke Cleo's ears. He closed his eyes and emptied his mind. Very softly he whispered, "Show me."

The world shifted. If he had not been ready for it, he might have fallen, but he braced himself against the desk as his perspective shifted, and he saw the world from close to the ground, moving swiftly, and then stopping.

Where he stood, mist swirled. His senses were nearly overwhelmed by scents and sounds that, had he stood in that very spot, he would not have been aware of. There was an animal musk that he somehow recognized. There was the soft perfume and light sweat of a woman. Ahead, in brighter light, there was a shack. He knew the place. He'd sat on the porch by moonlight once, a bottle of whiskey on the table.

There were three figures seated there. Cletus Diggs was staring at him, or at someone, or something just to the side of him. Amethyst and Nettie were talking. Donovan whispered a cryptic phrase in his mind. His focus narrowed. The two women's voices became clear, and he listened carefully.

"She is not trapped in stone," he heard her say. "It is wood, growing, living wood, and its roots extend beyond my control, not in this world, I think, but in another. I can't break them free, and they will not bend to my will. Even if I managed to loosen those roots long enough for her to escape, the tree would take another. It's a trap. That is how she ended up in the tree."

"I know," Amethyst said. "And that is why I didn't share my plan with Donovan, or with Cletus, before coming here. I intend to let that trap take me."

Donovan cursed softly and broke the connection, pulling back from Cleo, and the desk. He stumbled and would have fallen had Edgar not caught and supported him.

"We have to go," Donovan said. "Now."

"What did you see?" Edgar asked.

"I left someone I care about very deeply to look into Eleanor's curse. She is about to do something incredibly dangerous. I don't know if we can get there in time to stop her, but if we can, we must."

Edgar stared, just for a moment, and then nodded.

He moved around the room quickly, gathering a few books and papers and stuffing them into a worn leather pack. Donovan watched, already inching toward the door.

"I need one thing," Edgar said. "Without it, I believe we have little chance of success."

He pulled a sheaf of papers off one of the shelves, drew forth a small packet, and handed it to Donovan. Donovan read it, and then smiled, though the expression was weak and devoid of humor.

"I remember it well," he said, "and believe me when I tell you, not only do I have these words, but the one we are going to save has them as well. I have kept them safe since the day you entrusted them to me."

It was Edgar's turn to stare.

"I am flattered," he said. "It was a chance meeting. I knew you were more than you appeared, but I had no reason to suspect how much."

"I am not the only one," Donovan replied. "Everything we see or seem, eh?"

Edgar smiled thinly.

"So I have written. We must hurry then, and as we go you must tell me what has happened. I am good with a story, but I need to know the plot, and the characters to bring it to life."

Chapter Fourteen

The plane touched down at Louis Armstrong International just before noon. They avoided the major traffic and bustle, taxiing to a smaller, private hangar where they were met by a group of brown-clad workers, and a dark limousine. Bullfinch and Gunter descended a metal ladder, where they were ushered into the limo without a word.

Their bags were quickly stowed in the rear of the vehicle.

"We have a few hours," Bullfinch said. "It will not do to call on the two we are here to visit during the day. It would be impolite, at best."

"Of course," Gunter replied. His eyes twinkled with anticipation. "I must say, I was worried—quite concerned—that this might prove a bad idea. Now that we are here, though, I find I am much more curious than I am frightened. I am very eager to meet these undead."

Bullfinch laughed.

"I would contain that eagerness, my friend, and I would not call them undead, or vampire, or any of the old tropes. I would address them as Copper and Alicia. I believe you will find them very accommodating of your inquiries, but only if you can contain your exuberance."

Gunter nodded, but his smile did not waiver. "Of course. And our goal—we must keep that foremost. My studies and theories can evolve in their own time. We must learn what we can of Rathburg.

"I will need to review the data on this mission many times. The undead intrigue me, but talking birds, spirits trapped in trees? Just to understand the fundamental concepts of such a thing will take weeks, maybe a lifetime."

"You don't have to understand everything," Bullfinch said. "Now and then you can allow yourself a bit of childish wonder, or very mature awe. It's what being human is all about."

"If I don't continue to try and understand," Gunter said, his eyes wide and filled with the intensity that always set Bullfinch a bit on edge, "then I will go mad. There is so much. So many things we don't comprehend. As a mathematician, it is always on my mind. The number of years we have is an ever-diminishing quantity in the most important equation in history."

"As a man who has lived an inordinately long time," Bullfinch replied, "I can tell you that a lifetime of lifetimes will not answer all of those questions. If there were no questions, everything interesting would die."

Gunter fell silent, considering. "I believe you may be right," he said at last. "It changes nothing, but it does reduce the futility of inevitable failure."

Bullfinch laughed.

"I am glad that I could help," he said.

The limo pulled up to the curb, outside the Hotel Monteleone. Bullfinch led the way inside. It was a grand old place, not fake and glittery like so many modern hotels, but solid. Passing that threshold was like walking into another era, a sensation that Bullfinch appreciated more than most men. He remembered when the city had been young, when the gleaming white building had been new and exciting. It had aged well, as he liked to believe he had. It suited him, and he was happy to see that Gunter appeared to share his pleasure.

They checked in and took the elevators to adjoining rooms. One good thing about working for O.C.L.T. was that the funding was solid. When they had the leisure to actually stay overnight in nice accommodations, it was well-funded. Their employers included most of the world's super powers, several covert organizations, and the United Nations. Even when the mission—like this one—was not necessarily backed by a single entity, the network Mack had created, and the security elements it made available, paid for everything they needed and more several times over. None of them were in it for the money, but on the other hand, as Gunter had pointed out, life is short.

After freshening up and a short rest, Bullfinch and Gunter met in the hall outside their rooms. Gunter had a thin electronic tablet. Bullfinch carried a leather-bound notebook and several ballpoint pens protruded from his breast pocket. He felt as if these items were some sort of anachronism and wondered why he held on so tightly to his past, to a world long dead. If Gunter noticed, he did not mention it. Bullfinch sensed that the physicist spent more time inside his mind than out and wondered what it would be like to live that way, to experience so little but understand so much.

They made their way to the elevators and down to the first floor. They had arranged to meet with their guests at eight o'clock, and they did not want to be late. It was already a quarter till.

When they reached the dining room, however, they were informed that their party had already arrived and awaited them. Bullfinch frowned, shook his head, and smiled.

"It is their way," he said, turning to Gunter. "The mysterious appearance. The impossible disappearance. Keeping one guessing just what they are, and are not capable of, and what they are, and are not inclined toward. I should have known that they would surprise me. I thought they might make an entrance, but it seems, instead, that they would rather we come to them."

Gunter's eyes twinkled. "I would imagine that finding one's entertainment after so many years could become an obsession."

"Indeed," Bullfinch replied, aware of the irony. Gunter did not seem to acknowledge his own longevity in the same manner, though by this point, it must have become clear. How the man could be enamored of vampires and not question an apparently human man with centuries of memories was yet another anomaly in a long string.

They followed the host to their table, far to the rear of the dining area, window-lined, with faux marble tables, tan leather seats and lamps that appeared to be from an earlier age at each table. Seated and waiting was a tall, austere man with a mellow, light brown complexion, bright, intense eyes. Beside him sat a slightly darker skinned woman beautiful enough that, despite his years, and having been prepared for it, Bullfinch's breath caught for a moment in his throat, and he stared. He glanced to the side and noted that Gunter, who rarely showed emotion, stood blinking in surprise.

Copper rose and held out a hand, and with a great effort, Bullfinch stepped forward and shook it. He closed his eyes, just for a moment, and cleared his mind. No matter how many times he interacted with the undead, it was impossible to prepare mentally.

"Geoffrey?" Copper said. "So glad to meet you in person. I've been a fan of your writing for a very long time."

Bullfinch nodded. "I am flattered."

Alicia rose then and offered her hand. He took it and leaned down to brush his lips across her cold flesh.

"Enchanted," he said.

She laughed, and it was like tinkling bells—or a soft shattering of glass.

"Sit down," she said. "It has been a long time since anyone asked us about Rathburg or Rosa. I would say that it seems lifetimes ago, but in a way, it has been exactly that. We are not so old that we have nothing in common with you. In fact," she smiled a little more darkly, "I believe you may be a tad older than either of us."

It was Bullfinch's turn to bow slightly.

"You are probably correct," he said. "I have met many of your people over the years, and I sometimes forget that longevity still has a start and a finish."

Gunter blinked at him, then at Alicia, absolutely lost in the context.

They took the two empty seats, and the waiter, gracious and clearly impressed by the party he'd drawn, took their orders. Copper and Alicia ordered steak tartare and deep red wine. Gunter ordered steak as well, with potatoes. Bullfinch chose red beans and rice and a dark, rich beer. The fare was splendid and the service perfection.

"So," Copper said, after their drinks had been delivered, "You want to know about what happened in Rathburg? The answer to that, I'm afraid, is a very long one. So, I suppose the best first question would be, what exactly are you looking for?"

"There is a castle," Bullfinch replied. "On top of a mountain. A very long time ago, someone was abducted from that place. We are hoping to find out what you might know of it, of the family who lived there. There is a woman, older, I believe, than your Rosa, who also lived there She appears to command a good deal of magic."

Alicia smiled again, but this time more in curiosity than coquettishness. "Before Rosa? That *is* interesting. The villagers spoke of older times, of course. I heard their stories many times. I admit, my focus was always on Rosa, the moment at hand, and later, on Copper. But I may be able to help some. There are also people in the village itself who will know more, and who owe us both, possibly more than they could ever repay, though the part we played in all of it was small and happened mostly behind the scenes."

"Rosa's family lived in that castle," Copper said. "She had a sort of den in the lower levels, where she'd go to spend time with her memories."

"They were not the first generation, though," Bullfinch said. "Her family was old. Very old."

"She never spoke of anyone beyond her parents," Alicia said. "There was a sort of unspoken rule that her past was off limits, though she spent endless hours delving into ours. There was one time, though…"

Even Copper turned to Alicia at that, as if he also wanted this story from his own past for the first time as much as Bullfinch and Gunter did.

"It may, or may not mean anything," Alicia said. "She told me that her father had built a castle on the mountain, so far in the past that even her memories were blurred. She had an older sister, who disappeared at a very young age and under odd circumstances. When she was, taken—when she became what we are now—that castle had already stood a hundred years. She told me that the original palace had been torn down, destroyed by invaders, but that her father had rebuilt on its bones. By the time I saw the place, she had sealed off the main levels of the castle and created a place underneath it all, a place she'd been hoarding treasures from around the world for her own entertainment. I never saw it, was never invited that close, but she spoke of it that one time."

"Any more details on the sister?" Bullfinch asked. "I'm not certain, but she sounds like she might be the key. I'm trying to work out a timeline in my head, but it's difficult. This Rosa, she already had her den in the ruined castle when she met the musician, Klaus. If I recall the details, she also killed his parents, which takes it back a single generation. Donovan told me that Edgar—Poe, the poet—carried a copy of the fairy tales recorded by the brothers Grimm. Those stories were published in 1812, and the story that appears to be relevant is titled "The Raven." In that story, a girl was turned into a raven by a wicked stepmother who was also a sorceress. Edgar told a different story, involving a servant woman, but the basic details were the same. I am wondering if the princess in the story might have been the lost sister."

"This is fascinating," Copper said. "I am younger than any of the others associated with this story, and she rarely confided anything in me, particularly her past. I remember her saying that the place she'd carved out in one of the old dungeons was filled with musical instruments. I was never invited to visit, but the safe house we maintained below the Inn in Rathburg was similarly equipped. There was an entire wall of instruments, and she could play all of them. By the time my inclusion in anything beyond serving her was possible, or likely, things had begun to slide toward their inevitable end. I admit, I would love to see it now and to know."

"After all this time?" Alicia asked.

Copper nodded. "We are due for some travel. You have been promising to come with me to my ancestral home, very far away indeed, but maybe we start where we began? It sounds as if things are about to get interesting in Rathburg, and if we are present, it seems more likely the locals will open up. Remember how they treated Klaus and his band."

"They will be frightened. No matter what we may have done for them, they will remember earlier times. We are part of their nightmares."

"No one should always sleep soundly," Copper said.

"Excuse me," Gunter cut in. "Are you offering assistance? If so, I would, if I am not too forward, wish your indulgence? I am a man of science, and I am given to theories that are considered, at best, eccentric. I have some questions I would love to ask."

Bullfinch laughed.

"I believe we have a jet that would accommodate your particular needs," he said. We don't use it often, as you might imagine. If you can be ready to move by tomorrow, I will make the arrangements. Is there anything else you might require?"

Alicia pursed her lips, and then, she smiled. It was a beautiful smile, full of dark promise and mystery.

"It is settled then," she said. "We must arrange our affairs and prepare to travel. I will send word ahead to the Inn. I do not know what they have done with our 'quarters' there. We will need a safe place. Even with your protection."

They finished their meal and polished off the last of the bottle of wine Copper had ordered. It was very old, and exquisite. Bullfinch nursed a second beer.

"We will return to our hotel and await your call," he said at last. "I can log on and get the arrangements finalized. We will, of course, take off after sunset tomorrow, unless you need more time?"

"I think that will do," Copper said. "We've gone a bit more high-tech than our predecessors. You have to learn to change with the world if you want to blend in."

"Indeed," Bullfinch said.

Alicia laughed again. "You have made very little effort in that regard Geoffrey. I believe that might be the same jacket you were wearing the last time we met."

Bullfinch blushed.

"Academia," he said, "is thankfully is still moving at a snail's pace in the realm of style. I am fairly certain I'll never cut the sort of figure that looks good in skinny jeans or flannel."

They all laughed.

"You are dapper and handsome as always," Alicia said. "I am evil to tease you, but you do make it easy. I think this trip is going to be interesting on many levels. Tell me though, because you have piqued my interest. Why would you have a jet that could accommodate our kind? You often escort vampires on international flights?"

Bullfinch reddened again, but this time his embarrassment was more a deep discomfort.

"It has not often been used for pleasure," he said. "We picked it up from a para-military group. We had problems with their business practices. They had some hard-liner views on other-than-human races. When their operation folded, the government we were working for added the jet to our payment. We have since made modifications."

"So, it was used to transport captives," Copper said, brow furrowed.

"We freed those that we could," Bullfinch said.

There was a long moment of silent, and then Alicia and Copper rose. Alicia held out a hand, and Geoffrey took it gently. He glanced over at Copper. "A story for another time?"

Copper nodded. Then Alicia spoke.

"We do appreciate our friends, you know," she said. "There are all types of monsters in the world. One day, we will tell you the entire story of our time with Rosa and Alex. Not all of those who might have worked for the organization you mention would have been wrong. Freedom, for any race, is a right, but it is also a thing not to be taken for granted."

Gunter, who had been standing silently, taking in the exchange, blinked and actually held up his hand, as though he might be interrupting a lecture.

"I believe," he said, "that there are cycles to the universe. This jet, it was not created with a good purpose in mind, but now it may save lives—alter the future—redeem the past. It is so with many things, many bits and pieces of science, and knowledge. Your Rosa, she created you, in a manner of speaking. It was not for a good purpose, and yet, here we are. A thing is just a thing. It is up to men, and women, he nodded at Alicia, to provide the purpose."

"So, everything is like your Schrödinger's box," Copper said, winking at Gunter. "Until you measure it, it can be one thing—or another."

Gunter blinked. His eyes glazed over for just a second, as if processing something he found incredible. Then, very suddenly, he smiled.

"I am going to enjoy our talks," he said. "Very much. So much to learn, so little time."

"You may find," Alicia said, "that the lack of time is not the curse it may seem. It just takes a very great deal of *extra* time to put it in perspective."

She smiled and Copper nodded. Then he stared over Bullfinch's shoulder into the interior of the restaurant. The two humans turned reflexively to see what had caught his attention. When they turned back, they stood alone beside the table. The check lay on the silver tray the waiter had brought. Two crisp, hundred-dollar bills rested on top.

"Well then," Bullfinch said. "*That* happened."

"Like in the moving pictures," Gunter said. "So fast—"

Chapter Fifteen

Cletus was up at before sunrise. He'd spent the evening before eating buffalo wings at the Cotton Gin and chatting with Willow, but, in the end, had realized that barging in and telling her that the girl people claimed to see running around in the swamp with a bow-and-arrow and a giant deer—the one that hung out with Nettie? She said we should not name the boy Jasper, was a bad idea. The realization of such a thing had not often prevented him from stumbling on ahead, but this one time common sense prevailed. If it was going to happen, it was going to happen and just knowing was enough. If he was slated to spend the rest of his life with a woman, it was a damn-fool thing to give her reasons to scream at him and call him crazy before they'd even gotten started.

Instead, he'd had a beer, and told her a little bit about what he was doing, leaving out most of the details, just explaining he'd been out to see Nettie and that he'd been guiding someone for a friend. She listened, told him who'd been in, where the fish had been biting. It was pleasant, and before he rose to leave, she reached out and slapped him on the shoulder.

"We go on like an old married couple, Cletus."

He'd stood very still, and Willow had laughed.

"I'm not proposin', you goof."

"That would be my department." The words had come out before he'd had time to think about them, and because he hadn't wanted her to see how red his face was, he'd turned, and left. The tinkle of her laughter still echoed in the back of his mind, even as the worn old Mr. Coffee in his trailer burbled and brewed the lifeblood of a new day in the kitchen.

He poured the coffee into his thermos and stepped out into the fresh morning air. The sun wouldn't rise for another half hour, but there was a shimmer of light over the trees.

Dog followed him out, jumped down off the step, and stretched. Cletus checked the food bowl, still half-full, and ran some water from the spigot into a large metal bowl. Dog looked at him, then at the pickup, and took a few steps toward it.

"Not this time, buddy," Cletus said. "I've got to take a lady into the swamp, and she's got a cat. I know you'd behave yourself, but I don't *know* about the cat. You keep watch here. I'll call Jasper if I'm late; he'll come and let you in."

Dog stared at him, clearly not happy. Then, with a heavy sigh, turned and wandered over to the old rug by his food bowl, and flopped.

Cletus never tied him. Dog had wandered into his life one day out of nowhere, and he never strayed far. Besides, there were plenty of other animals out in the fields, the forest, and the swamp, and Cletus did not want to stake his buddy out like a sacred goat. They had an understanding, though if he thought about it too hard, he realized only Dog knew what it was.

With a quick wave, he climbed into his truck, fired up the engine and drove in a short circle, pointing back down the drive to the main road leading to Highway 17. He had to hit the One-Stop for provisions, and he didn't want to be late. He had an idea Amethyst and her cat might take off into the swamp on foot if he didn't stick to the schedule, and this was looking to be one of the more memorable days in his long life.

The morning sun trickled through the branches and drew intricate patterns of shadow on the road as Cletus and Amethyst wound their way along the boundaries of the Great Dismal Swamp. Lake Drummond was most easily reached through the state park trails off 17, by the tourist center, but they didn't want to be seen going in. They also knew Nettie wasn't coming within a country mile of that place, with its wood-planked walkways and tourist-trampled clearings. Some of the tamer animals wandered in and about the area, giving people a thrill, but it would still feel like a cancer to Nettie, and she was probably right. Farms, and roads, homes and men with their heavy equipment and big ideas that somehow missed the beauty they were erasing had already reached much too near the heart of the swamp.

Cletus knew the ins and outs of both the park and the swamp. It hadn't been so long since he, Jasper, and others had tracked a creature that should never have been alive in the first place deep into those waterways.

This wouldn't be anything like that. There was nothing particularly dangerous about reaching Lake Drummond or the tree. He'd been going there since he was a boy. It was around to one side, well off the normal beaten path, but anyone who'd spent time in the swamp could find it.

The key was going to be keeping it private. If they attracted attention from park rangers, or anyone else, whatever Amethyst had planned might be interrupted.

Considering that, if they could, the authorities would drag Nettie out of there for trespassing, it was likely the old woman would be as scarce as polar bears in the desert if they were discovered, whatever the danger to Amethyst or Cletus.

"So," he said, breaking the silence, "You haven't seen the cat since last night?"

"No," Amethyst said. "I'm nearly certain she went to Donovan. I don't know if he was in trouble, or if she thinks that I am, and that's why I need to hurry. If he gets here before I am finished, I have no idea what might happen, and I need to concentrate. Lenore's life almost certainly depends on it—and my own as well."

"Are you sure about this?" Cletus asked. "Seems to me you are doing pretty much what she did when she got trapped, and we know what kind of bad idea that turned out to be."

"I'm sure. She didn't know what was going to happen to her, and she had no training to protect herself. I'm not going into this blind."

"The one who put her there was powerful. Nettie is also powerful."

"You aren't going to fight me on this."

Cletus started to answer, and then, realized it was not a

question. He made the last turn and pulled in beneath a stand of trees a little way off the road. The truck wasn't completely concealed, but it would not be easily visible from the road. He killed the engine, took a deep breath, and shook his head.

"I've stepped into the ring for too many losing battles not to know when I'm overmatched. Let's get out there and see what you can do. I'll be there. If I can help, you let me know. If'n you just need me to shut the hell up, you tell me. One thing though."

She stared at him, waiting.

"You don't have anything in that bag of yours to protect me from Donovan if you get stuck, and we can't get you out? I like the swamp just fine, but I don't think I'd enjoy spending the rest of my life as a frog hopping along the bank of Lake Drummond."

Amethyst laughed.

"Sorry, Cletus, but you'll be on your own. I'm not sure I could protect you from Donovan if I was there when he was angry. That doesn't happen very often. He'll know there was nothing you could do, but I sense him now. It's faint, but he's getting closer. We have to hurry."

They grabbed her bags and Cletus's cooler and took off through the trees. There was a trail. It was not well-worn. It was hard to tell how long it might have been since anyone had walked along it, but it was there, and it only took about ten minutes to break into a clearing that brought them in sight of the lake.

"The tree is just over there," Cletus said. "To the right. You won't be able to miss it when…"

Amethyst was already moving—and fast. Something was drawing her, and all Cletus could do was fall in behind, try his best to run without tripping over the cooler, and keep up.

He didn't know at what point the deer appeared, or Nettie. One moment he was struggling through the tall grass, cursing under his breath and trying not to trip. The next, she was there, and at her side, the great stag. Something in her presence changed everything.

Cletus no longer struggled. He ran, and it felt graceful—powerful. The things he carried were of no consequence. He saw Amethyst, and the lake, and the distance between them melted away. He thought the younger girl was there too, but he couldn't see her, and there was no time to stop, or to look, or to speak, because as he slowed and dropped the cooler to the ground, he saw that Amethyst was already drawing patterns in the earth, planting crystals along the pattern. He heard her voice, but it was low and indistinct, and he could not make out any of the words.

He saw that there was now a circle, about six feet in diameter, circling the base of the tree. The water level was low, and there was enough dry earth on all sides. Within that circle, he saw she was completing the second circle and he remembered the story of her mother, and the creature she'd banished when she was only five.

This was different though. Cletus knew nothing of spells, or of magic, but he sensed that what was trapped within this circle was yet another trap, that the trunk of the tree itself was a circle in its own right. It had stood the test of time, and the attacks and invasions of powerful men and women for nearly a century—who knew how long before that?

He stepped forward, determined to get within the circle before Amethyst could close it, but thin, very strong fingers gripped him by his arm and held him back. He struggled, but a smaller hand, just as powerful, gripped his free arm.

"Let her be," Nettie whispered. "There is nothing you could do, and if the tree took you instead of her, as she plans, she might not be able to reverse it."

Cletus wanted to explain. He wanted to tell her about the circle within the circle, and what he feared, but when he met those clear, ancient eyes, he realized that she knew, had known all along, and might know more about what was going to happen even than Amethyst herself.

The girl who might be his daughter leaned close to his other ear.

"She is making a door. I don't know if she can hold it open, but the crystals, the stones, I feel them drawing energy from the earth, and from the swamp. She will make a portal in, and out, of that tree."

"Won't it take her?" Cletus said.

"Only if the portal closes," Nettie said. "That is the key. If she can keep that portal open, it will remain there, like a trap waiting to be sprung."

"Until when?"

"Until whatever holds it open fails," the girl said.

Colored lights crisscrossed the interior of the circle now, splashing against an invisible, cylindrical wall stretching up toward the clouds. Within those lights, Amethyst danced, a rhythmic, shuffling hop, arms weaving intricate patterns that dragged the lights behind, creating words and images that blinked, imprinted themselves on his mind, and flashed out of existence to be replaced by others.

It all made an odd humming sound, a band of vibration that blended so closely with the pattern you could see the sound. Each differently colored crystal had its own note, and those notes sounded in tandem with Amethyst's movements, seeming to emanate from each stone and terminate on a finger, or a feature of her face, or a glittering bit of quartz braided into her long, streaming red hair.

It was dazzling. Cletus had never seen anything quite so beautiful, and he might have dropped to his knees then, but the others steadied him. Then, breaking his concentration, voices sounded behind him. He heard footfalls and very slowly, barely able to drag his eyes from the tree and the lights and the dance, he turned.

Donovan and Edgar burst out of the trees like a black wave. Their long, dark jackets, very similar, the two dark birds gliding to either side, and Cleo, directly between them, gave the impression of a single entity bearing down on Cletus and the others. Donovan paid them no mind. His gaze was fixed on the circle behind them, and his expression was wild and filled with pain.

Nettie turned with Cletus and stood her ground. She held an old wooden staff, planted firmly in the soft lakeside ground. It seemed that Donovan would fly past them and crash into the circle of lights beyond, but she held up a hand and, with great effort, the tall, wild-eyed wizard drew back, and stopped, eyes blazing.

"What have you let her do?" he said. "How could you let this happen?"

"You know as well as I—likely better—that there is no *let* involved with that one," Nettie said firmly. "There was nothing I could have done that would have stopped her, and this one," she tilted her head toward Cletus, "is completely out of his league."

Donovan started to speak, thought better of it, and closed his eyes. He took a long, deep breath, and then turned to Cletus.

"Do you know what she is trying to do?" he asked.

"Not really," Cletus said. "I think Nettie might, but when they were talking last night, I was sort of distracted. Or blocked."

"She's going to trap herself in that tree," Donovan said. "She is planning on freeing Lenore, but…"

Nettie cut in. "It's not quite like that," she said. "At first, that's what I thought too, but she's a smart one. She's going to open a portal, as Lenore did so long ago, but this time she doesn't intend to let it close."

Donovan frowned. He stared through the lights to where Amethyst still moved gracefully, winding and binding the strings of light and power. As they all watched, she reached out and jabbed something into the trunk of the old tree. Then she moved on and did it again, and again. The points where she made contact continued to glitter after her hands passed on, and after only a few moments, it was clear she was forming a large, uneven ring of light.

"That spell is strong," Donovan said. "It is dangerous to stand between such magic and its purpose. Time can be stilled, and for short periods reversed, for instance, but it will snap back into place given the slightest chance and take whatever is holding it back at that moment along for the ride. It's the nature of this trap, as well."

"Then we'd better be thinking about what, or who, that's going to be," Nettie said, "instead of worrying about stopping something that is almost complete."

There was a sudden shift in the patterns nearest to the

tree. The colors, formerly gliding where they were guided by Amethyst's dance, picked up speed. They bent around the tree and circled like a whirlwind of color and sparks, but where the crystals had been pressed into the bark, the streaks of color bent. Cascades of blue and green and red light shot off like lasers to blast against the inside of the circle like a fireworks display gone mad. The spot on the tree darkened.

At first it was just a lack of color, a shadow against the brilliance, but as it spread and deepened, Cletus saw that it was more than that. As he watched, terrified and fascinated, a chasm opened in the bark, peeling back to all sides from the center. It was black and deep. Then things got really strange.

Donovan stood as still as stone. His entire being drew him toward the lights and the tree. It took every bit of his will not to dive through, and into the circle, to grab Amethyst and drag her out, or be trapped with her forever. Edgar stood by his side, eyes bright, but silent. He too appeared ready to reach out, or to dive forward.

Asmodeus and Grimm, who had been circling overhead, suddenly dove straight at Donovan's head. He waved his arms, backing away, stunned. They dove again, driving him back toward the trees. The two birds split then, curving around him on both sides, and took off for the trees, gliding fast and low to the ground.

"They want us to follow," Edgar cried.

Donovan stared at the tree, and the whirling lights. He could barely make out Amethyst's shadowed form, but he could hear nothing, only sense the power building and swelling against the bonds she'd created.

Asmodeus whirled and shot back. This time there was nothing hesitant. The raven crashed into the side of Donovan's head, claws out, hard enough to send him reeling, then spun without a sound and shot back toward the forest.

Cursing under his breath, Donovan turned and raced after it, closing the distance between himself and Edgar, who had been quicker to decide—and to react. They were heading back the way they'd come, toward the ruined hotel. It was not far, and considering their current speed, if neither he nor Edgar tripped and killed themselves on a rock, they'd be at the steps in only a few moments.

Edgar reached the steps first, nearly dove down and pressed his hand into the empty air. A wooden door appeared, and he pushed it inward, stepping through. Donovan nearly stopped to stare. His own method involved an intricate pattern of steps up and down that caused the portals to open. It seemed as if he might have to up his game.

The birds had soared into the torch-lit halls, swinging in a tight arc to the left and flashing into the distance. Edgar took a deep breath and followed, Donovan by his side. There was no time to count the doors they passed or to check locks. There was no time to pay attention to twists or turns. All that existed was the stone floor, and the speeding birds. Ahead, the ravens circled, like a black cyclone of feathers, before a door that, unlike the others, glowed at the cracks. The light was not a specific color or even brilliance. It rippled and pulsed.

Edgar started to slam into the door, as he'd done entering the labyrinth, but Donovan held him back.

"Wait," he said. "We have to be sure. If we burst through that door with no idea what we are facing, we could destroy everything—everyone. We could all be trapped.

"There is no time," Edgar said.

"But there is."

Donovan pulled the old watch from his pocket. Working quickly, he turned the longest stem back three clicks, reached out to take Edgar by the hand, and clicked the button on the watch.

Grimm and Asmodeus hung, like a surreal mobile halted in midflight. Just for a second, Donovan wished he had time to photograph it, the moment was so graceful and ancient and filled with power. He released Edgar's hand.

"Now!" he said. "Three minutes. We have three minutes."

To his credit, Poe did not hesitate. He pressed his hand into the wood of the door and stepped through. Donovan followed. The light around them had ceased all movement. It rippled like spun glass. Glints of light hung as if they were tiny, captured stars, or camera flashes caught on the film they intended to illuminate. As they moved through those brilliant threads, they could sense the lights, drifting like spider-webbing over their faces and tickling at their skin.

Donovan took in the situation at a glance. Directly in front of them, two women stood, facing one another. One was Amethyst, and she seemed to stare directly into Donovan's eyes, though obviously she did not see him at all. She was fixated on the woman before her. The two held hands, and it was impossible to tell if one were pulling the other out, or if it was reversed and they were both being dragged inward.

Edgar seemed oblivious to the moment. He moved quickly, his purpose fixed, and clear. He ran his hands around Eleanor's body—Donovan knew that's who it had to be though they had not met—and lifted, one arm beneath her knees, the other behind her back. Turning, he lunged for the door.

Amethyst was drawn after, floating through the brilliantly colored air as though through water or clear gelatin. Donovan slipped around Edgar, grabbed her wrists, and spun to the door. There was no time to check the watch. He thought he had time, but there was no way to know—no time to look or to be certain.

He staggered into the passageway, and Edgar, with almost surprising focus, spun and kicked it shut with a bang. The watch released them, and Amethyst's eyes flashed open. She took in the scene, Edgar, Lenore, Donovan, and the door. She saw the ravens dangling in mid-air, and with a frantic burst of energy, she yanked free of Donovan's grasp. She managed to land on her feet, and was already reaching for a pouch dangling from her side.

Donovan stepped back. He did not know what she was doing, but he'd caught the desperation, and the focus in her gaze. Something was about to happen. Whether that thing would be a good one, or a bad, likely rested in that small, jeweled pouch, and there was nothing he could do to help or prevent it.

She dumped the contents into her hand, grabbed something in the fingers of her other, and slammed something into the wood of the door. She did this again, and again, moving so quickly it was a blur, particularly with time still not back to normal, only beginning to return to normal. Donovan finally glanced at the watch. Twenty seconds.

He didn't take his eyes off the watch. If the time lapse ceased before she was done, he would grab her, hold on for everything he was worth, and whatever happened, would happen. If she did finish, he believed he would grab and hold her; Edgar was on his own.

Amethyst drew her hand back and slammed her palm into the wood. There was a flash of color, and a flutter of wings. Light shot around the odd, nearly circular shape she'd made by somehow pressing crystals into the wood of that door. They did not seem loose, or likely to fall, but instead were deeply embedded. The force it would have taken to do that should have driven them through her hand, but there was no blood. She fell back with a gasp, and sound hit Donovan from every side at once.

Something struck the far side of the door with the force of a sledgehammer. The sound echoed up and down the hallways, but the door held. The light shimmering between the crystals surged, grew brighter, and then steadied.

Donovan bent and put his arms beneath Amethyst's arms, lifting her to her feet and turning her into his embrace. Beside them, Edgar held Lenore just as tightly. She was trembling like very thin paper on a desk with a fan about to blow it away and flatten it against a wall. She seemed not quite able to stand, and her face was buried in Edgar's neck.

Donovan held Amethyst close, but he watched the door. There was another resounding thud, and it bowed ever so slightly, but, again, it held. The next crash was smaller, and the next smaller still. At last, the door was as still as they were. When everything was silent, he spoke.

"What, in the name of all that is or is not holy, have you done?"

Amethyst pulled back, but only slightly. She gazed up into his eyes.

"I have bought us time," she said. "It will hold but not forever. I have no idea what will happen when it fails. The tree is a very ancient, very powerful trap. For it to exist, there must be someone, or something, inside. It may take whoever is closest, it may reach through time, and space, for me, or for Eleanor, or even for the one that set it. But for the moment, we are free."

He kissed her. There were no words that would change what she'd said. He was afraid he'd accuse her, be angry. The thought of time, which had all but ignored him, closing in overwhelmed him. When she pulled back, slightly, she started to speak again, but he put a finger to her lips.

"We have to get out of here," he said. "We have to finish this. I don't know how, yet, but I think I know who needs to be in that tree, and if that is going to happen, we have things to discover, others to speak with. Nettie is waiting, and Cletus— they have no idea you are free."

Amethyst nodded. They both turned to find a pale but upright Eleanor leaning on Edgar's shoulder.

"We have to go," Donovan said.

Edgar nodded. "I know."

Asmodeus spun around them and headed back the way they'd come with Grimm gliding behind. They did not move as quickly as they had on the way in, as though afraid they'd lose their companions, but neither did they hesitate. They reached the door leading to the ruined hotel and the swamp beyond, and Donovan stepped aside. He knew he was going to have to talk to Edgar about the trick of the doors, but for the moment, the other man's method was simpler and much quicker.

When they were out, and standing in the sunlight, Donovan turned to Amethyst and put his hands on her shoulders.

"Wait here. Watch them. I will go and get Cletus, and I must warn Nettie. If that thing is in any danger of snapping closed and trapping someone, she needs to be aware. She should be able to put up wards of her own, and possibly to obscure it and prevent someone wandering up who is entirely unaware."

She leaned in, kissed him quickly, and turned to Edgar without a sound. Donovan took off into the swamp at a run for the second time that day, hoping the others had enough sense to remain clear of the tree and not to put themselves in more danger than they already were.

He knew Nettie would sense it—that she probably knew

more about the situation than he ever would, but he didn't slow down.

As it turned out, by the time he reached the shore of the lake, the others were already moving away from the tree. The shimmering, magical circle was gone. Cletus, Nettie, the younger girl, and the great stag approached him in a tight group. They saw Donovan, and he slowed, catching his breath.

"It took her," Cletus said. His eyes were glazed, and he was unsteady on his feet. He looked like a condemned man, and, suddenly, Donovan realized the man expected to be turned into a frog, or simply killed, for letting Amethyst become trapped.

"They're fine," Donovan said. "But we have to get as far away from that tree as possible. Nettie, it's still open. It is being held. I don't know for how long, nor does Amethyst. We have to go—to see this through to its end. I suspect that Edgar will tag along, and Eleanor too."

"Wait," Cletus said. "Edgar. That other guy in the long coat, that's Edgar—Poe?"

"The same," Donovan said. "Pretty sure we're going to need a ride out of here, so there will be plenty of time for you two to meet on the drive."

Cletus blinked.

Nettie was already turning away.

"Wait," Donovan said, taking a step after her. "Will you be okay? Can you watch it—hold it until we can figure out how to close it forever?"

The old woman turned. Her eyes were bright, and clear.

"I will hold it," she said. "I sensed what she'd done as soon as she disappeared, but I didn't know where."

"The birds," Donovan said. "They knew. They led us to a door."

"I suspect we see such things differently," Nettie said, "but I understand. The other end is sealed?"

"For now," Donovan said. "There is a lot of power behind that spell. It nearly broke Amethyst's ward—then it held."

Nettie nodded. "I can't seal it," she said, "any more than I could break it and free that woman, but I can lend my strength to what she's done. It will hold until you return, but don't be long, Magic Man. I would not be happy if one of my own was lost."

Donovan nodded. "You have my word," he said. "For now, we will follow the trail of the one who set the trap in the first place. If there is an answer to be found, she will have it."

"Take care," Nettie said. "That one is old, and powerful. She may not know you are coming, and that is in your favor, but she will realize that it is possible, that *someone* is coming, or might be, and she will be prepared. There is not much left in her but the hatred and the evil. I hope you find what you seek, but either way, I expect you to return."

"My word," he repeated.

Nettie nodded. She turned away again and moved with surprising quickness toward the trees. The girl followed without a word, though she and Cletus exchanged a glance as she passed. The stag took three leaps and was simply not there.

"I'll never get used to that," Cletus said. "What do you mean, they're okay?"

"Let's get moving," Donovan said, turning toward the trees, and the trail leading back to the ruined hotel, and the highway beyond. "I will do my best to explain it, but I'm really not sure it will make any sense. I'm not completely certain how it all works myself. But yes, they are fine for the moment. Or, at least, Amethyst and Edgar are fine. Eleanor has been a prisoner for longer than you've been alive, so…"

"Let's get them to the truck and out of here," Cletus said. "We can call ahead and get another room at the bed and breakfast, so she can rest, or talk, or eat, or whatever floats her boat."

"Perfect." Donovan said. "While she does, I can take that time to reach out to the others we're working with and to plan the next step. We can't leave a magic ticking time bomb in the middle of Nettie's swamp, particularly since you will be the only one of us left, in the end, to bear the brunt of her anger. I don't believe I'd like to piss that lady off."

Chapter Sixteen

The satellite phone on the jet rang quietly, and a light blinked to notify Bullfinch that the call was for him. Gunter was lost in one of the articles on his tablet, and though no sunlight could penetrate the skin of the jet, Copper and Alicia had retreated to their cabin to rest.

"Yes?" Bullfinch said.

The signal was very clear, despite their altitude and speed.

"It's me, Donovan. I have others with me. Amethyst is here. Edgar and Eleanor are in the next room."

"You freed her?" Bullfinch said.

"No, Amethyst did, but it's not complete. Listen, Geoffrey, I don't know what, if anything, you have learned, but we are short on time. For the moment, everyone is free, but that tree, that evil, ancient trap, is still open."

"Well," Geoffrey said, "We will be in Germany by this evening. We should make it to Rathburg shortly after that—I've arranged for vehicles."

"Wait for us," Donovan said. "Don't go up the mountain without me. I'm going to risk the labyrinth to get me to my home, and then to you. I don't know exactly where we'll exit, but we'll find you. I have to get some things, but it's dangerous to go anywhere near those byways until we have ended this."

"Do you have a plan?"

"I have part of a plan," Donovan said. "Do me a favor, think back to that version of "The Raven" by the Brothers Grimm, the one Edgar recited to me. Then check it against the original. In magic, things are very seldom as clear as they may seem, but I believe there were certain items that were necessary to free the princess. And, not that I'm committing to any team, but can you get us a ride out of San Valencez?"

"I'll have a jet waiting on you," Bullfinch said. "I'll text details."

"Thank you," Donovan said. "And Geoffrey?"

"Yes?"

"Be careful. Whatever is on that mountain, it is old, powerful, and without a doubt insane."

"From one long-lived fellow to another," Bullfinch said with a chuckle, "I didn't get this far by being a fool. We'll take precautions and I will see you—?"

"Hopefully by tomorrow. If you find anything in that story, anything at all, send that along too. I will be packing a war chest of sorts, and it would be helpful to have a better idea what it should contain."

Donovan ended the call and turned to the others.

"We should get some rest and head out in the morning. We can stay at the bed and breakfast, and Cletus can get us back out here in the morning. We're going to have to use those passages, and that means moving quickly, and avoiding the door that Amethyst jammed open like Hades itself was on the other side."

He turned to Edgar, and Eleanor.

"I'll understand if you don't join us."

"I'm afraid that is a choice not afforded us," Edgar said, his features grave. "If there is still a chance of Lenore, or myself, or even one of you being sucked back into that trap—particularly when traversing the roads below—I must remain a part of the solution until the end. And we two will not be parted again—if I have any say in the matter—so I believe you have two traveling companions, if you will have us."

"I cannot imagine a better way to spend a flight overseas than listening to stories told by, well, you," Amethyst said, laughing. "And, of course, you are both welcome."

"Flight?" Eleanor said, speaking up from where she was seated on the bed of the truck.

"A great deal has changed in the world," Edgar told her.

"That odd vehicle that brought us here from the swamp is but a tiny glimpse."

"Wait until you see cable TV," Cletus chimed in. "And, just for the record, if it's all the same with you, Donovan, I'll be staying here in Old Mill. I've had a good bit of change in my own life these past few days, and it needs sorting. Also, I think I'd like to be here if Nettie needs me. Don't know what kind of help I could offer, but—"

"Of course," Donovan said. "We all have our parts to play. One day, maybe you'll let me take you and show you a bit more of the world, but this time you are needed here. I have the strangest urge to tell you something, about Jasper. Something I heard in the swamp, before Nettie and the others left."

"I know, I know," Cletus muttered. "Tell Willow not to name him Jasper."

He turned in the direction of the swamp and frowned. The others laughed, though only Amethyst truly knew why.

They climbed into his old Bronco and headed off toward Old Mill.

Chapter Seventeen

The flight to Germany was uneventful. The jet set down just after sunset, and a long, sleek limousine with jet black windows pulled up to greet them. The crew transferred what baggage they'd brought with them, except for Gunter and Bullfinch's carry-on bags, which the O.C.L.T. agents kept close to hand.

It was a couple of hours drive to Rathburg. Mack had managed to contact the Inn and arrange rooms for the two agents, and had also, somehow, conveyed that they would not be traveling alone. It seemed that the accommodations Copper and Alicia had once shared with their sire had been maintained. In fact, there had since been upgrades for comfort and safety.

Clearly, though they were terrified of the notion, the citizens of that remote village remembered their past. Neither Copper nor Alicia had played a major part in removing the curse that Rosa had represented, and the two had been a part of the horror prior to that. Things had changed. Since moving to the United States, back to Alicia's home in New Orleans, the two had been in contact with the villager more than once. They'd sent money, supported local charities, and even the local Church; everyone involved saw the irony in that.

Rosa's death had been as much a release for them as for the people she'd terrified for so many generations. It was not possible to make amends for such crimes, but over time they had convinced the villagers that the crimes had not really been theirs by free will. Still, had they not been accompanied by Bullfinch, and Gunter, things might have been different. As it was, they found the doors to the underground garage open, and Bullfinch pulled the limousine inside. No one was there to greet them, but that was no great surprise.

"It is fine," Copper said. "Who could blame them? We will be safe and comfortable. Perhaps you will come down and share a drink before you rest?"

Bullfinch smiled.

"I would like nothing better," he said.

Gunter nodded excitedly. "Oh, yes. I still have many questions."

"For tonight, I think," Alicia said, "we simply drink and talk. Maybe share a few stories."

Before they could close the garage door, a voice called to them from the shadows. It was an older voice, strong and rich.

"If you have room," the man said, stepping into the moonlight, "I would like to join you? You may or may not remember me. I believe I saw you burst through that very garage door many years ago. You were driving very quickly. I had my hands full."

"Father Adolph?" Alicia said, stepping forward. "Is it really you?"

"In the flesh. I wanted to thank you in person for your generosity over the years, and to put a face to the names I've come to know. If there are going to be stories told, I believe that I have details you might be interested in, and I am absolutely certain you can fill in some of the blanks in my own understanding."

"More, and more interesting," Bullfinch said. "I am suddenly glad that Donovan won't be here until tomorrow. We'll have time to catch up while we wait for him."

The group entered the garage and Copper pressed the switch that closed off the world beyond. Once inside, Alicia moved through an inner doorway and returned with a lit candle on a small silver holder. They followed her through the doorway, and she circled the room slowly, lighting more candles as she went. Before long, the room was well lit and warm.

The walls were lined with divans and couches. They were dark and rather gothic in design. Copper turned slowly, took it all in, and then laughed.

"My God," he said. "They believe we *are* Rosa. This—" he waved his arms vaguely, "it's almost too much."

Alicia's laughter joined his. "You'll have to pardon us," she said. "Rosa was very old, and she loved playing on the idea of Victorian vampires. Believe it or not, she read Anne Rice's books, and any others she could get her hands on. We have very good memories. At times she would act out scenes, play parts. This furniture, this décor—she would have liked it very much."

"And you?" Father Adolph asked.

"We have more Bohemian tastes," she said. "While I don't mind a good role-play now and then, I like to think I define myself, rather than allowing my condition to do it for me."

"It does bring back memories, though," Copper said. He walked into the next room and returned with a violin.

"The instruments. They aren't the same ones, obviously, but they have replaced what was damaged. I think Alex's flute is still here."

"Alex was a problem," Alicia added. "Imagine a pet dog that wanted to be the only pet. Then give it super speed and strength, jealousy, and a horrible temper. He hated everyone but himself and Rosa."

Copper raised the instrument to his chin, dropped the bow onto the strings, and played a flurry of notes with crystalline precision. Then he turned, headed back into the other room, and returned without the violin.

"We seem to have entered something of a time warp," Alicia said. "Perfect backdrop for story time, I suppose. I almost expect Rosa to slip up behind me and whisper in my ear, or Alex to burst out of the other room, make some macho move at one of us to prove how terrifying he is, and at the same time to prevent us from seeing how insecure and terrified he was."

"It sounds to me," Geoffrey said, sitting back, "as if life among the undead is not really so different from what the rest of us experience, though without some of the borders and with new ones imposed."

"The differences are not subtle," Copper said, "and this is where that life began for me. I had been with them for some time, stolen from my home very, very far from here, a lifetime, to be her servant. When that band, Von Kroft, came to the mountain, I was the driver, the watcher. I made payments during the daytime when it was necessary. I fed on Rosa's blood but had not been turned."

"You were so beautiful," Alicia said, smiling. "When Rosa allowed me to..."

"There may be time for that story one day," Copper said, cutting her off. He sounded embarrassed, but the shadowed room, his dark complexion, and possibly some supernatural quality they did not understand due to his lack of circulation, made it impossible to know if he blushed. "I think we need to stick to the main facts tonight. There is little time, and a lot to tell."

"You are right, of course," Alicia said. "Pour everyone a drink, and I'll see if I can abridge it properly. While I know there was a lot happening that was of little importance going forward, what I don't know is which pieces might be vital. For one thing, there was that song."

"Ah, yes," Father Adolph said. "That wonderful, magical song. I have often wondered about it. I spoke with the other members of the band several times, and they alluded to some sort of mystical story behind it."

"I thought it was just a game," Alicia said. "Rosa started that so far in the past. She visited Sebastian, the keyboardist when he was young and in school. He heard her play a version of it on a harp, and after that it was stuck in his head. Later, she led him to his 'chance' meeting with Klaus Von Kroft, and a new life that brought them inevitably here. Back to her own beginnings, her own past. That was when she shared it a second time, with Klaus.

"I don't know if she created it—if it was a simple melody that she wove into a spell—or if it was older than she, it was inherited from somewhere in her past. We hunted on the mountain for so many years, off and on, that I cannot remember the first time I visited this place. In all that time, she never took me more than halfway up. I never saw the castle or the rooms beneath it.

"I heard stories. Some of those that I took..."

Alicia hesitated, and Copper took the opportunity to offer tumblers of Brandy all around.

"It was different," he said. "We do not feed in that way, and would not have, I think, without Rosa's influence, and Alex's maddening challenges. We cannot change the past, even those of us who have too much of it."

Alicia took the brandy, sipped, and nodded.

"You are right, but I am never certain how much to say in the company of the living. I do not want to offend, nor do I want to awaken to a stake through my heart or be dragged into the sunlight. This time, though, it is a part of the tale.

"Those I met here on the mountain were terrified of Rosa, but it was not just because we came here, and we hunted. Their parents, and their grandparents, told stories. There were sometimes decades between our visits, and we never stayed long. But that was often enough to bring nightmares to the younger families, tales to frighten children off the mountain at night. It still didn't account for the way the old ones treated her. This safe place; they created it at her request. They watched over it. When we were here, even though they knew full well what we were, and what we would do, they protected her—because they were truly frightened for their souls.

"The undead, as some of you are aware, can be a very frightening bunch. We have speed, power, strength—sometimes magic. For all of that, we can be stopped, killed, destroyed. They could have done it at almost any point, thrown open the doors by the light of day and marched in with fire, but they did not. Whatever Rosa's family and that castle instilled in their hearts, it was a fear beyond anything normal, or even paranormal, that I have ever experienced."

"It does seem odd," Bullfinch said. "I've encountered your kind on more occasions than I'd care to get into, and it has not always been pleasant, but in the end, the situation was resolved either by some form of cultural peace, or the frightened rising to the occasion. Even the worst situations came to an end. It's a cycle that has been repeating as long as your race has existed."

"And one day, perhaps," Alicia replied, "we'll understand when yours created us, and how."

There was silence for a bit, then Alicia continued.

"I don't know all of what happened here that night so long ago. I was distracted by my sudden connection with Copper, and by the need to protect him from Alex until they became more equal. Rosa had her game in play, and she shared very little of it with us. She did take us to Von Kroft's concert on the mountain. By then she had the entire band enthralled with that song, had given it to them to pass that magic on to the gathered audience. Alex was wandering through the crowds, being Alex. We were lost in our own world and not invited to the end game.

"When she took Klaus up the mountain, we were here, which is likely a large part of why we were able to escape in the end."

"I believe I can fill in some blanks at this point," Father Adolph said. He stared at the brandy in his tumbler for a moment, then continued. "When they took Klaus, we followed. Not immediately, and we were a rag-tag bunch, at best. There was more to that game than you realize.

"Rosa knew Klaus' father. She tried the same seductive routine with him that she did with Klaus, but the father—he was in love. He was married, and he had a son. In the end, as powerful as she was, and as beautiful as she was, he turned away from her. That, I believe, was the beginning of it all. It was more than she could bear."

"That would do it," Copper said. "I cannot imagine such a man—truly. He resisted her." It wasn't a question.

"He did. Klaus was not so lucky, but then, he was not in love. She lured him with her beauty and with the music. That song— He thought she was doing it for him. He thought she was bringing him to that place on the mountain to share her life. Even when he came to realize what she was—I think—and what he was going to become, he believed she wanted him for himself. But what she wanted was revenge."

Father Adolph turned to Alicia, and then to Copper. "Do you know? Do you know what she'd kept secret on that mountain for so long—what she showed him? Do you know what we found?"

Copper shook his head.

"No. We know that whatever happened, Klaus turned on her. We know that someone, one of you, perhaps Klaus himself, hurt her and drove her back down the mountain. She came here, but this time, when she clawed her way into the shadows, they came for her. *You* came for her, and she was ended."

Father Adolph nodded. "That is all true. It was a great cleansing. The lives of the villagers changed that night, everything changed, but before that, there was another place. It was not at the top of the mountain, but about halfway down. It was off the main track. I don't believe they passed it on their way up, and by the time they were coming back, by the time Klaus realized we were coming after him, it was too late.

"She had them, you see. Klaus' parents. They were trapped in an old stone cottage, shackled to benches they could not break free of. I don't know if your kind can live indefinitely in such a state, or if she'd been feeding them, just a bit, for a very long time. They were starving, out of their minds. She brought him to them to show them how she had betrayed him, and that she still owned him; she brought him there to show his parents what they had lost."

"It was possibly the vilest thing I have encountered in my long life…" he glanced around the room and chuckled taking another sip of brandy. "Okay, a relatively long life. I won't go into the details of that night here, but suffice it to say, his parents were freed, and Rosa, in the end, was defeated."

"I have heard stories," Alicia said, "of what happened to Klaus, but none of them sound right. Do you know? Were you there?"

"I was," Father Adolph said. "As I have stated that the way she held his parents was the single most evil thing I have encountered, that next morning may have been the single most noble, and beautiful, thing I've ever witnessed.

"They played that song. Klaus, and his parents, stood on that stone stage they'd made on the mountain in the early, dark hours of morning, and they played. They played that song together and on Rosa's instruments. They stood there, and then, when the sun rose, and fell full on them, they stood a moment more and—together—dove into that burning light. I suppose that was the end of the game, but it was Klaus, and his family, who won."

The room was silent, for a moment after that. It might have stayed that way for a long time, except, for the first time since entering that dark place, Gunter Krieg spoke up.

"I would love," he said, almost as if speaking to himself,

"to hear that song. I wish I could have seen that moment, how the sunlight ended it. There is so much in this world I do not understand, so many things to be fascinated with that sometimes, if I let myself think about it for too long, I am completely overwhelmed. There is simply not enough life."

Then the silence returned, and they finished their drinks. Copper, who had been oddly moved by Gunter's short speech, crossed the room and took a seat beside the old man.

"When this is over," he said, "we will talk. I will tell you what I know, and what I have learned, and I will listen to your theories. I do not know what may come of that, but there is a thing that I would dearly love."

Gunter turned and blinked. "Of course," he said. "But what?"

"I would like to see the sun, and then I would like to continue to live."

The two gazed into one another's eyes, the old physicist deep in thought, and the dark skinned, handsome vampire steady and sincere."

"It will be," Gunter said at last, "my pleasure to try. My very great pleasure."

They all rose then. Bullfinch, Gunter, and Father Adolph said their goodnights, and Copper closed first the outer doors of the garage, and then the inner doors behind them. The moon was still high, but no one had the inclination for more stories, speech, or anything but rest.

"Interesting times," Father Adolph said. "I am an old man." He chuckled again and shook his head. "But I spend a lot of time on that mountain. If I can be of any help, as guide or even a rather slow pack mule, I would love to accompany you."

"Of course," Bullfinch said. He clapped the priest on the shoulder. "There are others coming, some as amazing, or more so, than those you've just met. When they are here, I will feel my years as well. If you keep books, you might want to see if you have anything by Edgar Allen Poe and brush up on it."

Father Adolph shook his head, smiled, and turned away. Geoffrey and Gunter watched until he disappeared into the shadows, then they turned back to the Inn, and headed inside.

Chapter Eighteen

Donovan and the others did not waste any time. They were up before dawn, gathering what they could carry of Amethyst's thing, and arranging with the front desk to ship the rest back to San Valencez. When they were done, they climbed into the rental Amethyst had been driving with Cletus behind the wheel.

"I'll drop it off tomorrow," he told Donovan. "I'll have to get Jasper to follow me down and get me back to my truck."

"Thanks, my friend," Donovan said. "I don't know when we'll come back, but I know that when we do, we will either have good news, or need serious help, and fast, so it's good to know you're here."

"All my life," Cletus said grinning. "Haven't even been on a decent double-D Goddam vacation since my parents took me to Disney World."

"I told you," Donovan said, "I'm going to drag you away one day soon. Adventures happen all over, not just in your swamp."

"I've had about enough adventure for three lifetimes," Cletus said, "but damned if I'm not intrigued."

Donovan laughed. He was in the back seat with Amethyst and Edgar. Cleo was curled contentedly on his lap. Eleanor had climbed carefully into the seat beside Cletus, and he helped her with the seat belt. She was clearly still fatigued and confused by how much the world had changed.

"I thought magic would be the most amazing thing I encountered," she said. "Even after all these years of being trapped, of watching the sun and moon shift through the sky, of hearing voices, and seeing men and women and children living their lives, I never could have dreamed anything as wonderful as this."

"There is little difference between science and magic," Donovan said, "but believe me when I tell you that it's not all flowers and sunshine. For every useful, entertaining, magical thing man has created, there are four that cause misery, damage the planet, or draw us all closer to the brink of destruction. Necessity may be the mother of invention, but it is seldom accompanied by restraint."

"It is going to take some getting used to," Eleanor said.

"We are not trapped in this time," Edgar said. "There are many roads to follow. Or, there once were."

"And there will be again," Amethyst said. "Whoever that woman is who started this, she's built up a lot of negative credit at the karma bank. You are always saying, Donovan, that magic has consequences, and that the more it is out of line with reality, the stronger those consequences are likely to be. I'd say she's due for a cosmic slap in the face."

"And," Edgar added, "do not forget that the princess had her entire life stolen several times over, and has likely never known freedom in any time or place. When this is done, I will have to record that in a poem."

"Maybe that's what those Grimm brothers were doing," Cletus said, backing out of the parking space and turning toward Highway 17. "Making sure that her story did not end with the princess trapped forever. You know, by writing it down?"

"I think you're right," Donovan said. "At least, I hope you are. We're counting on that story leading us to the things that can help us free her."

"I know it well," Edgar said. "There are three keys, but if it is a literal tale, I fear we are going to be in for some trouble."

"Yes," Donovan agreed. "I've read it recently. I could probably create a cloak that would make me invisible—I know spells that will serve—but it would take time, and preparation, and we'd have to know in advance the exact moment it was necessary."

"That would be child's play next to the horse that can take you anywhere you want to go," Edgar said. "Not to mention the last thing, the key that will open any lock."

"Dibs on the horse," Amethyst said. Then, without warning, she burst into peals of laughter.

"What?" Donovan said.

"Are you kidding me? A magic horse? A universal key? Oh, and the cloak from Harry Potter. What could be simpler?"

"Harry who?" Eleanor asked.

Amethyst glanced up and saw the expression of utter confusion on the other woman's face. She tried to rein in her mirth, but all she managed was to turn the laughter into a sputter that left her gasping, leaning on Donovan's shoulder. Cleo reached up and batted at her reproachfully with a paw, but Amethyst barely noticed.

"If it's any consolation at all," Edgar said to Eleanor. "I have no idea what she is talking about either. If this Potter has the cloak we need, though, could we not simply ask for his help?"

"If y'all keep that up," Cletus said, his voice quavering, "I am going to wreck this truck, and I'm pretty sure no one wants that to happen."

He turned to Eleanor. "Those two think they are funny," he said. "Harry Potter is something Edgar would be familiar with, though. He's a character in a novel about a school where they teach magic. He even had a bird."

"An owl, not a raven," Amethyst said helpfully, stifling another burst of laughter by biting her lip.

Cletus shook his head. It wasn't far to the Highway 17 bypass, and he hit the gas.

They all fell silent as the truck sped up. Eleanor stared out the window, watching the trees passing and wondering at the speed. In the distance, on the left, a long line of tall wind turbines spun lazily in the air.

"What are those?" she asked.

"They catch the wind," Cletus said. "Like pinwheels. But they use that motion to create electricity."

"More magic," she said softly.

"That's what I think," Cletus said. "I don't fully understand how they work, but I believe in them. They are helping the world by creating power in new ways. This truck? It runs on gasoline. It spits out a sort of poison gas into the air. Over a very long time, that's become a bad thing for the Earth, so we have to find new magic."

"They are amazing," Edgar said. "Both the truck, and the windmills. Don Quixote would have found these a bit more challenging, I think."

Cletus laughed. "For all the world has changed," he said, "there are people who believe the damned things are creating wind and blowing it at their homes, or that the vibrations are causing infestations of snakes to rise up. People have always reacted the same way to magic; it just comes at them faster these days."

"You," Amethyst said, leaning forward to put a hand on Cletus' shoulder, "are much smarter than you appear to be."

He didn't answer. They turned onto Highway 17 and rolled on toward the old road that led back to the ruined hotel. It wasn't marked, and there was so little of the place left that most people didn't know it was there. Cletus had known there were ruins, but until Donovan had explained what they were, he'd never given it much thought.

Since then he'd spent some time down at the library in Hertford, studying in the little room where they kept the references on local history. The hotel had been wild, and unique—the kind of story out of American history people passed down from family to family until the facts changed into legends.

Eleanor stared at the trees as they rolled slowly in.

"The waterway is near here," she said. "Everything has changed, but I sense it."

"Right around the corner up ahead," Cletus said. "There's nothing left of the hotel but rubble, but you can see the waterway from there. It's been running from one end of the country to the other since George Washington was a surveyor."

He parked, and they all climbed out of the SUV. Donovan and Edgar started hauling out the things they had with them. Eleanor, with Amethyst at her side, headed straight past the ruins to the edge of the water. She stood on the bank, staring first one way, and the other. She glanced up into the trees.

"It was there," she said, pointing across the water to two particularly tall trees. "I saw the faces there that I was drawing, when I met Edgar, when this all began. They were trapped, and we set them free."

"Maybe it's a sign," Amethyst said. "A theme for this journey. Freedom. Are you frightened?"

"I would be a fool if I were not, but not for myself," Eleanor said. "The tree holds no horror for me that I am not familiar with, that has not become a part of who I am. I have seen the seasons come and go. I have watched boys come to fish, boys who grew to men and brought their lovers here. I have seen Nettie and her great stag, and heard her stories, and I've listened when Edgar came to sit by my side and tell me of his travels and read his poetry. I am afraid that it will take someone close to me instead, or that something far worse will happen when we find the one responsible. I am afraid for the girl—the princess—for Donovan and Edgar, and for you."

"We are not alone," Amethyst said. "Donovan has powerful friends, as do I. Edgar has not only been wandering, he has read, and studied. You can see it in his eyes, sense it in his presence."

"Maybe we're all just part of a story, in the end," Eleanor said. "If it proves so, I hope that it is someone like Edgar, or even your friend Cletus, who is writing it. Good men. Men who believe in hope and magic."

"I've read a lot of stories with evil sorcerers in them," Amethyst said. "I've even lived through a couple with Donovan. Almost every one of them ended well—or at the very least, ended with hope."

Eleanor smiled. "You have not read enough of Edgar's stories, I think," she said. "Still, I take your meaning."

"We have to get started," Donovan said. "It won't take long—that's not how the labyrinth works—but we're going to need rest when we get to San Valencez, and I have some serious preparation to get through."

They all shook hands with Cletus, grabbed their bags, and headed for the ruins.

"You lead the way, Edgar," Donovan said. "You are going

to have to try and explain to me how you work those doors one day, but this is not that day."

With twin cries, Asmodeus and Grimm dropped from the trees to circle the group and land on the two men's shoulders. Cletus watched them move slowly away, and thought it was the closest thing he'd ever see to a real life rendition of *The Lord of the Rings*—or maybe *The Game of Thrones*: the wizard, the poet, the witch, the artist, the twin dark birds, and the strange, intelligent cat, heading into the unknown on a double-D goddam *quest* to save a princess from an evil sorceress. He shook his head and blinked. And in that instant, they were simply gone.

Chapter Nineteen

Donovan sat in his den, staring into the glow of his computer screen and frowning. On the corner of the desk, Cleo rested, idly batting at the ancient Chinese coins dangling from the violet-shaded lamp on the desk's corner. Grimm and Asmodeus were perched on opposite sides of the mantel that rose above the fireplace, preening themselves.

The room was an endless bookshelf. The floor was covered in boxes filled with more books, papers, bound manuscripts, and scrolls. It wasn't completely disorganized, but there was considerably less living space than there might have been.

The others had disappeared, one by one, into the various bedrooms off his main hall. At first glance, it seemed short and narrow, but as with so many other features of the brownstone, that perception was deceiving. The hall stretched the length of the thirteenth floor. There were many rooms, some filled with more piles of paper and books waiting to be filed. Others held artifacts and crates of magical apparatus. There were also several well-presented bedrooms. Over the years, Donovan had played host to all manner of guests, and he was well prepared for a small invasion force.

Edgar and Eleanor had chosen a darkly paneled room with polished wood furniture, an intricate Arabic rug, and a roll-top desk. Amethyst had stayed awake as long as she could, but her efforts at freeing Lenore had drained her, and it was not long before she slipped off to Donovan's own chambers and fell into a deep sleep.

Donovan rarely slept. He tired, of course, and rested, but often in the form of deep thought, or simple meditation. He did not know if it was a feature of his longevity or a secondary gift from a liqueur he'd received for assisting the local undead in a particularly messy kidnapping case. The need for actual sleep had been slowly slipping away for some time.

He still gave into sleep occasionally, particularly when Amethyst was over for a visit, or he was staying with her, but this night he was wide awake and intent on the files flashing across his screen.

The journey through the labyrinth had been uneventful. They had not come near to the dangerously wedged portal they'd created, and he hoped that—if others still walked those passages—they would also steer clear until things have been sorted. He'd left glyphs at every turn that, when touched, activated a whispered warning for any who might encounter them. It wasn't much, but it was all he'd had time for.

Now, with Bullfinch's jet arriving the next day, it felt as if time was slipping away too quickly. He'd brought up every file he had on the Brothers Grimm, searched invisibility cloaks and spells, gathered legends about locks and keys, but for some reason it just was not clicking. He knew he was missing something, probably something vital, and he did not want to rush off to Germany without answers.

It felt too much like they were caught up in an arcane plot, playing preordained parts, but without the opportunity to exercise their own wills in the solution. That was unacceptable. There was always an answer, and more often than not it was found when you properly formulated the question.

He had gotten as far as he could with the notion of being invisible, so he concentrated on the second thing. In "The Raven," by the brothers Grimm, the hero had set out to rescue his lover. She'd been spirited away to an inaccessible castle, but the mount he rode was able to get him there despite the apparent impossibility of it. How this was accomplished was not really explained in the story, as fairy-tale plot devices so seldom were.

If I were trying to get somewhere that I did not know how to reach, he thought. *What would I...?*

It hit him with such sudden clarity that he gasped.

The Labyrinth. He'd just come from there, walking along and explaining what he knew of the paths and tunnels to the others, how they opened to nearly anywhere or when, if you knew the proper pattern and chose the correct door. Why not a ruined castle in Germany? Why not the very tower of such a place? And did the sorceress know? Would the way be blocked, warded, or impassible?

The more he thought of it, the more certain he was that he was correct. It was only one of the three elements required to complete their quest, but it felt like a great burden lifting from his heart. His companions had vast stores of knowledge, some overlapping with his, but a great deal of it not. Between them, they would find the key they needed. The invisibility was going to prove tricky, though. There were too many variables.

Did it mean not being seen by the sorceress? In the story, the hero had used one item to achieve the next, stealing the horse then finding the key. If that was the pattern, then the key might rest beneath the tower, in the Labyrinth itself. None of it would matter if they did not figure out the who, what, and when the invisibility referred to.

"Nothing is ever easy," he said, turning to Cleo and scratching between her ears.

He rose then, poured himself two fingers of bourbon, and opened the cabinet in his bookshelves where he kept the items he most depended on. Amulets, charms, a few spells bound in ribbon that would disappear once used—all gifts from previous clients. He emptied the pockets of his coat onto the bottom shelf and began sorting through them, keeping some things, returning others to their proper place in the cabinet to be replaced by others.

His jacket, which he wore no matter the situation or the weather, had many pockets. Amethyst had accused him on more than one occasion of enchanting it so that the objects that appeared to be drawn from within were stored somewhere else.

"Like a bag of holding?" he had asked her, earning a hard punch to his shoulder. Then a grin.

"Well," she'd said, "When you put it that way, yes. Exactly like that."

Sadly, though her words had sparked an interest in figuring it out, there was no such link between Donovan and his supplies. He had to guess what would be useful in any given situation and plan accordingly. He rummaged carefully through the pendants, stones, crystals, and magical objects, quickly filling the gaps he'd created in his pockets. The watch was always with him, as was a string of crystals that Amethyst had given him that could be whirled and used as a soft of magical shield. It was more difficult choosing those objects that were good for a single use, many of them irreplaceable.

He'd also filled a portable hard drive with records, spells, and his night's research. He thought maybe he'd have a chance to share some of it with Bullfinch when they arrived, and crosscheck it with the O. C. L. T. network. Donovan might not want to join up and be part of their team, but he appreciated their resources, and he trusted most of the agents he'd met. He had issues with Isabella, an Italian monster hunter who had previously worked for the Vatican, because her methods leaned more toward kill and worry about the consequences later than it did toward diplomacy. Bullfinch said she'd mellowed considerably since joining the O.C.L.T., but instinct is a hard thing to change. He was glad she would not be along on this trip, though there might come a point near the end where he wished otherwise.

Satisfied that he was ready as he was likely to get, he carried his bourbon over to the big leather chair by the fire. It was tall, backed with deep cushions and sweeping arms. He placed his drink on a coaster on the side table and leaned back. He had a couple of hours to rest, and he needed to clear his mind. The bourbon helped. Normally, he would have chosen cognac or brandy, but he'd been thinking about the swamp and Nettie, and the bourbon had seemed more appropriate. It had a satisfying, smoky bite.

Cleo hopped off the desk and padded over to climb onto his lap and settle in. As he finished the drink and closed his eyes, he heard the soft flutter of wings, and he knew that Asmodeus had joined them. Grimm would likely remain where he was until Edgar reappeared. He tolerated Donovan, and seemed close to

Asmodeus, but his bond was with Edgar. One day, that was a story he was going to have to hear.

A few moments later, as if she'd sensed him settling, Amethyst appeared at the end of the hallway, leaning on the door frame. She held out her hand, and he smiled. Gently placing Cleo in the chair, he rose and left the computer, the books, and everything else behind. The two passed silently down the hall, entered his chambers, and climbed into the huge, ornate bed. Donovan wrapped her in his arms, and she lay back against him. Within moments she was asleep, and he lay quietly, holding her, breathing in the scent of her hair, and letting everything else in the universe wash away.

He didn't stir until the sun broke over the city skyline. There was no way to see it from inside his rooms, but he sensed it. Very gently, he untangled himself from Amethyst, who did not fully awaken. He rose and headed into his bathroom for a quick shower. There were still a couple of hours before they had to leave, and he thought everyone might need coffee and breakfast. As difficult as the past few days had been for everyone, he knew they had to be worse for Eleanor and Edgar. As close as they were, it had been a very long time since they'd spoken face to face, and though Edgar had some idea of what was happening in the modern world, it might as well have been another planet to Eleanor.

After he was freshened up and dressed, he slipped down the hall to the kitchen, flipping on the lights and going through his morning routine. He didn't really need coffee—but he loved the ritual of it, the scent, and the taste. He poured dark beans into the grinder and pulled a large, clear carafe from a shelf over his stove. Normally, he used a much smaller pot, but it wouldn't do for guests.

He added a filter to the top of the carafe and put his kettle on the stove. He could have had a fancy espresso machine or a Mr. Coffee, but he liked doing it all by hand. He had several French presses, and an intricate set of beakers and tubes that looked as if they had come from an alchemist's lab and that could brew to perfection, but time was limited. He poured the hot water slowly and evenly over the grounds, watching it drip slowly but steadily through the filter into the carafe, and he smiled. He was glad he'd started before Amethyst woke, because she would have wanted to go to Starbucks, and he thought that, this day in particular, was a time for older ways.

"Something smells good," Edgar said.

Donovan turned and smiled.

"Wait until the bacon starts to fry," he said.

Eleanor stepped up behind Edgar, and Donovan suddenly realized that he'd been a very bad host.

"There are showers and a second bath down the hall," he said, catching himself. "I have towels, even some clothing. I've collected a lot over the years. Amethyst can show you."

Eleanor laughed, and it was like music, crashing through the awkward moment with ease.

"That sounds wonderful," she said. "But if I could, I would rather start with a cup of whatever that is you are brewing. It smells like heaven."

Donovan bowed, and pulled several mugs down from another shelf. He removed the grounds and the filter, then poured four steaming mugs of hot, fresh coffee.

"My pleasure," he said handing the two of them each a mug.

Amethyst appeared a moment later, hair sticking out in all directions, her eyes heavy with sleep. He handed her one of the mugs and ran his fingers through her long, red hair to straighten it.

"We do not," he said with a chuckle, "in *any* way resemble a team of powerful heroes."

"Surely we will fare better after a meal?" Edgar said with a grin. "I have always been more of the tragic hero, but today, for some reason, I am feeling the call of a truly happy ending."

They all laughed, sipped the coffee, and enjoyed the moment.

"I did some packing for us last night," Donovan said. "Once Amethyst helps Eleanor choose some suitable attire, I think we'll be as ready as we can expect to be. Also, I took the liberty of gathering a package that I hope will ease the transition from past, to being trapped in a tree, to all of this."

He set his coffee down and left the kitchen, returning a

moment later with a leather pouch. He handed it to Eleanor. She set her own drink on the counter and opened it. She pulled out a spiral bound pad of paper and a box of drawing pencils. She studied them, turning them over and examining the examples on the box of what each pencil's hardness was capable of, and intended for.

"Thank you," she said at last. "More than I can say. I have a lot to work through, and a lot of things that I must clear from my memory. I can think of no better way to do so."

"I hope you will share what you create," Amethyst said. "I've heard a great deal about your talent, but I admit I am curious to see the reality."

"We'll see," Eleanor said. "It has been so long, and even when I first started, I never drew for myself. The things I saw, the lost, the trapped, those images frightened my parents, my teachers. They told me that I had talent, but the things that I spent that talent on, the images that spoke to me, were always dark. I know they will still need me and will still speak to my mind and my heart. First, though, I need to try and create something more personal."

"The gift is without price," Donovan said. "Fill the pages with whatever feels right. The patterns, the memories. If it helps even a little bit in setting things right in your mind, I will be happy."

She smiled and tucked the pencils and the pad back into the leather pouch. She grabbed her mug and held it up.

"To the future," she said. "To the years, the adventures, the memories—and to love. May it be enough to see us through."

As odd as it seemed, they all lifted their cups and drank, as if the dark coffee was expensive brandy.

Chapter Twenty

The jet that met Donovan and his party at San Valencez International was a bit more standard than the darkened version that had carried Bullfinch, Gunter, and their two undead guests. It was sleek, dark blue, and bore only the minimal markings required for licensing and the law. The crew was courteous and efficient. Had Donovan not known that they worked for one of the most powerful and secretive organizations on the planet, they would have seemed nothing more than a private travel crew on a routine mission.

The luggage was stowed quickly, and they rode a small cart out to where the gangway had been lowered to the tarmac. Donovan watched Edgar and Eleanor as they inspected the sleek aircraft, and gazed in wonder at the runways beyond, where other machines were landing and taking off.

"It's wonderful," Eleanor said. "And terrifying. That men and women actually climb into those machines and fly like birds."

"Many times faster than birds," Donovan said. "We will be in Germany in a matter of hours."

"If only Verne could see this," Edgar said. "I am not sure if you are familiar with his work, another author."

"I know him well," Donovan said. "It will probably come as no surprise that I've met him, but we'll have to add that story to the pile of the many we will share at another time. I wish he could see this too, to know how close he came so many times to predicting the future. Did you know that he predicted the skyscrapers, stretching to the sky, lit up at night—and even the elevators that would carry passengers from the bottom to the top? He was a true visionary, and we are living in that vision."

They mounted the steps and climbed into the jet. The hatch was sealed behind them, and they took their seats. There were no rows of uncomfortable bucket-style chairs. All pretense of the normal craft exhibited by the exterior dropped away the moment they entered the main cabin. There were padded leather seats with rounded tables, drink holders to prevent spillage, and docking stations for laptops and phones.

"We have high speed Internet access," a young man said, standing in the doorway. "There is a fully stocked bar, and lunch will be served in a couple of hours. We'll be in to take your orders soon. If you need anything, there is an intercom button by each seat. In the unlikely case of an emergency, oxygen masks will deploy from the compartments above your seats. We are fully protected, though, in more ways than I have time to explain."

"I sense that," Donovan said. "The wards are strong, and I suspect from the sensations they bring that Rebecca York had something to do with them."

The young man smiled. "Indeed," he said. "My name is Andrew. I've been with the organization for several years, and I've worked with Ms. York extensively. She is very talented."

He left them alone then, and they settled in. Amethyst sat beside Eleanor, explaining things as simply as she could and making sure the seatbelts were fastened securely. She explained about the force of the take-off and how it would press them into their seats. Eleanor listened, but kept glancing out the window into the sunlit morning. Donovan watched from his seat beside Edgar, trying to gauge whether she was in shock, or merely taking it all in and processing it slowly.

"Once we are in flight," he said, turning back to Edgar, "I believe I'll avail myself of that bar. We have several hours until we land, and though it's early here to be drinking, it will not be when we arrive in Germany. Travel of this sort causes strange shifts in your internal timekeeping. Best to pretend it is the time you most prefer it to be and go with that."

Edgar nodded. He sat a bit stiffly, and Donovan noted that he gripped the arm of his seat tightly. The first time in a jet was difficult, even for modern men and women who experienced wonders like flight, and high-speed trains on a daily basis.

"Once we are in the air," he said, "you'll barely notice. The landing and the takeoff are both a bit jarring, and now and then there is a bit of wind turbulence that shakes things up, but for the most part, the flight itself does not feel much different than being in the cabin of an airship. I believe you may have some experience in that realm, Edgar? At least judging from that story… "The Balloon Hoax"? If I am a judge of how your stories come to light, I must assume the original experience was very real."

Again, Edgar nodded, but did not speak. Donovan leaned back, glanced out the window, and watched as they pulled slowly away from the terminal and nosed out onto one of the runways. The sunlight glinted off the wings and glass of other aircraft like tiny stars.

A few moments later, after a slow turn to line the jet up with the runway, he felt the familiar rumble of the engines gathering strength. They started forward and picked up speed. The craft shuddered slightly as they neared the far end of the strip, and then there was the soft lifting sensation, the upward swing of the craft's nose, and they were soaring into the morning sunlight.

It was only moments until they breached the clouds and leveled off. Edgar took several long, slow breaths, and then glanced out his window. His eyes widened, but to his credit, he simply watched.

Eleanor stared, rapt. She reached out with a finger to run it over the glass of the window. The sunlight on the tops of the clouds lent a glow that was simply beautiful to behold. After a moment, she reached down to where she'd lain her few belongings and found the leather bag Donovan had given her. Without a word, she pulled out the sketchpad and pencils, and began to draw, tentatively at first, then with growing confidence and speed.

Donovan saw Amethyst glance, just once, at the paper, and then win the battle with her curiosity and look away.

"I believe," Edgar said, finding his voice at last, "that I could use a brandy, if one is to be had. That was exhilarating."

Donovan laughed. He unbuckled himself and walked carefully across the cabin.

"Coffee for me," Amethyst said, "please."

Eleanor glanced up, pausing just for a second in her work. "Do we have tea? She asked. "It has been a very long time."

"If Geoffrey Bullfinch has ever been on this jet," Donovan said, "There will be tea aplenty, and it will be quality stuff. I will check."

He checked the shelves, the bar, and the rest of the cabinets quickly, took stock, and set to work. There were a variety of tea bags available. He chose an Earl Grey, knowing it would be most like what she remembered. He poured two snifters of brandy, and brewed a dark, aromatic cup of coffee in the single cup brewer. He opened the small refrigerator, smiled when he saw the cream, and added a teaspoon of that, and two of sugar, just as Amethyst liked it.

Moments later he'd delivered the drinks and returned to his seat.

"We will have to go over what we know before we land," Edgar said. "It is a shame that we can't involve those who are waiting for us."

Donovan smiled again and shook his head.

"I am afraid that there are still wonders to share," he said. "Give me a moment to contact Bullfinch and I'll see what I can arrange."

He pulled out his laptop and flipped the lid so that it stood like a tripod with the screen facing them on the table. He then opened an application Geoffrey had given him and tapped a few keys. There was a soft buzz, and moments later, the screen filled with an image of a quaint, European hotel room. Seated on a chair facing them was Geoffrey Bullfinch

"Hello, Geoffrey," Donovan said.

"Good morning, my boy," Geoffrey said. "I thought you might give us a call. Give me a moment and I'll see if I can find Gunter. The others are indisposed at this hour. I believe you'll have to await your arrival to meet them face to face."

Edgar had leaned forward and was examining the computer

screen carefully. He sat back, at last, shaking his head.

"He—you," he corrected, "are in a hotel room in Germany. I am hurtling through the sky faster than I can conceive of from any point of perspective available to my experience, and yet, we are speaking as if…"

"As if we were in the same point in time and space," Bullfinch finished. "Yes, miraculous, is it not? You must be Edgar. I have to say, I have long enjoyed your work. I don't know what Donovan has told you of me, but we are nearly contemporaries in a way. You might have known me as Thomas."

Poe blinked, and his eyes widened a bit further, if that was possible. "The Thomas Bullfinch who wrote so eloquently of mythology?"

"I don't know about the eloquence," Bullfinch said, "but that book was mine. I have had to change my name from time to time after a certain number of years. It's best to allow the perception of generations passing to accompany your life and affairs, if you don't wish to draw attention. It is a great pleasure to make your acquaintance."

"And yours, as well," Edgar said, sitting back. He raised a hand to rub his forehead, as if stricken with a sudden headache.

Bullfinch rose and left the room. A moment later, he returned with a tall man in his mid-forties with hair that appeared to defy any suggestions posed by a comb or brush. The man's glasses sat a little crookedly on his nose. The two seated themselves so that they were both clearly visible on the screen.

"Donovan, Edgar, I'd like you to meet a colleague of mine, Gunter Krieg."

"We're here too, Geoffrey," Amethyst called out. She rose and stood behind Donovan, leaning down so that she showed on screen. Eleanor remained seated. She was leaning over the sketchpad, drawing furiously, as though unaware anything around her had changed."

"Eleanor is here, as well," Donovan added. "She is busy currently but can hear you."

"Astonishing," Geoffrey said. "Truly."

"Talk to me, Geoffrey," Donovan said. "Tell me you have something? I believe I may have worked out one third of the puzzle, but I admit that I'm concerned about parts one and three."

"Nothing specific," Bullfinch said. "We have learned a great deal from our companions about this mountain, and about the castle. There is another man, a Father Adolph, who was a part of the group who confronted the vampire Rosa. He provided details even Copper and Alicia were unaware of. I think we have an idea where to go first when we get to the mountain but getting into the castle proper may prove a bit of an enigma.

"When Rosa created her little nook beneath the main building, she sealed off the entrances to the main halls. We're not certain from the sketchy legends we've heard whether she was trying to keep things in, or out."

"That's the part of the puzzle I think I have a handle on," Donovan said. "I'll explain that when we get there. What we need to focus on is how invisibility plays into this, and what represents the key."

"Excuse me," Gunter cut in, "But are you saying you are bringing a horse?"

Donovan fell silent, processing this, and then broke into a huge grin.

"No, my very literal friend, no horse. I believe that the items in the story are metaphorical—symbolic representations of the things the hero of the story used in his quest. My belief is that the place I call the Labyrinth, which would take me a very long time to explain, particularly to a physicist, is the horse. It is a series of passageways and doors that appears differently to different travelers. There are infinite doors, it seems, opening to other places and times, and if you have a means of navigating those ways, you can open a door to just about anywhere."

Gunter blinked, once, and then smiled. "As different as our minds are in their methods of processing the fantastic," he said, "I believe what you are describing is a phenomenon long theorized by my more Avant Garde contemporaries. There are many names for it, the theory of alternate dimensions is one. I prefer the term so familiar to and embraced by fantasists and mystics: the multiverse. In this theory, it is posited that any choice that occurs offers multiple outcomes, and therefore, the possibility that alternate realities diverge from that one point."

"If that were true," Edgar said, his brow furrowed, "then what Donovan calls the Labyrinth would be some sort of focal point, or crux. A place where lines of possibility cross, and where some formula, some ritual, allows one to choose from those infinite possible realities."

He stopped speaking, just for a moment, then glanced up to meet Gunter's eyes across the screens.

"How do we know, after having walked those ways so many times, into so many stories and places, and back again, that we are the same men who entered—or that this is the same world we left behind."

"That is why they call it a theory, young man," Gunter said. Then he laughed at the absurdity. "Sometimes, until we have studied a thing long enough, we must accept that it simply 'works' and let time lead us to the how and why."

"But…" Edgar started to speak, then stopped.

"You see it, do you not?" Gunter smiled. "It is so much like what you do—your mind, your fantasies and poetry and adventures that never happened. They could exist in another pattern of the universe."

"They do," Edgar replied simply. "I have walked among them, as has Donovan—and very recently."

"All that we see or seem," Bullfinch said softly.

Edgar turned to him. "It is odd that those words haunt me now. I wrote them so very long ago, but those close to me seem moved to repeat them at the oddest moments."

"There is nothing more powerful than words that contain truth," Donovan said. "All the spells in the history of the world are proof of that. More often than most, my friend," he set his hand on Edgar's arm, "you see the true pattern."

Edgar stared for a moment and then looked away.

There was a knock on the cabin door, and the young man who'd welcomed them aboard the aircraft stuck his head in.

"Lunch will be served in about ten minutes," he said.

"We will see you in a few hours, Geoffrey," Donovan said. "Go back through that story and see if anything occurs to you, any small thing that we might have missed."

"We will comb through," Bullfinch promised. "If there is anything to find, I believe one of us will see it."

"It was particularly helpful," Gunter added, "that you explained the metaphorical nature of the objects. I feel much more confident in the outcome after hearing that. I am not fond of horses."

They all laughed, and Donovan cut the connection. His screen went dark, then returned to its normal display. He shut it down, closed the top, and packed it carefully away. Then they all returned to their seats to await their meal.

As if just noticing their presence, Eleanor looked up from her work, setting her pencil aside. Without a word, she turned the sketchpad so that they could see. It was a bank of clouds, sunlight gleaming in carefully wrought highlights. Among those rolling, billowing bits of mist, very clearly, she had drawn a string of faces.

"When this is done," she said simply, "I must find a way to help them. So many—"

The others sat stunned.

"That," Amethyst said, taking the drawing and examining it carefully, "will be a very large task. If we can, of course, we will help you. First, though, we have to concentrate on getting you past the danger at hand."

Eleanor nodded, but she glanced out the window once more. When she turned back, she closed the sketchbook, and stowed the pencils and erasers carefully. The scent of roasted chicken floated in through the door, and after a few moments, they all managed to clear their thoughts and eat. The remainder of the flight was spent in silence.

Chapter Twenty-One

"So," Donovan said, spreading the map out before him over the top of a square dining table. "We're agreed that our best move is to come at her from more than one angle. We don't know everything, yet, but if we keep her busy and distracted, we may buy the time we need to figure it out."

They were gathered in the lower chamber of the Inn, where Copper and Alicia had waited out the daylight hours. The sun was setting beyond the mountain, and they were gathered in a tight group.

Father Adolph had joined them, bringing their number to nine.

"We also agree," Donovan continued, "that the Labyrinth is the most likely representation of our mystical horse. If we are correct, and the Brothers Grimm left the clues we need, it's all going to tie in with passageways."

"Which are, of course," Amethyst said, "less safe than ever at present. The good thing is we are nearly certain that our friend on the mountain is unaware that her trap is even partially sprung. It may well be that Eleanor's freedom is either the missing key, or the fact that—though she surely knows others have come to the mountain—the fact Eleanor is among us is hidden—or invisible. This is a lot less certain than our interpretation of the horse. A lot of our answers probably exist at the top of that mountain."

"Our plan," Donovan continued, "depends on getting Eleanor up as close to the tower as possible without notice, and keeping her there, out of sight, until we are certain of our next move.

"Copper, I'm hoping you and Alicia can help with this. The fact that Rosa sealed herself off from that castle would seem to indicate she was aware that it might contain a threat at some point. It also seems reasonable that she either prepared defenses or was aware of those already in place that would help her to avoid unwanted notice. If you can, I'd like the two of you and Edgar to try and get Eleanor there safely and keep her protected and out of sight. I think it's important to separate myself from Edgar because we two are the most capable of opening and using the Labyrinth. You'll have Grimm, of course, Asmodeus will be with me—my eyes when I get higher up. Cleo can accompany the third group.

"Geoffrey, I'm going to ask you to take possibly the most dangerous path—straight up the mountain with Gunter. I want you to just wander directly up the main trails toward the castle, as if you have nothing more in mind than sightseeing or exploring. Father Adolph, if you are planning on tagging along, this would be the group for you, perhaps posing as a guide? It's something of a risk, but it might prove enough of a distraction for Amethyst and me to slip around to another side of the castle and mount a more direct attack.

"I don't know what kind of wards she'll have in place, or what dangers we'll be facing, but I'm confident, at the least, that we can protect ourselves and keep her busy. If, by some miracle, we manage to get inside, I'll send Asmodeus to you. If you discover anything, you'll have Cleo. She and I are always connected on some level."

"Thank you for that," Bullfinch said. "I know she's only met me once or twice, but I will feel much better if we aren't the only ones without a way into those passageways of yours, or a way to reach you should anyone be in need. I should have no trouble playing the part of a doddering old explorer. I've a few years' experience at doing just that, but I believe if it comes to trouble that three old men could certainly use a bit of backup."

Donovan turned to Cleo and raised an eyebrow.

Without hesitation she walked over and wound herself first around Geoffrey's legs, then Gunter's. She came to rest leaning against Father Adolph's knee.

"That much is settled, then," Donovan laughed.

"While I hate to miss a good fight," Copper said, "I have been curious about that mountain den for a very long time. It will be my pleasure to play escort, and body guard as well. It's also possible that we'll be able to provide some insight into what Rosa was doing and what she might have known. You're right in saying if there was a power in that castle tower, she would have been aware of it. If you are also right in your thought that the stolen princess might be a long-lost sister or some other relative. It seems possible that if she had information that could prove valuable, should we be able to locate it.

"Good point, and one I had not considered," Donovan said. "She may prove an unexpected ally after all these years.

"So, Amethyst and I are going to take off immediately. I'd suggest that the three of you, Geoffrey, start your wander next, while Copper and Alicia lead the others on beyond the normal trails and upward through the forest. With luck, you'll be moving quickly enough that you'll be up the mountain before it occurs to whoever is up there to pay attention. We want her to see Geoffrey, but keeping the rest of us out of sight is the key."

"The lower slopes are not so steep," Father Adolph said. "I think, though, that we will not be doing any running. The main path should be well lit by the moon, and I think it will not seem so strange, at least at first, that I am up there, even with companions. Ever since Rosa passed, it has been a particular pleasure of mine to walk there. The darkness held such fear for the people of Rathburg for so long. When I first came here, I did not believe the stories. The villagers would not speak of their fears, but they did not go to that mountain after sunset.

"Now the worst there is to fear is that a young woman might spend too much time out of sight of her parents with her boyfriend. That you might fall and twist your ankle. Men and women walk those paths by day and night, and hunters roam among the trees. I have even performed weddings in the small garden where Rosa and Klaus first worked on that song."

"Now, there is another darkness," Gunter said softly. "When I was a boy, we had our creatures of the night—our shadows. I have never visited this mountain, but I have seen the homes of many of the human monsters who haunt us. I do not want these simple men and women to find how easy it is to fall back into a world of fear. My homeland has been a place of great tragedy, but it is healing. It has been many years since I last set foot here; I would be saddened if it ended in yet another memory of evil."

They all grew silent, just for a moment.

"Let's do it then," Donovan said. "Amethyst, are you ready for an adventure?"

"You know it, Magic Man," she said. "Let's see if we can't put a chink in her armor."

They turned then, grabbed their bags, and slipped out into the night. The moon was nearly full, and there was plenty of light.

"Let's approach from the right," Donovan said. "The map shows that the main entrance faces the village, but there was a large gate on the side, as well, made for visiting troops and to bring cattle and peasants inside in case of an attack."

"A real castle," Amethyst said. "You sure know how to show a girl a good time.

There was a loud flutter of wings, and a soft caw. Asmodeus took flight and whirled across the moon before disappearing into the trees. They followed his lead and started up the mountain at a light trot. It was cool, and the breeze brought unfamiliar scents down from above, and out from the interior of the Inn, and the homes of the citizens of Rathburg. It was a very long way to San Valencez.

Copper slid the branches aside carefully and led Edgar and Eleanor forward. Alicia had gone ahead, and his heightened senses told him she'd shifted form, taking to all fours as a wolf to make better speed. He wished that he could join her, but the others would never find their way unguarded, and he was certain they would react poorly to yet another crazy revelation. They were holding up well, but he knew how disorienting the changes that had reformed the world around them must seem.

When Rosa had first found him, he'd lived in the jungles of Africa. His tribe had been primitive, and though he was intelligent and a quick study, the life she'd dragged him into had been one huge shock after another.

"It's beautiful here," Eleanor said softly. "I've never been out of America until now. What traveling I have done was very slow and limited. It's hard to believe I'm on the far side of an ocean."

"The world is much the same, wherever you find yourself," Edgar said. "It is the same with the people you will meet on your journeys. There are the good, the bad, the ugly, and the stunningly beautiful."

Copper said nothing. He concentrated on Alicia's scent, tracking her up the mountain, and doing what he could to make the climb easier for his charges. If they were having trouble with a simple shift in continents, he was having an equally different time wrapping his head around the fact that the man trailing behind him was Edgar Allan Poe, and the woman was his lost Lenore. Rosa had been ravenous for entertainment. Books, poetry, the music, anything that would give her something that she'd not already experienced.

They had read Poe's works to one another in the early hours of countless mornings, trying to find something new each time. He realized with a start that he could probably recite more of the man's verse than Poe himself. It was yet another surreal moment, and one that—despite all she had done to him—he owed to Rosa.

They had been moving steadily for about an hour and a half when he heard a motion, and Alicia melted from the shadows.

"It's not far," she said. "I found the way in, and I checked to be certain it was empty. No one has been there in a very long time—not even animals. I believe the Magic Man was right. She has some sort of protective spell guarding the place. We should be safe there."

They followed her farther up the mountain, struggling a bit as the terrain grew rougher and steeper. It was nearly impassable, and the reason was soon clear. The spot she led them through hid a low-slung cut in the stone of the cliff. At first, it seemed nothing more than an overhang. They had to duck under a rocky outcrop that was completely hidden from the surrounding landscape by brush and trees to gain entrance, and even then, they stood in complete darkness.

Edgar felt a rush of wind, and, as he stood up inside, he felt Grimm drop heavily to his shoulder, choosing not to remain in flight in the closed quarters.

"Wait," Copper said. A moment later there was the soft snap of a match igniting, and the light of a candle guttered, and then grew, illuminating a small chamber. Again, once you were inside, it seemed that you'd reached the end of the line.

"Around here," Alicia said, leading the way. There was a rounded boulder at the very back of the chamber, and when they stepped past it, they found a narrow passage. Copper followed Alicia, the candle held aloft, and the others fell in behind. It was tight and claustrophobic, making the few yards it contained stretch endlessly. At the far end, a sudden brighter light appeared, and when Edgar stepped into the chamber, he saw that Alicia had found and lit a very old oil lamp.

The chamber's interior was one of the most eerie, uncanny sights Edgar had ever witnessed, and in the journeys through his many tales, he'd seen some very strange things. The room was not cold, but there was a chill in the air all the same. There was no film of dust, or sign of decay. The furnishings were lavish and gave the impression that the owner might walk in at any moment. There were even wine glasses on a table, though the wine in the bottle beside them long dried to dark dust.

Grimm lifted off, circled the room, and lit atop one of the ancient chairs circling a fireplace. There was wood resting on a grate as if waiting for someone to pull out a tinderbox and strike a fire with their flint. The chamber felt ancient, and yet, somehow timeless.

There were divans and couches along the walls. Tapestries dangled from hooks near the ceiling. It was like a great, royal version of the smaller space Rosa had built beneath the Rathburg Inn at the base of the mountain. Clearly, at one point this had been a lower level of the greater structure above, or perhaps a remnant of the previous castle, the bones upon which the newer structure had been built. There was a sensation of absolute separation from the world in every inch of the place.

One wall, as in the chamber beneath the Inn, was lined with musical instruments. Despite having been left untouched for decades, they glistened in the flickering light of the lamp and candle. They were beautiful, and very old.

Edgar stepped closer and ran a finger gently over the surface of one of the violins. "I am not an expert by any means," he said with awe, "but I believe this is a Stradivarius."

"I would be shocked if it were not," Alicia said. "You will not find an instrument here that is not worth the price of a modern orchestra. She knew them, you see. She taunted them and haunted them. She played their music, and their instruments, and left them bits and pieces of songs. For me, the time apart from her has been much shorter than our time together, and I am still shocked when I hear, or see, or find some trace of her. She walked the world and lived like a dark flame. She left a mark."

"So it would seem," Edgar said, still admiring the instruments.

"We need to start searching," Copper said. "There is a lot here, and very little time to get through it. Look for books, journals, chests; look anywhere she might have tucked something away to keep it out of sight. I don't believe she'd go to any great length to hide anything here, because she did not believe anyone would ever be without her."

"Until now, that was true," Alicia said. "But what we are looking for—it would be hidden so that, at some point, it *could* be found without her, or what would be the point?"

There was another wall that seemed to be one continuous bookshelf. Gleaming bindings of dark leather winked at her. There was a shelf with more modern volumes, and there were alcoves filled with papers and folders, packets of parchment—scrolls. It was overwhelming.

Eleanor was drawn to a large tapestry. At first glance it seemed to be nothing more than a beautiful landscape. Something about it was off, though, something that did not seem quite in line with the intricate detail. She started at one end and moved slowly along it, half certain she'd see a face beseeching her in some splash of color, a trapped soul who would draw her in, but there was nothing; at least, there was nothing obvious.

She turned and watched the others for a moment. Edgar was

fingering the strings of a very old guitar, and Copper had found a desk in a far corner. He was shuffling quickly and efficiently through a pile of letters, and documents. Alicia had made it about halfway down the length of the bookshelves. They were so well ordered, so symmetrical, that the pattern created by their spines was nearly hypnotic.

Eleanor turned back to the tapestry, and she saw it. The hillside she was staring at with its even rows of crops, perfectly symmetrical roads, buildings of stone cut into such perfect blocks they seemed impossible—it formed a pattern. All of it. The same pattern as the bookshelves across the room.

Except on the tapestry, there was a road, a spiraling trail leading to an object just a bit shy of the center. It was a rendering of an ornate iron gate decorated with a wrought iron sculpture shaped like a bell. On second glance, it reminded her more of a birdcage. Atop it, staring at her, sat a single raven, its eyes dark with bright highlights, its talons wrapped tightly about the iron of the gate.

She let out a gasp and stepped back, nearly tripping. With uncanny speed, Alicia was at her side, steadying her.

"What is it? Did you find something?"

"I—I think so. Look. Tell me if you see it."

Eleanor pointed at the gate and the raven. Alicia glanced at it, and her eyes widened as she swept her gaze from side to side. She took Eleanor by the arm and guided her quickly to the shelves on the far wall. She reached up without hesitation and dragged a single volume free.

It was bound in leather, very old, but not by a professional bindery. It was more like a journal, wrapped in leather straps that held a flap in place, protecting the contents. As Edgar and Copper joined them, Alicia handed the book to Eleanor.

"You found it," she said with a smile. "Let's see what Rosa has left for us—a clue, or just another dark joke."

Alicia unknotted the old leather straps with trembling fingers and drew back the flap. The interior pages were covered in hand-scribed lines of text, and carefully drawn diagrams and images, but the language was not English. Eleanor stared for a moment, shook her head, and looked to the others for help.

"It's German," Copper said, reading over her shoulder. "See here, on the first page? It's a note explaining that these are collected notes and research. This last line—"

He pointed, and Alicia read softly "die Brüder Grimm. The Brothers Grimm."

Eleanor handed the book to Copper, and the tall vampire flipped through the pages rapidly. He barely seemed to glance at the words, but there was an intensity in his expression that belied this. A moment later he came to a halt on a page with a sketch of a tall tower and a mountain. At the top of the page were the words "die raben."

"The Raven," Edgar said.

Eleanor turned to him, surprised.

"I have seen and done much since we were last together," Edgar explained, smiling thinly. "I am far from fluent, but there are certain words I might not be forgiven for mistaking in any language, all things considered."

Copper continued to read. Now and then he stopped, and explained what he'd found. What was recorded on the pages was not so much a complete story, as it was a series of notes and scribbles, but there were drawings, and, on the final page, there was a detailed map of a tower.

"Is that this place?" Alicia asked.

Copper nodded slowly. "I think so. If not, it's very similar. We need to see if we can figure out if there is anything helpful in it. Rosa seems to have known someone would come here and find this."

"My God," Edgar said softly, as a sudden epiphany hit him. "Do you know what you are holding in your hands?"

Copper turned and raised an eyebrow.

"It's their notes," Edgar said. "The Grimm brothers were not just writers; they traveled and collected folklore and fables. They interviewed people to gather the oral traditions of the old stories. That book, that journal, is the resource behind their fables."

"I wonder," Alicia said, "if one of those they interviewed wasn't a much younger Rosa? If all we have guessed is true, it could be that we have been looking at this entire thing in a completely skewed manner. What if the brothers Grimm left no clues at all? What if they had no idea what was going on in the tower, never knew there was a real princess. What if Rosa fed it to them?

"Think about it. It's exactly what she'd always done. She found creatives. She drew them to her until they could think of literally nothing else, and then she fed off their energy. She gave that bit of song to Sebastian, the keyboardist from Klaus' band, and she may have given the answers to our quest, hundreds of years before it was certain who would find or use them.

"It could be that, though she did not have the power, or possibly enough actual concern, to try and save her lost sister, or aunt, or whoever that girl is, she did care enough to leave a means for someone else to do it."

"If so," Copper said, "I am certain she intended to be around to watch it unfold."

"None of that matters now," Eleanor said. "Bring that book over here to the light where Edgar and I can see it as well as the two of you. Let's see if the notes—or the diagram of the tower—shows us a way in. It seems to me that since your Rosa sealed this place away from the castle, the key to breaking that seal—or slipping past it—is likely here. No one goes to the elaborate trouble of a thing like that tapestry for no reason."

"I thought it was a little too perfect when we came in," Copper said, glancing at the magnificent wall hanging. "Now that you have said it, I can see her hand in every stitch. It would take a man or a woman years to create such a thing, but she probably did it in a week."

They all dropped onto one of the long couches beside the flickering oil lamp to study the pages of the ancient book. Grimm, as if anticipating some change, glided down to rest on Edgar's shoulder. They read in silence, each taking a turn at studying the diagram. They knew there was little time.

Chapter Twenty-Two

It did not take Father Adolph long to lead his two companions to a set of stone steps that led to a level clearing, where what could have been a small garden, or even an ancient altar, still stood. There were stone benches, and they all sat gratefully.

"This is where Klaus came to meet with Rosa," Father Adolph said, "When she showed him what she was and introduced him to the others. The one they called Alex surely wanted to kill him. Klaus. Alex was arrogant and jealous, and very, very much alone. He would not have lasted a week without the others, at least not in such a small community."

They glanced around, took in the face of moon and the clouds shifting across it.

"We can't wait long," Bullfinch said. "Coming this far, as you said before, won't be seen as much of an anomaly."

"Of course."

"Are you okay, Gunter?" Bullfinch asked.

Gunter turned to stare at him, as if just becoming aware he was not alone on a strange mountainside, studying the stars.

"Yes. Yes, of course," he said. "I have done a lot of hiking and climbing in my day. And walking. I quite like a long, quiet walk where I can think without distraction."

"I can't promise this hike will be distraction-free," Bullfinch said, "but it's going to be long, and as we move upward, it's going to get steeper and more difficult. I suggest that as we near the castle, we continue to speak—as loudly as we can without it sounding forced. We won't talk about what we're doing here, of course, but maybe the good Father will tell us more about the times when Rosa and her minions prowled the forest."

"Of course. It's quite the story, and it stretches farther back than even Alicia knew. It was interesting to meet them after all this time. They caused their own share of trouble here, but I can see that they have made different choices since their liberation."

"I have spent more than a little time among the undead," Bullfinch said. "For the most part, those who have survived into modern times have found ways to fit in and remain in the shadows. Donovan's city is home to their council. They have quite the intricate social structure for creatures our myths and fables would have leading solitary existences and sleeping in coffins."

"Every time I sit in my tiny office in my secluded church and begin to feel that the world is shrinking around me, something, or someone, widens it once more. Do you know, Geoffrey, how hard it was for me to accept?"

"Rosa?"

"All of it."

Father Adolph rose and turned to walk up the path but continued talking.

"Vampires. Evil. When I came here, the villagers tried to tell me. They warned me. It was a very long time after that before I had even the first tickle of belief. I believed in my God and my church. I thought the local men and women had told their children stories about evil creatures to keep them home at night for so long that they had forgotten they were only stories.

"Then that band came, Von Kroft. One of their members, his name was Sebastian, came to see me. He sat with me, and we talked. He knew something was happening to his friend. He suspected that it was more than just an obsession with a song, or with a woman, but he could not put a name to it.

"If I had been more vigilant before they arrived, and less arrogant in my knowledge of the world, I might have helped him sooner. We might have found a different outcome. His friend? Who knows?"

"You might also have inadvertently left Klaus' parents tied alone and starving into dust for eternity," Bullfinch said. "It's very easy to look back in time and see the twists and turns you might have made, but much more difficult to turn them around again, and see how each might have twisted the present."

"The multiverse, again, I think," Gunter said. "An infinite number of choices, none right, or wrong. Just different. Your church teaches that free will was the gift of their God, and yet, the exercising of that gift was man's greatest sin. It is a paradox I have never quite wrapped my mind around."

"It is one of the most difficult problems of faith," Father Adolph agreed. "You are free to act as you wish, but if you do not wish to act as you were created to act, you are damned."

"My perception of this comes down to the same truth every time," Gunter said. "The concepts of organized religion start with good teaching, and good intentions, but as soon as they are out of the hands of God and into the hands of men they are manipulated, twisted, and turned into something entirely different. It is enough to concentrate on living one's life in the best manner possible without spending time and thought on talking snakes and what happens if you choose the wrong apple."

They walked in silence for a moment, and then Father Adolph began to laugh. He turned to each of his companions, and then stopped, just for a moment, staring up at the mountain before them.

"This," he said, "Is going to prove one of the most interesting walks of my life, I believe. Even if we do not run afoul of evil queens or get caught in the crossfire of some occult battle. I believe my soul, for the moment, is in good hands."

"I have always wondered," Gunter said, as if none of the previous conversation had occurred, "about the nature of a soul. If we are all pure energy, and all connected, perhaps there is but one soul, and we share it. Perhaps they stretch between worlds and dimensions, and we have one, but share that one with thousands, perhaps billions of others."

Bullfinch turned to Father Adolph.

"Do *not* ask him about his theory on the nature of vampires. This is beginning to sound suspiciously similar to it, and the next thing we'll be discussing is whether Alicia and Copper are siphoning off bits of their doppelgangers' souls to keep them alive, and, if so, the spiritual consequences of such a bond."

"I would be lying," Father Adolph replied, "if I tried to tell you that did not sound fascinating."

Bullfinch laughed and trudged on. "Then it would seem," he said, "that I am doomed to greater understanding when all I sought was a pleasant, moonlight stroll."

The path, at least at its lower levels, was smooth and recently worn. There were footprints and signs of recent visitors, a thing that seemed to lift Father Adolph's spirits even further.

"Let me tell you about Sebastian," he said. "He was a very talented young man, well-spoken and intelligent. I often hope that he will return one day."

"I'll make you a deal," Bullfinch said. "If we get through this, I'll see if the organization can't track them all down. The band, I mean. Maybe a reunion would bring some kind of closure. Particularly since the story wasn't really over when they left."

"I would like that very much. For now, though, my story."

As they walked on, he told them of Sebastian, Devan, and the rest of the band, the girls they'd brought, the stage on the mountain with its great speakers and huge crowd. All the time, the moon shone down on them, illuminating the path ahead, and making them easily visible to anyone far above.

Donovan moved rapidly up the mountain, not quite at a run, but very close to it. Amethyst paced him, seeming not to feel the effort at all. They had left the cleared path miles back, shifting steadily to the right and climbing in a wide arcing spiral to come at the castle from the side.

"It must have been a very long time since the place crumbled," Amethyst said. "If there was a road here for moving cattle, supplies, and troops, there's no sign of it."

She was right. The trees were uniformly tall and thick. Nearer to the ground the trunks were slightly farther apart than one might expect, but they had clearly grown undisturbed for a hundred years or more. Moonlight trickled down through the branches and drizzled dancing glimmers across the underbrush and grass.

The higher they went, the clearer the land. Apparently, things grew at a slower pace higher up. Eventually they saw that they were going to be exposed by the time they reached the last slope upward, and they paused.

"This would have been a good time for that cloak of invisibility," Donovan said, frowning. "I'm pretty sure we can hold our own, but I'd be a lot *more* confident if I thought she wasn't going to see us coming."

"I might be able to get us across that last open stretch," Amethyst said. "You're not the only one with a bag of tricks, but once we're there, we still have a good way to climb, and we're going to be pretty exposed."

Asmodeus whirled overhead. He circled once, and then wheeled in close to the slope. He spun away at the last second, glided across the scrub brush and rocks, then took another long, circling dive—and disappeared.

Donovan glanced at Amethyst, then back at the side of the mountain. About a hundred yards up, the old bird rose, just for a moment, then dove back out of sight.

Donovan grinned.

Amethyst frowned. "If you say, 'Hey, I think Lassie is trying to tell us something,' I am ending you."

Donovan laughed. "Get us in close," he said. "I think he's telling us that the road into the castle is still there, or part of it, and that it's cut down into the mountain. If that's true, we'll have some cover most of the way up. Then all we have to do is either scale the walls of a ruined castle, open an ancient door that's probably not even there anymore, or bust through solid rock."

"You make it sound fun," she said.

Amethyst pulled out two long, slender chains. One end of each was attached by a hook to a leather handle, and on the other dangled long, slender smoky crystals. She handed one to Donovan, and he held it up, letting the stone hang like a pendulum.

"This looks familiar," he said.

"It should," she told him. "The other crystal that you have is for protection. This one is made with smoky quartz. I made them years ago. They have to be exposed for long periods to fog and smoke, and there is a ritual that must be performed over several weeks. I take them running with me in the mornings for the mist."

Donovan whirled the chain in a slow circle. He watched carefully.

"I don't see anything," he said, letting it slow to a halt. "Are you sure?"

He caught her expression and bowed his head. "Okay," he said. "Let's go."

"Over your head," she said, stepping into the lead. She started flicking her crystal in a tight circle over her head while walking slowly, but steadily, across the last open stretch toward the mountain.

Donovan stood for a moment, getting the rhythm of the moment down, and set off after her. It was impossible to tell what effect the stones and chains were having. Asmodeus had climbed and whirled again, circling back behind them. He dove again, heading for what Donovan now saw was a sort of wide crevasse cut into the earth and stone. Some of the crevasse's side walls had crumbled, but in other places hand-placed stone was visible, the remnant of the road itself.

He was so caught up in thinking about this, imagining the traffic in and out of the castle, that he nearly missed it when Asmodeus, continuing his dive, headed straight for him. He turned, saw the bird, and cried out, releasing his grip on the chain and diving forward to avoid a direct collision.

The bird rose sharply, letting out a startled cry.

That settles that question, Donovan thought. It was working.

He crawled over to where the chain had fallen and picked it up. There were only a few yards separating him from the entrance to the road, so he tucked it into his pocket and continued on his hands and knees until he saw Amethyst crouching ahead behind a cracked boulder.

"Very graceful," she said.

Donovan didn't reply. He was studying the slope above them for any sign of movement, of any indication that he'd been spotted. Nothing had changed. It was dark, and only bats crossed the bright face of the moon. Asmodeus had dropped to perch on his shoulder.

"You'd better stay close, old friend," he said. "She may be evil, but she's not stupid, and she knows birds. Not many of you are comfortable flying by night."

The old raven ruffled his feathers and settled.

"Let's see where this takes us," Amethyst said, turning and starting up the old road. "Maybe we'll find a ghost along the way to show us the servant's entrance."

"We should be so lucky," Donovan said. "Anyway, I remember Edgar's version of the story, the one he saw in his vision. The sorceress *was* a servant, or was disguising herself as one, so that would probably not be our best point of entry."

The way was surprisingly clear, and up ahead he saw the lower-level entrance, which had once been a massive iron gate, but was now reduced by time to strips of rust entwined with clinging vines. It was mostly blocked by the vines, and there was a gnarled tree growing up through the tines of the gate. Very few leaves remained, and the tree seemed mostly dead, but it gave him an idea.

"I think we might be able to get over at the tree," he said. "Once we're on the other side, we'll have better cover. If we have to do something drastic to get in, at least we'll have a few minutes to prepare."

Amethyst nodded.

"You first, Magic Man," she said.

He grinned, took a short run up the last slope, which set Asmodeus' wings fluttering again, and leaped. He caught the bottom branch of the tree and swung up. There was a loud creak, and for a moment he thought it would break and send him back onto the rocks, but the ancient gate braced it, and it held. He quickly scrambled up, and after glancing over the top to be certain the ground was clear on the far side, he waved to Amethyst to follow and dropped into the shadows.

Moments later she was at his side again, and they took stock of the situation. The road continued up to the side of the mountain. An arched passageway led into deeper shadows, but there did not seem to be a door or gate barring the way.

"Seems too easy," Amethyst said.

"Which is why we are going to assume it's a trap," Donovan said. "We still have to go in."

She nodded. She pulled another stone from a pocket in her jacket, but kept it cupped tightly between her palms.

"It will help with the darkness," she explained. "But first we need to get inside. It's kind of bright, but I think at this point our chance at sneaking in is nearly gone. Better to see whatever is coming at us so we know how to defend ourselves."

"Right then," Donovan said. "Let's do it.

They moved a few yards into the shadows, and then Amethyst opened her hands slowly, letting the light from the crystal illuminate the passageway. The stone was set on a leather thong, which she looped over her head, freeing her hands.

Donovan glanced down at the light, then grinned.

"Eyes on the prize," Amethyst growled. "Happy as it seems to be making you, don't let that be the last thing you see."

He laughed and turned away. They moved farther in. The passage hooked to the right, and they approached the turn slowly.

"Maybe she's arrogant, or crazy enough, not to worry about someone finding this way in," Amethyst said.

Almost as if on cue, they heard a loud, scraping sound, like metal grinding against stone, and both stopped cold.

"Well, hell," Amethyst said. "I should have known better."

They continued more slowly, and as they did so, Donovan began to speak softly, chanting words he'd memorized decades before. He felt energy seeping up from the ground at his feet and from the walls around them. It was like a silvery web of light, and he searched along those threads, reaching out to the shadows, to whatever waited around the corner. When he finally made contact, he stopped and stood very still. He reached out, grabbed Amethyst's arm and pulled her back. She turned to him and he reached out with one finger and brushed it across her eyes. One of the silvery strands trailed his finger and attached to her lashes, like spider silk. And then she saw.

The passageway grew so silent that when Grimm pecked softly at his neck, it sounded like a hammer blow.

The creature blocking their way moved again, and the silence was shattered by the grate of scales on stone. As one, they ducked, and ran forward, and cried out. Asmodeus squawked and took to the air. The bird barely managed to slip past the striking head as a great serpent slid further into view, and then everything went to hell.

Chapter Twenty-Three

Edgar finally turned away from the diagram and stood. He walked back around the corner and stared at a stretch of wall. There were no shelves there, and it was clear of tapestries, hangings, and instrument racks. It was, in fact, the only part of any of the walls that was just—a wall.

"What is it?" Alicia asked, glancing up from the pages of the book Copper still held.

"I think we're being too literal," he said, "which no doubt sounds odd coming from a man who has spent his life in the company of words. We are looking for a doorway, or a stair, or a place where an entrance might have been bricked in. When we came here, though, we were already convinced that Donovan's Labyrinth, the road I have traveled for decades, was the key. What we should be looking for is the point where this place and that other meet. I have the sense that if I were to simply touch this wall—"

He did so, and, rather than brushing against stone, his fingers pressed inward on a door, heavy wood, and dark. Beyond it, lit by the same flickering light as the room where he stood, a corridor stretched off into the shadows on either side.

Edgar turned and raised an eyebrow. "Shall we?" he said.

They closed the book and rose. Copper tucked the old volume into his waistband beneath his coat.

"Just in case," he said.

Then they stepped past Edgar, who held the door, and into the passage beyond. Edgar followed, and the door closed behind them with a soft *snick*!

"This is new," Edgar said. He had stopped at one of the entryways to the right of the passageway. It opened onto a spiral stairway, leading upward. "I have never seen a stairway like this, and I have never seen an entrance, or an exit, without an actual door."

"Do you think it's a trap?" Copper asked. He stepped up beside Edgar and leaned in, looking upward.

"No way to know," Edgar said. "I never know where the doorways will lead; I only know the one I am meant to take."

"And this is it?" Eleanor asked.

He nodded. "For better or worse, it is."

"Then," Alicia said with a smile, "lead the way, Mr. Poe. I very much want to see how this ends."

Copper grinned and said, ""Deep into that darkness peering, long I stood there, wondering, fearing, doubting, dreaming dreams no mortal ever dared to dream before.'"

Edgar stood very still, then turned. "When this is finished, we are going to have a talk, friend Copper. You have impeccable taste in literature. For now, though, if that woman is at the end of this stair, I have scores to settle."

He stepped through into the shadows, and the others followed.

There was a hunter's cabin about halfway up the mountain, and Father Adolph led the group there. It was very old, with walls of stone and roof that showed years of wear. The windows were boarded, and the place had an ominous chill hanging about it, giving it the aspect of a cave or a tomb.

"I have an idea," the old priest said. "If it is our intention to draw attention to ourselves, we may want more than an electric torch to light the way. I believe we can find what we need here for some actual torches. I admit my sense of drama compels me. This all reminds me of that novel by Mary Shelley."

"Indeed!" Bullfinch said with a grin. "We are the villagers, storming the castle to roust the monster. Something like that?"

"Exactly," Father Adolph said. "It is also much steeper and rougher from here on up. When there was a castle there, I suspect the trails were clear of brush, but now the only people who travel beyond this are hunters—and the more intrepid hikers and climbers. They tend to leave less trace of themselves in passing and are not much bothered by hard going. The torchlight will be brighter and could prevent my falling and breaking a hip. I am not a young man."

Cleo, who had been stalking along the side of the path, just out of sight, took that moment to wrap herself around his legs. He stumbled slightly, but she moved—so quickly it was hard to tell if she had shifted, or if he'd been incorrect about her initial position. The big cat nudged him, and he regained his balance.

"Point taken," the old priest said. He knelt and stroked Cleo's ear. "I have never been one for pets," he said, "but somehow, I sense, you are no man's pet. I am pleased to be your companion, and even more pleased to have you looking out for me."

Cleo let out a soft meow and began washing her paw.

Bullfinch laughed. "I believe you have made a friend," he said.

"I wonder," Gunter said, cutting in. "Is this the place? From your story? The parents?"

"No," Father Adolph said, his mood darkening perceptibly at the memory. "I will not return to that place. It's not far from here, but it is off the regularly traveled paths. Rosa couldn't take a chance on someone stumbling across them and either making the mistake of releasing them, or—for her purposes even worse—killing them. They were well hidden.

"This structure, though, is very similar. The design is almost the same. Inside is a fireplace, and there will be tinder, logs, and some oil for the lamp, as well as a supply of drinkable water and dried meat. There are a couple of cots, a table, and some chairs. Parties of hunters use it as a base so they can extend the range of their hunts without returning to Rathburg."

"How do you know the place?" Bullfinch asked. "You don't strike me as a hunter; did they have you come up to bless it?"

Father Adolph laughed.

"No. As I told you, I walk up these paths quite a lot. More than once I've encountered hunting parties here in my wanderings. I often stop just to see if someone is here before going any farther up. Prevents turning myself into a target, or, at least it gives me advance warning. Also, at my age, it's not a good idea to travel too far up a mountain without anyone knowing you are gone."

They entered the old cabin and located the firewood and oil. Father Adolph found a pile of rags in one corner and tore them into strips. Bullfinch walked back outside and returned with three stout branches. He cleared them of leaves and twigs, and the three of them set to work binding the bits of rag around the top of each. They were crude but serviceable. When they had tied as much material to each branch as they could, they took the oil out to the path and soaked the rags thoroughly.

"That should do it," Bullfinch said.

Gunter returned the oil to its place, and they left the cabin, closing its door carefully behind them.

"We've lost enough time," Father Adolph said. "It is time to make ourselves visible and make some noise. I don't know what will happen, what we might bring down upon ourselves, but I'm feeling a bit adventurous."

Gunter tilted his head. "Odd," he said. "I feel no differently than before, but I very much want to meet an ancient sorceress, if such a being exists, and I rather like watching the chemical reactions of fire."

Bullfinch laughed and pulled out a lighter. He lit the torch Father Adolph held, and it flickered to life, flared, then settled to a steady burn.

"One at a time should do the trick," he said. "They will last longer that way."

They started up the mountain again, moving as quickly as they could. The torch lit their way better than the flashlights had, and despite the rougher, steeper trail, they made good time.

The moon was very bright, but the circle of light from the torch lengthened the shadows around them. The trail was littered with protruding stones, fallen limbs, and brush. Bullfinch studied it carefully.

"This was a major road at one time," he said, "These stones— see how they have settled with their corners jutting up out of the earth? They are very large and would have taken a good deal of work to set in place. For the mountain to have settled sufficiently to cause these breaks means they must have been placed several centuries ago, at least."

"Is it normal for them to settle into a mountain?" Gunter asked. "I would have thought the stone beneath impervious to such shifting."

"It's actually more likely here than on a straight, level plain," Bullfinch said. "Mountains give the impression of solidity and timelessness, but they are initially formed by the motion of huge planes beneath the earth's surface. This never stops. They evolve, grow, sink, fall apart."

"Like lives," Gunter said. Then his gaze returned to the mountain, and it was hard to tell from his expression if he was still thinking about mountains and lives, or if he'd gone to some other place entirely within his mind.

The road wound upward in a long curve, and as they passed the last row of tall trees before the forest fell away, they saw the full face of the peak and the castle that crowned it. The sight was awe-inspiring in its grandeur, and its entropy. The bones of the place were intact. The tallest towers still stretched up toward the moon, but their edges were blunted. The sharp lines of cut stone had gone softer, and parts of the battlements simply did not exist.

"I wonder," Father Adolph said, stopping to stare, "what it was like when it was young. It must have taken years of labor just to cut the foundation into the mountain, and to drag the stones up and raise them into—this."

He fell silent.

There was no entrance evident on the ground level. There must once have been a gate, and it would have been tall, but the walls to either side had crumbled, and where the road had been cut from the mountain, the sides had poured in and filled it. The trail stopped at that pile of rubble. Almost as if planned by some cosmic interference, that rubble led up at a slant toward the walls, almost directly to windows on the second level.

"Looks like getting in is not going to be a problem," Bullfinch said. "I don't suppose she's left the way clear, but one can always hope."

"That seems like such a random way to conduct business," Gunter said. "*Hope*, I mean. It's like creating an equation missing most of the numbers and trusting that the few you have will see you through to a solution."

Bullfinch shook his head.

"You," he said, "are a font of optimism, my friend."

"Am I? I don't mean to be. Actually."

Before the old physicist could say more, Bullfinch started up the slope toward the open windows and the castle beyond. The others followed, and, as they stepped over the threshold of the first window into the shadows, he called out.

"Hello! Anybody home?"

There was no answer, but for just a moment the wind grew slightly colder, and the moonlight dimmed. They lit the second torch from the first.

Cleo scampered up beside him and leaped past into the passage beyond. Bullfinch laughed, and lifted his torch, following.

"Onward into the breach!" he said and started down the hall in search of a way upward.

The darkness closed in behind them like a curtain as soon as the torch was out of range.

Chapter Twenty-Four

The serpent struck without hesitation. Its great red eyes were focused on Donovan, and that is the only reason he survived. Amethyst dove in from the side, slipped a thin dark blade from her boot and drove it into the side of the creature's head. It reared back, slammed into the stone wall, and thrashed violently, before sliding back to the floor. The sound of its scales slipping over one another was like shifting sand in a storm, and Donovan knew it wasn't dead, but coiling and regrouping.

"What," Amethyst said, breathing heavily and drawing forth two more blades, "was that?"

"I'm not sure," Donovan said, "but whatever it is, it's not happy to see us."

"How do we kill it?"

"I'd rather not," he said. "If I'm correct, it's not from around here. I'd rather send it home."

"To giant *snakeland*?"

"Something like that," he said.

Donovan pulled a vial from one of the deep pockets of his jacket.

"We have to distract it," he said. "I need a moment to prepare this. Any ideas?"

Amethyst didn't answer. She pulled a second blade from her belt, and, with one knife in each hand, dove into the center of the passage. As she hit, she rolled, came back to her feet, and, as the creature struck again, she hit the wall and kept going. She ran up the side of the wall, and, as the snake's head slammed into the stone where she'd been, she leapt, coming down on top of its head and jabbing the twin blades into the flesh behind its eyes.

Where the blades met skin, they glowed, one red, and one blue. There was a vibration—not really a sound, but a scream that came from someplace beyond sound—but she held on tightly.

Donovan ran to the wall where the serpent had struck. He pulled the cork from the vial in his hand and swept his arm in an arc that splashed some sort of liquid that drew a semicircle of light on the surface of the stone. He leaped back and called out a sequence of words that brightened the light. Then, with a quick flick of his wrist, he was gone. Seconds later he appeared in the center of the circle.

He called out to Amethyst: "Get free! Let it go!"

He had no way of knowing if she heard, or if she did as he asked. One moment the serpent was coiled, eyes flashing like deep, red-hot embers, and the next it drove forward. Apparently, it believed that if it failed to close its fangs on his flesh, killing him by driving him back through the stone was the next best thing.

Except when it struck, Donovan was not there. His image flickered, wavered, and disappeared, and as the massive creature struck what should have been a solid wall, it drove straight through and disappeared into a pool of brightening light.

Donovan saw it try to slow its momentum, but, wherever it had come out on the other side, there must have been a slope or a drop-off. The rest of its body passed through, picking up speed, until, finally, it disappeared completely.

With a blinding flash of light and energy, the circle closed. Donovan shielded his eyes, steadied himself against the force of the blast, and turned, already moving toward where Amethyst should have fallen.

She was there, rising groggily from the floor of the passageway. She still held the two blades, both dripping dark, thick blood.

"I hate snakes," she said. "Where did you send it?"

"Back to wherever it calls home," Donovan said. "The potion I used to create the portal drew upon the creature's essence and, basically, used the same spell that had originally summoned it here to create a breach. A change in dimensions is always simpler when you are putting things back the way they were originally, than when you are drawing from one to another."

"Good to know," Amethyst said. She rubbed the knives in the dirt to cleanse them of the serpent's blood. They glittered in the dim light.

"You'll have to tell me about those one of these days," Donovan said. "For the moment, I suggest we get moving before our host decides one giant snake isn't enough."

"I wonder what kind of connection she has with her spells," Amethyst said, sheathing her blades and starting around the corner. "It would help if we could tell whether she knows we're coming."

"We'll have to assume that on some level, she does," Donovan said. "If we're lucky, she'll already be distracted. I'm not sure how the others are doing, but I can sense that Cleo is near, so Bullfinch and his group must have reached the castle."

"I hope they don't' find anything like we did waiting for them," Amethyst said. "I don't know about Bullfinch, but I doubt Gunter or Father Adolph are carrying any dimensional portals."

"I don't think she'll see them as that kind of threat," Donovan said, "and I don't believe she'll have the same level of protection on the main entrance to the castle. There is too much chance that people from the village might wander up and try to get inside, and the last thing she wants is to draw the attention of the outside world."

"I hope you're right."

"She'll also have Edgar and the others to worry about. I know she's old and powerful, but our undead friends are no slouches, and Edgar himself seems to be able to do things without effort that I've spent years perfecting."

They ran down another hallway and found an opening to the left that led to stairs. It was a narrow entrance, and the steps were steep. The two climbed as quickly as they could without being reckless.

"These must have been for servants, or possibly guards," Donovan said. "This isn't the sort of entrance a noble would use. Not by choice, anyway."

"Perfect for a couple of modern warriors then," Amethyst said. "How far up do you think that tower is?"

"From the outside, I'd guess there are at least four levels. The ceilings below were high, and that was just the antechamber. When we reach the upper levels, where people would have lived, and where visiting dignitaries would be allowed, things will be more open—and grander."

"At least there will be room to fight."

They climbed, avoiding crumbled steps and clambering over small piles of rubble. There was no sign that any other had passed the way in years. The way was clear, though, and they eventually stepped out into what must have been a kitchen. One wall was lined with stone ovens, and there was a long table, broken and canted to the side, but still basically intact despite its age. Donovan didn't hesitate. He skirted the near wall, passed by the first exit he saw, followed the wall to a point just short of the ovens, then slipped through a second entrance.

"How do you know this is the way?" Amethyst asked, following.

"I don't, but Asmodeus went this way. He was ahead of us, but I sense him. It's sort of like a thin thread of a spiderweb. He is sure, and that's enough for me. Without his help we could be wandering around these halls for hours."

The second set of stairs was clear from bottom to top, and at the top they entered a wide hallway. It stretched off into the distance and appeared to lead to a line of bed chamber doors. Some of the doors had rotted and fallen into the hallway, others were still in place. Donovan continued down the center of the hall, heading for a wide stair at the far end. It stretched up to either side with a platform in the middle.

Above them, Asmodeus circled into view. The ceilings were even higher than they'd been on the lower levels, and the bird had plenty of room to maneuver. He wheeled about and headed directly up the right-hand branch of the grand stair. Donovan and Amethyst followed, picking up speed.

"Do you feel it?" Amethyst asked.

Donovan did not turn to her; he concentrated on the ancient, crumbling stairs. "Feel what?"

"Maybe it's just me, and the stone, sometimes I can channel vibrations. There is power here, and it's strengthening. I don't know if that's because we're getting closer to it, or if something is about to happen. Be ready."

They reached a landing and Donovan grabbed her arm, slowing her. The stairs continued up to the right at a sharp angle.

"Wait," he said. "If you can sense her, or something, can you magnify it? If we are still, and not running, is it something you can focus?"

Amethyst said nothing, but she drew forth one of the many crystals dangling on cords and chains around her neck and held it in the palm of her hand. It was a sphere, about an inch in diameter. She stood very still and breathed on the tiny ball. Her breath fogged in the chill air. Then she closed her eyes. When she opened them, the fog from her breath was fading, revealing an image in the crystal sphere.

Details were hard to make out, but there was a room with windows. They saw very old furniture, a flickering lamp, and shelves lined with books. The place was not worn or falling apart. It was furnished with chairs, a table, and a bed with a canopy. To the side of that bed stood a very large, ornate cage. It was like something you would have for a bird, except, it stood nearly six feet in height, and inside they could make out the figure of a girl.

Then darkness swirled across the face of the crystal, and Amethyst dropped it with a start, shaking her hands and blowing on them.

"Damn it!" she said.

"She knows someone is here now," Donovan said. "Was it me, or did that room not look like it was somewhere in this castle?"

Amethyst nodded. "It was either a very powerful glamour, or she has sealed it off from—from time? Or just protected it? Moved it?"

"No way to know until we're there," Donovan said. "Since she was able to summon that serpent, I think we can assume she's familiar with the Labyrinth. She is old, as well, and it's likely that the wizards and sorcerers of her time were closer to the roots of that sort of magic. Our advantage, as well as our disadvantage, is that we come from different eras. What we have learned, she may not have found interesting enough to keep up with, but what she knows is likely entwined with a lot of powerful things that have been forgotten, destroyed, or banished."

"I'm starting to feel like we're caught up in an epic game of Dungeons and Dragons," Amethyst said. "If there is a gelatinous cube ahead, you are paying my cleaning bill."

Donovan laughed, and they started up again, more slowly, but only slightly. They had at least one more level before they would find stairs leading to that tower, and a large chamber meant another possibility of a trap. As they climbed, an odd sound echoed above them, like whispered voices and laughter.

"Seems our host may be throwing a party," Donovan said.

"By all means, then," Amethyst said, "let's not keep them waiting. If I read those voices correctly, we're going to be the life of the party."

Chapter Twenty-Five

A s Edgar led the way up the stone stairs, he became aware of a shimmer of light ahead. It did not seem to come from a lamp, candle, or torch, but it gave off a faint hum. Grimm had settled onto his shoulder, and remained there, still, and waiting. As they approached the first landing on the stairs, the source of both light and sound became apparent.

Beyond the landing, and through what seemed a tear in reality itself, the steps continued upward. They were no longer made of stone, however, but were old and wooden. Above them, dangling from a single cord, was a very old incandescent bulb, glowing dimly. It had no shade, and there was no railing on the stairs, which led toward a rectangle of brighter light above.

They all stopped and stared upward.

"I believe," Edgar said softly, "that you may all be about to experience the answer to an author's most oft-posed question. 'Where do you get your ideas?'"

"I do not smell wine or sherry," Copper said, obviously intrigued.

Edgar turned and raised an eyebrow. Then, without a further word, he started up the stairs.

As they stepped through the shimmering haze, the air became damper and mustier. The temperature rose slightly. The stairs, solid only moments before, bowed slightly under their weight, and they moved more slowly. The walls also changed. They were wooden and farther away from the sides of the stairs. The lack of a railing was jarring, at least to Edgar and Eleanor, who felt the vertigo from the surrounding shadows and invisible depths beneath them instantly.

Copper and Alicia were unconcerned and gently steadied their companions. Edgar took the steps as quickly as he dared, keeping his gaze fixed on the exit at the top. As they neared their goal, his steps quickened slightly, and his nerves steadied.

At that moment, darting like a small demon, a dark shape flew through the doorway at the top and headed straight for his feet. Edgar started, and began to topple to the side. Copper gripped him by the arm. Something brushed past his feet, and then there was a gasp behind him, followed by an odd mewling sound. Edgar sprinted up the final steps onto a wooden-floored Juliet balcony, partway up and overlooking the hall below. Ahead was a window sill with an upholstered cushion, beyond which large windows presented a view of dark sky and brilliant, blinking stars.

The others tumbled up behind him, and he turned. Everyone had made it safely, and, as Alicia, who had brought up the rear, stepped through, the stairs behind them disappeared. Cuddled in her arms, she held a large black cat. There was a small white tuft of hair at its throat.

Copper and Edgar glanced at one another.

"If I were you," Copper said. "I would not get too close."

Edgar nodded. He turned and headed down the hallway. There were windows to either side, but it was dark beyond them, and there were no exterior lights. The musty smell of the stairs had given way to that of cobwebs and dust. They rounded a corner—and stopped.

There was sound coming from ahead of them. No one was in sight, so they knew it must be emanating from one of the doors to their left. It couldn't be coming from the right side of the hall because it appeared to be an exterior wall, and it was lined with windows facing the doors on the left.

The sound began as an odd scrape. It continued, and then there was a moist sound, like something being spooned from a great kettle. A moment later, the scraping returned.

Edgar continued cautiously. This had the feel of one of his adventures in the Labyrinth, and, at the same time, did not. Something about it was off—empty and hurried—like a parody, or perhaps an unfinished outline. There was soft light coming from the last room, and he stopped just shy of the door, peering inside, but not entering.

The site that met his eyes was eerie, and vague. There was a hole in the wall to the right of the door. On the floor a man knelt by an old metal bucket. He appeared to be applying plaster to the break in the wall, mending the hole. As Edgar stepped into the room, the man glanced up.

It was himself he faced, as he had so many times before, and yet, this time, it was also not. The features were vague, like a chiaroscuro watercolor wash of a man.

"This is not right," Edgar said softly. "I have written this tale. I know both the ending I showed to the world, and how it came to pass, and this is not mine."

The cat broke free of Alicia's grip with a yowl and dashed into the room. Before anyone could move it had leaped over the kneeling man and into the void beyond the wall.

"Help me," the man said. His voice was a whisper of dried paper caught in an uneven, coughing-fit breeze and about to tear. "Come to the wall and help me. She is dead, and…"

Edgar turned away before his doppelganger could finish. He continued down the hall without a backward glance, and as he did so, Grimm took flight, just for a moment, circling a point directly above them in the ceiling. The old bird whirled back to Edgar's shoulder, and the four of them glanced upward.

Above, there was a rectangular crack showing, like the frame of a drop-down stairway, leading to an attic. There was no handle, and no chain, but on one side there were two ornate hasps from which dangled gaudy filigreed locks.

Behind them, the scraping began anew, and the whispered voice still called to them.

"What is he? A trap?" Eleanor asked. She shivered, and Edgar put an arm around her shoulder.

"I believe so," Edgar said. "Whoever created that illusion put only casual effort behind it, and thought very little of my mental capacities, which may play in our favor. There is a certain arrogance about our foe that will serve her poorly in the end, I think. For now, we must turn our attention to those locks, and that door. I believe we will find it leads to another stairway, and then, perhaps, to our tower.

"Grimm is restless. I sense it. The others are not so far away, and something of import is upon us. Good, or ill, I cannot say, but since the steps we climbed to reach this point have vanished, there is little else to do but follow the story to its conclusion."

Alicia laughed, and the sound of it broke through the rasping cries for help and the scrape of the trowel on broken plaster.

"I believe we may find that growing up near New Orleans is going to come in handy here," she said. "Copper?"

He moved so quickly that he seemed to magically appear, standing beneath the locks, and Alicia slid up him as if he were a solid pole. She perched on his shoulders, so easily balanced that she might have still been on the floor, and pulled a long, wicked-looking pin from her hair. She set to work on the first of the locks, her head cocked to one side, one hand steadying the hasp, and the other working that pin. Within seconds, there was a loud snap and it popped open. She pulled it free and handed it to Copper.

At that moment, the half-Edgar in the other room stumbled to the door. Perhaps he was more fully formed than they'd believed and had heard the click of the lock. Or possibly it was part of his malformed story line. Edgar glanced back and wondered if there was any way he could already have closed the cat into the wall. It was such a poorly wrought attempt at baiting him into a diversion that he now wondered if that, itself, was the trap.

"Help me," the man said softly.

Edgar shook his head. "There is nothing any man nor spirit can do for such as you. You should not have killed her."

The man stared at him, then stumbled into the hall. Eleanor was at the back of the group, and with a sudden clumsy lunge, the thing launched itself at her.

"I have not," it whispered, the words whistling as if through rice paper, "killed her. Yet—"

Alicia glanced over, but she was hard at work on the second lock, and Copper could not move. It was up to Edgar. And Grimm.

The bird launched with a cry and dove directly at the apparition's face, talons first. The creature was moving quickly, but inefficiently, as if it barely had enough coherence to remain solid. It had a dagger in one hand, though, and it was raised.

Grimm slashed right through the nebulous face, and the creature screamed. Edgar was on him in that instant, grabbing the wrist with the dagger and slamming it forward into the wall. The blade clattered to the ground, and the apparition crashed into, and through, the window glass. For an instant it hung as in stop-motion; shreds of its frail form clung to shattered bits of glass, hung on the frame, and then, caught in a wind that suddenly roared past that opening, it was sucked into the darkness. It gave a long wail and was gone.

Edgar grabbed Eleanor and drew her close. Grimm circled angrily once, and then came back to settle once more on his shoulder. The wind ruffled his feathers, and before their eyes the walls morphed from paneled wood to stone. The glass in the window disappeared. The floor revealed itself as rough stone. They no longer walked down a hallway in an old home, but along a corridor on an upper level of the castle.

The hatch in the ceiling remained basically the same though. It was still formed of dark wooden planks, and the lock was just as it has been—with one exception. Alicia yanked on it, and it came free with a soft snick. The door was unlocked, but it didn't open immediately. Alicia stood still, staring at it, and then, with a sudden motion slammed her hand, fingers first, into the wood, which splintered and crumbled. She gripped the hole she had made as if with steel claws and yanked the door downward.

Copper sank to his knees, and she leaped to the side as the door opened and a stairway pivoted downward on ancient metal hinges. There was a screech, as if it had not moved in a very long time, but seconds later, they were faced by steps that led up into the darkness.

There was another sound behind them, a scrabbling noise. Edgar turned and strode into the room where his poor doppelganger had been. The hole was still there, but it was rubble—as if a sledge had knocked through the stone walls, dislodging the ancient mortar.

He stepped closer and pulled aside one of the stones to expose the niche behind it. When he did so, the cat sprang out, narrowly missing him in passing. It rushed out of the room, and before any of the startled group could react, was up the ladder and gone into the darkness.

"I suppose," Edgar said, standing in the doorway and staring thoughtfully at the stairs, "that we should follow."

Alicia darted up the stairs after the cat, and Copper followed. Their speed gave them a better chance of dealing with anything waiting at the top. Edgar waited and let Eleanor climb before him. He glanced out into the darkness beyond the castle, then back at the room with the broken wall. He was suddenly glad he had not checked to see if there was body in that hole.

Chapter Twenty-Six

As it turned out, Bullfinch, Gunter, and Father Adolph did not have far to go to know that their presence had been noticed. The second-floor hallway that they entered through the window opened onto a grander hall. A crumbling table that must have stretched forty feet in its day canted slightly to one side in the center, and just beyond the head, sat a tall, very ornate chair, and beyond that was a grand fireplace.

Dust clung to every surface. The walls, once adorned in tapestries and paintings, were mostly bare. Shreds of material more like cobweb than silk still dangled in places. Broken sconces hung crooked from rusted spikes, and wind whipped in through high windows. There was absolutely no sign of any recent inhabitance, and though it had been cold outside, it was frigid within, despite the fact much of the wind was blocked by what remained of the walls.

Cleo, who had bounded in ahead of them, prowled along the length of the table, and then stopped. She tilted her head to one side, let out a low growling hiss, and circled back, winding around Bullfinch's legs protectively and glaring at the fireplace.

The three men closed in. Bullfinch held up his torch, but it was a tiny light in a huge cathedral-sized room, and the wind threatened to snuff it. Gunter held the remaining, unlit torch before him, and Bullfinch noticed with surprise that his stance showed signs of having worked with a staff.

Father Adolph stood calmly, but close.

"What is it?" he asked. "What does she sense? Is it really colder in here than it was out there, or are my old bones just failing me?"

"It is," Gunter said. "It is fascinating. I know of no phenomena that..."

His words died away as the wall behind the fireplace dissolved into a silver mist, and a tall, dark-haired woman stepped through. She was beautiful in the way an ice sculpture is beautiful. Her expression was devoid of emotion—except for her eyes. They were bright blue, and though the torchlight was weak and insignificant in the vastness of the chamber, they managed to catch it and glitter like diamonds.

Bullfinch watched her carefully. He noted that Cleo, who had stayed close during the woman's approach, had disappeared into the shadows. He did not know whether to be concerned, or comforted by her departure, but there was no time to consider it.

"Why have you come?" the woman said, striding toward them. "Why are you here?"

"We wanted to see the castle," Bullfinch said. It was the truth, and he hoped it would come across as such, were she probing his mind in some way, without giving too much away. "The good Father," he gestured at Father Adolph, "was kind enough to act as our guide."

"You cannot see the castle in the middle of the night," she said. "I will ask you again. Why have you come?"

"I have been here many times," Father Adolph said, stepping forward without concern. "If you have been here all along, you must know that?"

"You have never entered the castle," she said.

"So I have not," Father Adolph said. "But I have been around all sides and have wondered what I would find inside. I knew another who lived here, long ago, though not in these upper levels."

"Rosa," the woman said softly. "You knew the girl."

"Girl?" Gunter said. He looked suddenly confused. "I was led to understand she was old."

"She was not young," the woman said, "but she was not old. I tolerated her presence, because she did not intrude upon mine, as you have done."

"Estrella," Bullfinch said. "I have to say, even though I have heard the stories, I was not quite prepared for that entrance. Very dramatic."

Her expression didn't flicker. It was a wash of boredom, disdain, and contempt. Despite all of that, it was captivating. "You climbed a mountain to flatter me—before I kill you?" she said.

Gunter stepped forward. Bullfinch grabbed his arm, but the old German pulled free. His eyes were bright.

"You have created a portal," he said, "where solid matter existed. There is a law I learned as a young man, one you may, or may not know—the law of conservatism. I wonder if you understand it?"

She stared at him as if confronted by a suddenly fascinating bug she had not noticed. Estrella cocked her head.

"I have never been much concerned with laws," she said.

"Oh, but you are," Gunter said. "You could not have done that—without laws? If you could, everyone would do this, yes? We would walk to Paris in the morning for tea instead of requiring a jet and obeying the laws of aerodynamics. Everything, then, abides by some law. The goal of any scientist, or I think, magician, must be to discover that law, and then to envision how it can be used, or manipulated.

"I wonder. You so easily passed through matter; can you do the same with time? This hall, this place. It must once have been remarkable, yes? Magnificent, even. I should very much like to see?"

She didn't answer, but moved her hands in a quick, intricate pattern. The air shimmered. The wind around them died, and the table stood, perfect and intact, with chairs around it, and upon it, platters of food and pitchers of ale and wine. Music filled the air, strange, lilting music from another age. Even the scent of the feast permeated the air, drawing them in.

Estrella stood at the head of the table. Around her men and women spoke, laughed, danced. There was a throne near the fireplace, one that had not been present seconds before. A man sat there, and to his right, on a slightly less impressive seat, a very regal woman rested, her arm curled through his, watching the proceedings with a slight frown. The man roared with laughter, leaning to the left to clap a young warrior on the shoulder, nearly spilling the man's drink.

It was surreal, and the three men stared. Bullfinch caught motion to his left and turned. Father Adolph was making the sign of the cross, and Geoffrey could see the man's lips moving rapidly. On his other side, Gunter stared as if mesmerized. He did not remove his eyes from the sorceress, even to examine the room, or to marvel at the scents and sounds finding their way to his senses from the deep past.

"And the princess," Gunter said. "You have truly taken her, from this," he waved a hand absently at the scene unfolding around them, "through time, and space, combined her spirit with that of a bird, and brought her home again? Such power!"

Estrella's eyes sparked. It was the first moment of actual engagement that Bullfinch had seen. He had no idea what to do, how to distract her—or stop her. Her hands flew, and the fireplace opened once more, so that they saw through the wall to what lay beyond it—except that wasn't quite right, because they were only on the second level of the castle, but the place they saw must surely have been the tower.

They saw the room, the cage, and the girl, who stared back at them in terror, and still, all around them, the music played, and men and women ate, sang, and danced. Estrella stepped up by the fireplace and Gunter's gaze followed her, locked to her hands, her fingers, their motions.

"Are you satisfied, old man?" she asked. "Do you believe now? Your science is nothing. The things you believe, the laws you adhere to, are insignificant. I can be wherever, whenever, I choose."

Bullfinch was on the verge of trying something, anything, to draw her attention away from Gunter. He caught sight of Cleo beneath the corner of the table. He did not speak, but he closed his eyes and concentrated. He thought about Donovan. He tried to reach the mind of the old familiar, to tell her to escape, to find her partner, to pass on what they had seen and learned. When he opened his eyes, Cleo was gone.

Believing he'd done all that he could, he turned, ready to launch himself at Estrella, buy them a couple of seconds before she blasted them out of existence, or sent them to another dimension.

Before he could act, Gunter was moving. His hands were a blur of gestures, but his gaze still fixed dead center on the face of their antagonist. Bullfinch frowned, and then, a moment later almost cried out in shock and surprise. He saw Estrella's eyes go wide. Saw her sway and try to regain her balance, but she was as shocked as Geoffrey. Gunter grunted something, some phrase that Bullfinch could not make out, and finished the pattern he'd been weaving with his hands. As if feeling it needed a final flourish, he flipped his wrists up and pushed his palms forward toward the fireplace and the room beyond.

With a cry, Estrella shimmered, struggled, and then with sudden speed and energy, was sucked backward. She disappeared through the portal she'd opened, and it slammed behind her with such a resounding snap of energy that it nearly drove the three men to their knees. The images flashed out of existence. Reality crashed around them so absolutely, so quickly, that it numbed Geoffrey's thoughts and blinded him momentarily. He took a deep breath, and then another.

"We have to get out of here," he said. "I have no idea what you did, or how you did it, but if she returns."

"Yes," Gunter said. "I believe she will kill us."

Bullfinch straightened and turned. Father Adolph still stared at the fireplace, but his eyes were clear.

"Father" Geoffrey said. "Are you—?"

"I'm fine." He said. "Come, I believe that our part in this is completed. Your friend Donovan asked us to get her attention. I believe we have done that, though I confess I have no idea what just happened."

"I watched her," Gunter said simply. "The patterns she used to open the portal to the tower. My memory, it is eidetic you know, like a photograph? I simply reversed her pattern. I was not certain that it would work, but the basis of scientific experimentation is to achieve a result and then, to prove that it can be repeated. So, I repeated it."

"You," Bullfinch said, poking a finger into his companion's chest and breaking into a deep laugh. "You are a very interesting man."

Gunter blinked. "I do not know if that is true," he said. "I very much wish that I had my notebooks. I must record this. There will be patterns.

"Later," Geoffrey said. "Much later."

The three turned, and, without a glance behind them, ran toward the hall and the window through which they'd entered.

"Assuming we survive this," Father Adolph said, a bit out of breath, "You are going to have to explain the law of conservatism to me. I have a vague notion that it was taught to me in school, but I believe that when *you* explain a thing, it is likely to stick."

"I have many students," Gunter said, "who would tend to disagree, but I will be happy to explain."

They scrambled down the rubble outside and started back down the mountain.

Bullfinch glanced back.

"It's all you, old man," he said softly, willing the words to somehow reach Donovan. "Bring the princess home."

Chapter Twenty-Seven

Donovan nearly went tumbling as Cleo dashed down the stairway, straight at him. Amethyst was a step behind, and she saw the cat coming. Without a thought she leaned forward and pushed Donovan down flat onto the steps. Cleo leaped into his arms, and Asmodeus took off in an explosion of feathers.

"What—?"

He didn't get the rest of the words out. Cleo lifted a paw and whapped him across the cheek, then she whirled in his arms, squirmed free, and headed back up the stairs at a run.

Donovan grunted, stood, and followed, taking the first few steps on hands and feet, and then running. The sounds from above had grown louder. There was the loud murmur of many voices, and music, but above that he thought he also heard other, more familiar voices. He couldn't make out what they were saying, but something told him it was not going to be a long conversation.

"Do you hear that?" Amethyst asked, following right on his heels.

"I do," he said. "Sounds like a party we weren't invited to."

"Yes, but if Cleo is here—?"

"I know," he said. "Then Bullfinch and the others must be up there. I didn't think they'd be in the direct path of this. Geoffrey is old, and wise, and he has tricks. She's not using tricks. She has power."

He sped a bit more, rounding a corner. Ahead were the crumbled remains of a door. Cleo was already out of sight. They scrambled up the last few steps, but the sounds had died away. They clambered through the broken doorframe and entered a large, empty hall.

They saw the broken table and the tattered wall hangings. Cleo stood at the rear of the hall, paws up on a low platform beneath a window overlooking the side of the mountain and the trail below.

Donovan ran over to the window and stared out. He caught movement in the dim light and concentrated. There were three sets of footsteps. Someone was speaking. Gunter.

"They escaped," he said. "Whatever happened here, the three of them are on the way back down.

Amethyst circled the old table. She had a blue lens in her hand, and she scanned the floor with it.

"Something big is what happened," she said. "Can you sense it? There is a residual energy sort of infusing the air? I have to say, if something this big went down, and your man Bullfinch is walking away, maybe he knows more than a few tricks."

"Assuming we make it down the mountain as well," Donovan said, "I'm sure there's going to be a good story. Can you see where the energy is concentrated? I do sense it, but it feels to me as if it comes from everywhere—I can't use it to track anything."

"I might be able to. Let me…"

Amethyst fell silent, and Donovan glanced up. He followed her gaze to the old fireplace, and saw that Cleo was sitting in front of it, casually wetting her paw and washing her face.

"Or," Amethyst said, "We could just look there."

They walked down the length of the broken table. Donovan stopped, leaned down, and rubbed a finger on the floor, then brought it to his tongue. There was a small puddle at his feet.

"What are you?"

"It's mead," he said. "And not any type of mead that's been brewed in the last hundred years."

"I don't see anything."

He glanced up at her, then back at the ground. The puddle was gone. "Residuals," he said.

When they reached the fireplace, Donovan stared at it and the wall beyond, intently. He reached out and ran a finger over the stone of the ancient mantel. Then he glanced down at Cleo.

"Through here?" he asked.

The old cat let out a soft mewling sound, turned, and pawed at the side of the fireplace.

"We know where, then," Donovan said. "We just need to figure out how."

"She's in the tower, right?" Amethyst said. "This may be how she came, and went, from that place, but is it the only way?"

"Probably not," Donovan said, "but consider this: You saw how she guarded the other points of entrance. Despite whatever just happened with Bullfinch and the others, I think it's likely that this is her private entrance, and she does not believe anyone is apt to use it. The one thing I can't figure out is that there are two power signatures here. One is very old, and very powerful, and it matches that mead on the floor. The other is odd, and I can't place it."

"Bullfinch?"

"Maybe, but anyway, I think this is our best bet. We need to figure out a way in."

"Or maybe," Amethyst said softly, "we need to get her to come out. I have an idea, and it might be the only thing to save Lenore."

"I'm all ears then," Donovan said. "Talk to me."

Amethyst explained, while digging through her pockets. Donovan listened, nodding, but he never took his gaze, or his full concentration, off the fireplace. He'd been taken by surprise one too many times for his taste.

He heard a flutter from above, and almost ignored it. Then he realized Asmodeus was resting on his shoulder. He glanced up. Grimm was sailing down from above. It was impossible to tell if the old bird had come through a window, out of a stair or hall, or simply dropped through some portal in mid-air, but there he was.

Amethyst glanced up too and frowned.

"Okay," she said. "First Cleo and now Grimm? I wonder if we're the last wall standing?"

"I don't think so," Donovan said. "Grimm would sense it if something was truly wrong, but there's a reason why he's here. How close are you to finding what you need?"

"I thought you weren't listening."

A Midnight Dreary   *199*

"I was, of course," Donovan said. "I just feel jumpy. We have been the ones surprised every time tonight, and it would be nice if just once I felt as if we were doing something—anything—that she had not anticipated."

"I am fairly certain," Amethyst said, "that she will not see this. Also, I get the distinct sense that, whatever it was that happened here, she didn't see that coming either. Whatever was going on in here had the sound of a victory celebration, but that's not how it ended. You've mentioned several times how old she is; it's possible she is also very disconnected from reality. She may believe that nothing can touch her, that she has covered every angle. She doesn't strike me as the cautious type."

"All good points," Donovan said.

Grimm dropped onto his free shoulder. Without preamble, the raven leaned in and tugged at his earlobe. It was an odd sensation. He reached up to pull the bird away, but before he could do so, his mind was flooded with a series of images and sounds, voices and bits of memory. It was a muddled mess, which he attributed to the fact that Grimm was Edgar's familiar, and not his own. He closed his eyes and tried to concentrate.

"What is it?" Amethyst said.

"I'm not sure," he said. "There is another stair, and a room. There was a cat, but not Cleo—a black cat—and a room. I see a very old book, and it feels important, but I can't see the cover or make out the words. They are close. Edgar, Eleanor, Copper, and Alicia are nearer to Estrella than we are, and they are closing in."

"That could go badly," Amethyst said. "For all his accidental magic, Edgar is no match for Estrella, and as old and powerful as the vampires might be, I can't imagine she doesn't know how to deal with them. She knew Rosa, or, at least, she must have known *of* her."

"Let's get this done," Donovan said. "If we can get it in place, and you are right, we may be able to find a different way in for ourselves. She does not know what we can do, or what we understand. We need to be there for our friends, and to be certain that the girl is made safe—and that Eleanor *remains* safe."

"You know the odds of all of us getting through this aren't

good, right?" Amethyst said. "I've read most of the fairy tales written by the Grimm brothers. They almost never ended well for anyone. People dancing themselves to death. Children being eaten by witches. Theirs was not a world of happy endings and rose gardens."

"We weren't a part of that world," Donovan said. "If they had been able to deal with someone like Estrella, I like to think that they would have, rather than just writing a story. The fact they apparently embedded clues in that story for someone to find, to follow, and to use to save the princess, leads me to believe they at least had hope that someone would follow who would not only understand but would have the power and spirit to make it happen.

"I wish they were around to see how the story comes out, you know"

"Who knows," Amethyst said. "There is the Labyrinth. If we manage to get through this, there is still a lot of exploring to do. If you can go into that place and find the library of Edgar Allan Poe, who is to say you can't go down a different path and find the Brothers Grimm?"

Donovan laughed.

Amethyst let out a quick "Yes!" and turned back to the fireplace. She had a bag in her hand closed at the top with leather straps. She unbound the straps and dumped the contents of the bag onto the ancient hearth.

"Time for us to get to work," she said.

Donovan knelt beside her, hoping they were not too late.

Chapter Twenty-Eight

Unlike the retractable stairways in modern homes, the one that had dropped from the ceiling of the castle's hallway was solid. The steps were solid, but the wood that had once lined them had crumbled away. Each was braced by a metal plate, and these were intact. The vampires had followed the cat so quickly they were gone before Eleanor's foot touched the first rung. She followed more slowly, and Edgar brought up the rear, stopping every now and then to glance over his shoulder and be certain they were not being followed.

Moments later he stepped into a narrow hall with no doors or windows.

"This must have been for the servants," Alicia said. "Castles like this often had hidden passages so that the wait staff and maids could go about their work unnoticed, not bothering their lords and ladies. I'm guessing that this one leads to the tower."

"According to the story," Lenore said, "that is where Estrella took the princess, and where she locked her away."

"Just like a fairy tale," Edgar said. "So very much like. You almost expect hair to dangle to the ground for an easy escape."

Grimm, who had settled nervously back onto Edgar's shoulder, uncomfortable in the enclosed space, ruffled his wings and pecked gently at the poet's head.

Edgar turned slightly and cocked his head.

Then he turned back to the stairs.

"The others, Donovan and Amethyst, I believe, are near. They are very close to her, and Grimm senses that her attention is turning to them. I believe we have a situation here. As old and powerful as the two of you may be," he nodded to Alicia and Copper, and as many strange adventures as Grimm and I have encountered, I believe those two are what you would call our 'big guns'. If she is about to turn to them, then I believe the best use of our time will be in creating something of a diversion. I supposed we'd better find our way to the top of the stairs and see about finding or creating an entrance."

The stairs were very narrow, and there was no light. Copper had a flashlight, and Edgar saw it bobbing along ahead, but it barely gave enough illumination to keep them from missing a step. These, at least, were stone, and very solid.

"Something is strange here," Copper said as he climbed. "Below, when we were in the main hall, things were older. They were aged, like you'd expect them to be. But here—?"

The shadows had cloaked it, but Edgar realized it was true. He should have noticed, and would have, except for the dim light. The stairs were clear and clean. The walls were smooth, as if the stones they were formed from had been recently carved. Even the air seemed fresher.

"It is like one of my adventures," he said, "but unlike, at the same time. This story is not of my making, it is hers. I believe we have passed through all the glamours and entered the first levels of her stronghold."

"Can she sense us?" Eleanor asked.

"I'm not sure," Edgar said. "Certainly, she could if she tried, but she may be distracted. A lot is going to depend on chance, and fate, from here on out. I have lived through many such adventures, and it heartens me to know that I have walked through the other side of all of them. If Donovan is making a move, we need to do the same. She might be able to repel, or even destroy one group, but if we divide her attentions, we have a chance."

"I think we've talked enough," Copper said. "I'm ready for some action, even if it's the last I ever see. I might say something trite like, 'It's a good day to die,' but I've been there, done that, and have the t-shirt. Seriously. It says, 'I died—it didn't take.' It's back home in New Orleans."

They all laughed.

"You talk too much," Alicia said. She took off up the stairs, and the others followed in a tight group. The shadows deepened, but oddly this allowed the pool of light from Copper's flashlight to spread. Their shadows were long, but they could see their way.

Ahead was a door. There was no handle, no latch, only ornately carved wooden panels, and what appeared to be a window about face level. Beneath that was a slot, blocked by bars that could be lifted upward with a handle.

"In the story," Eleanor said, "she was trapped inside. Now, she has secluded herself. This must be how they passed her food."

"But how did the door open?" Alicia asked.

"I do not believe that matters in this time, or this place," Edgar said. "Such doors either open or they do not"

He stepped forward, placed a hand on the center panel, and, without hesitation, pushed it open and stepped through into the chamber beyond.

The room was lit only by a candle and an oil lamp, but after the shadowed passage they were nearly blinded. At least, Edgar and Eleanor were. Copper slipped in to the left of the door, and Alicia to the right, the two fanning out to surround the center of the room.

Estrella stood inside. They knew it was her, tall, elegant, dressed in a floor-length gown that should have seemed dated and ridiculous but hung like shimmering jewels instead. Her hair was tied back, and she held a glass of wine.

Against one wall there was a tall, canopied bed, and beside that stood a large ornate cage. Something about that cage was off, something fundamental. It looked like a very large birdcage, but inside, a young woman stood. She gripped the bars and stared, wild-eyed.

"You," she cried. "I remember you. I…"

"Yes, yes," Estrella said. "They freed you from the raven. They saved you, don't you see? The freedom? It's all because of them."

"I see why you locked yourself up," Copper said, circling slowly. "It's the personality."

"A vampire?" Estrella said. "Interesting, and Rosa—do I smell her? Is she here too?"

"She's dead, witch," Alicia said from across the room. She was making her way closer to the caged princess. "She burned not far from here. I'm surprised you missed the fireworks."

"I don't generally bother myself with the lives, or deaths, of others. Particularly those who already had a death and lacked the good sense to accept it. I have my own concerns. A pity you decided to become one of them, if you managed to escape her control."

"Fine words for one whose fame rests in a fairy tale," Edgar said. He stepped forward, seemingly unconcerned, and she watched him, sipping her wine.

"The poet," she said. Then her gaze slipped past him, and she stopped drinking. She stared at Eleanor as if she'd seen a ghost, then actually took a step back.

"You." she said. "You cannot be here. The tree, the spell is not broken. You cannot be—"

"Free?" Eleanor said. "If you recall, that is exactly what I have brought to others all of my life. Freedom. Is it so surprising your flawed magic was unable to hold me?"

She stepped up behind Edgar and ran her arm through his.

"It does not matter," Estrella said. There was a slight tremor in her voice, but it evened out as she continued speaking. "You are right to say that I have locked myself away. It is very secure, and while you managed to get in, as you might recall from your stay in the tree, it is a much more difficult thing to get out."

"Doors swing both ways," Edgar said. "So my experience tells me."

"We shall see," Estrella said.

"I sense your power," Alicia said softly. "I come from a place of power, a city of power. My mother, my grandmother, and her grandmother, have walked the bayous. We have seen the *Bocors* raise the dead and sent them home again. How long, I wonder, since you were tested? How long since you just did what you wanted and believed there was no one to stand against you? When they locked you in this tower, you had your power, and they were mortals."

"Two of you are mortals, as well," Estrella said, turning slowly, concentrating on the two vampires, but not letting

Edgar, or Alicia, out of her sight for long. "Two of you are not, but I don't believe the magic is strong in you either. You are fast, formidable even, but…"

Alicia had begun to speak. The words were very soft, spoken under her breath, and rhythmic. Then Alicia moved, very quickly, raising her hands over her head and flinging her fingers out in a slow, glittering arc. Tendrils of light, like spider's silk, shot out from her fingertips and engulfed the sorceress. The strands dropped loosely about her, and Alicia yanked back hard. The light-cords tightened like some weird, luminescent Chinese finger trap, shattering the wine glass in Estrella's hand and sending splinters of glass tinkling to the floor.

Copper moved in that instant as well, diving at her and slamming her to the ground. He reared back, ready to slam his fist down on her trapped face, but the light went flat beneath him, becoming no more than rays on the stone floor, and dark laughter rose around them.

"I underestimated you," Estrella said. The voice came from behind Copper, and he dove forward, narrowly missing a piercing beam of white light that split the air where his heart had been seconds before. "Unfortunately, you have done the same, if you think your swamp magic and charms can hold me."

Estrella had reappeared outside of Alicia's cocoon of light, with her hands raised. The tips of her fingers glowed, as did her eyes. She turned slowly again, watching them all.

"Keep moving," Edgar said. "Circle."

Estrella laughed again. "What a clever man. Make me chase, try to confuse me, and then, what? Attack? Take me down?" Her laughter rang out loud and brittle, and none of them made a move to challenge her. However, it was clear Copper was looking for any opening.

"You are fast, dark one," she said. "I know this. I know your kind. I watched the one who made you. It is not enough. It was never enough. If it had been, she would have killed me—you know that. She would not have allowed me here, so close to her, if she believed she could end me.

"I knew her before, you know, when she was a baby, a small girl. I knew her long after this one," she gestured at the girl in the cage, who had yet to speak, "was long gone and only a memory to her. And I knew her after her father returned from war, after he rebuilt this castle on the stones of the one that was destroyed in his absence. I knew her when he took her, and it was I who killed him and let her live.

"Some of you are old in the eyes of the world. But to me, all of you are young. You are too slow, too weak, and too late. This one is mine, and has always been, as you all are now. Did you stop to think why it was so easy to enter, or why I did not prevent you?"

"It's a trap," the princess cried out. "She is going to trap us all here forever. Don't let her."

Estrella flicked a finger at the cage and the girl's words were choked off. Her breath stopped, and she gripped some invisible binding digging into the flesh of her throat. Copper lunged, but he made it only a couple of strides before a second finger raised some sort of wall that he slammed into hard enough to stun him.

The others continued to circle while watching her carefully. The princess gasped, regaining her breath, but she did not speak again. It seemed to be a standoff, but Edgar was certain this was an illusion. At least, he was certain until he heard the soft rustle of wings—and until he heard deep, rumbling growl that could in no way have originated from the black cat. Until one of the walls began to shimmer, and everything changed.

Chapter Twenty-Nine

Amethyst placed the last crystal and stepped back. She closed her eyes and murmured words Donovan didn't even try to make out. He stood back and watched. He knew that what they were doing was dangerous, and he knew, as well, that it was likely that nothing happened in this tower beneath the scrutiny of the one they sought.

When Amethyst finished, Donovan laid his hand on her shoulder and spoke in a low tone, as if afraid of being overheard. "This feels like a trap," he said. "You know that is her portal, and she will know that we can sense it, and that we will use it. If we go waltzing in through there…"

"That is why we will not," Amethyst said. "I have no intention of using this portal. We have to find another way in, and quickly. It is vital that we come in with everything we have, and I mean that very literally. If you have something powerful saved in that coat for the final battle of the universe, you should pull it out now and be ready to cast it."

"But how do we get in then?" Donovan asked.

Cleo turned with a soft growl, padded across to the wall and stopped twenty feet or so away. She clawed gently at the wall. Donovan followed and examined the stone where the cat had indicated. There was nothing to distinguish it from any of the surrounding walls, except that there was no hanging lamp. Nor were there any remnants of tapestries or other ornamentation. It was an oddly blank stretch where, if you stepped back and studied it, you might have expected a door or a stair.

"Good job," he said leaning to pet the old cat. "This was a doorway," he said. "It has been sealed—I don't know how long ago—but if there was a mortal passage here, we can use it as a portal. We can use it to enter the Labyrinth."

"Stop talking and start moving," Amethyst said. "We have one chance, and there is so much energy rippling through this place right now it feels like it might explode. Something is happening up there, and that means our friends are facing her alone."

Donovan closed his eyes. He started taking steps, three back, two forward, then one back. He repeated the pattern several times, growing ever closer to the wall each time Just as it seemed as if he would have to plant his face into solid stone, a door snapped into view. It was old, wooden, with a solid handle. He gripped it without looking and pushed inward.

In that moment so many things happened it was difficult to sort them—and better not to try. He had already dropped his free hand into his pocket and wrapped it around a very old stone. It had rested there since a long-past day in Chicago, when he'd taken it from the basement of a very evil building. It was not black magic, but it cut straight through the gray lines of neutrality. It could be used for good, or for ill, but it had a single purpose, and it was very old and powerful.

If used on a human, he was nearly certain that person would simply cease to be. He had almost used it on a vampire once but had thought twice and let it pass, because he feared it meant an even more certain damnation than rising from death. He had never had a reason to use it on another man or woman of power. If he did, he knew that moment would be a turning point, and the result would depend upon a balance. His power—that of the stone itself—against another. His research was inconclusive, but he believed that there were two very singular possible outcomes. Only one of them allowed him to walk away.

Cleo didn't hesitate. She let out a sound, a deep primal growl that Donovan had never heard, more tiger than cat, ancient and powerful. Amethyst followed with the two crystal daggers in her hands. The door closed behind them as they rushed up the ancient stairs and into the room beyond.

Cleo leapt. No hesitation. At that same moment, as though their minds were joined by some invisible, mystical cord, Grimm and Asmodeus dropped from the rafters of the room, straight at Estrella's head. The black cat, who had stood by Alicia, mirroring her motions around the room, growled and sprang at the same moment, and there was Donovan, standing in a circle of dark light, with the stone held tightly in his hand—pulsing with a shadow so dark it flowed over his hand and wrist and arm.

The sorceress whirled. She took it all in, let out a screech of rage, and dove forward. Without a word she ducked under Grimm's attack, cast Eleanor to the side, and dove for the wall. Donovan was poised to strike, but Amethyst slammed into him, destroying his concentration.

Estrella glanced over her shoulder.

"You will rot here," she screamed. "The world will be mine."

And with a snap, she dove through her portal. It slammed closed with such force that everyone in the room was shaken. Donovan toppled and fell, as did Edgar. Copper managed to catch Eleanor as she started to drop. Amethyst fell into a tuck-and-roll, and Alicia caught her before she hit the wall. The princess was thrown against the bars of her cage, but they held her upright. The birds and the cats stood their ground as if carved from stone.

"She escaped!" Alicia cried, diving for the wall. Amethyst caught her arm.

"No," she said. "She did not. She did exactly what I hoped she would do." She turned to Eleanor. "I told you, I would end this. You are safe."

Everyone turned to her then.

"On the far side of that wall, I placed a trap," she said. A portal leading to the wedged-open doorway to the tree. I counted on our entrance, if not frightening, at least startling her into flight. The second she passed through…"

"She was trapped," Eleanor said softly. "The other portal?"

"Closed as soon as anything passed through. She isn't coming out of there anytime soon. Possibly not until the end of the world. She is Nettie's problem now, and somehow I believe that will turn out fine."

"It does not matter," a voice said softly from across the room. "She has trapped us all here, as well. Did you not hear?"

Everyone turned to where the girl stood in the cage, trembling. Donovan crossed quickly to her and undid the latch, freeing her. He took her arm and helped her to the bed along one wall. Everyone remained silent for a moment, then as if by some shared thought, both Grimm and Asmodeus dropped down beside her, and the two cats, Cleo and the black stranger with the white patch at his neck, hopped up as well.

Edgar laughed. "I believe that they are trying to tell you," he said, "that we are not trapped. She might well have done so, were it just myself, or even just one of the others, but I assure you, between us we will soon sort the proper doorway and walk free of this place. Even if I did not feel that myself, Grimm has whispered it in my ear just a moment ago.

"Grimm would be correct," Amethyst said. "It was in the story, all of it, but it's only now that it is clear enough to explain, I think. There was only one thing necessary to free you from this place, despite what the brothers wrote in their fable."

"Fable?" the girl said. "What are you talking about?"

"Adela?" Eleanor said, stepping forward. "That is your name, yes?"

The girl glanced up at her and nodded. "Yes, but..."

"It is a very long story," Eleanor said. It involves two brothers from a very long time ago, a raven, the sorceress, and so many other things that I'm uncertain I have it all clear in my own mind, let alone the ability to shorten it enough to repeat it here. Suffice it to say, Estrella is gone. I suspect that when we piece all of this together, you will know a good deal more than we do about the beginnings, and we will be able to explain the middle. The ending is yet to be written, as you are now free."

"Free to do what? Everything and everyone that I have ever known are gone. I have no home, no family that I am aware of."

"I have some thoughts on that," Donovan said, "but for the moment, you must come with us. We will get you down off this mountain, get some rest, and in a day or so we will take our leave of this place and leave this mountain behind. I believe I know someone who would be happy to know you—someone you have met at least once—but first..."

Cleo walked over to the spot in the wall where Donovan

and Amethyst had entered, and he followed. Edgar stepped up beside them. Donovan was just closing his eyes when the poet spoke.

"Amazing. Just a moment ago, I did not see it, but..."

The poet reached out and pressed his hand against the wall. The others watched in various states of amazement as a door appeared, and, under his gentle pressure, swung open. He held it and winked at Donovan.

"After you, my friend."

Donovan stared, and shook his head, then stepped through and began descending a broad stairway, different from the one he'd stormed up moments before.

"You are going to have to show me how you do that," he muttered.

Edgar laughed, and held the door as the others followed Donovan out and down. Moments later, they stepped into the open air at the very foot of the castle, and as the black cat leaped free, following Amethyst, the door behind them simply disappeared. As they stood, staring down the mountain, the cat wrapped itself around Amethyst's legs and began to purr. She reached down and picked it up, and as she did, a strange, far-away look came into her eyes. She gasped, but rather than dropping the animal, pulled it closer to her heart.

"Ah," Donovan said. "It appears your family has grown by one. He has chosen you."

"Chosen?" Eleanor said.

Donovan turned to her. "Edgar can explain this, as well, I believe. Some of us who travel roads a bit different from the rest of humanity find companions along the way. There is a bond—a sort of mental exchange—that happens. Cleo is what the witches of old would call my familiar. Asmodeus, as well. They are very, very old creatures. We do not choose them to share our paths, but instead, we were chosen. It's a great honor."

Edgar walked over to stroke the cat's head and stared long and hard at the mark on its neck. It resembled gallows, with a dangling noose.

"I know you," he said. "You have shared at least one of my tales."

"Does he have a name then?" Adela asked shyly.

Amethyst turned to her and smiled. "He does now. How can I not call him Pluto?"

The girl's frown made them all laugh. Edgar bowed, and Copper seemed particularly tickled.

"We need to get moving," Alicia said. "The rest of you can wander down at your own pace, but Copper and I are on a schedule. It would be best if we reached Rathburg well ahead of the sun."

"Of course," Donovan said. "We will see the two of you below then."

"It's a good walk to the bottom of the mountain," Eleanor said, laying her hand on Adela's arm. "Are you strong enough?"

The girl smiled.

"I've been in that cage, or one like it, for so long I can barely remember walking freely. I would run with the dark ones, but I would simply get lost. I will be fine."

"Onward then," Edgar said. "If we are truly blessed, Bullfinch and the good Father will have a pot of tea and a bottle of something much stronger waiting for us."

As they started off, Donovan pulled out his cell phone, tapped the screen, and smiled as he saw two bars appear. Apparently, they were not so far away from civilization.

"I'll just call ahead and place your order," he said. I believe, for one night, that we've left more than enough to chance."

They walked in silence, lost in private thoughts, but staying close together. The two ravens took to the sky, wheeling and dancing in the waning moonlight, and the cats chased one another through the trees, threatening more than once to trip one or another of their companions as they darted across the trail.

Above, and behind them, the ruined castle loomed, but most of its dread, and glamour, had dropped away. Now it resembled only what it was: an ancient, crumbling pile of stone.

Chapter Thirty

"So," Father Adolph said, his face bright with interest, "you traveled, in the guise of a crow all the days from when you met Edgar, until you came to the dismal swamp together."

Adela nodded. "Now that my memories are sorting themselves, I remember the brothers as well, Jacob and Carl. They came to Rathburg to gather their tales. They were working on a grand project to collect the stories of monsters, magic, and strange creatures. They came long after Estrella joined me to the bird—to Grimm? You call him Grimm? I have known him by several names. I think I visited one of those brothers in their sleep. I know they came to the mountain while I stayed there. They climbed through the castle, it was much more solid then but already abandoned."

"But why?" Bullfinch said. "That is a part of this story that I have yet to understand. What happened to the father? The mother? Was Rosa truly your sister?"

"My much younger sister," Adela said. "When I disappeared, my father was angry. He was angry most of the time, but particularly when Estrella was long gone, and he had only my mother's strange tale to explain why I was not there. He wanted a son, but instead, he got Rosa.

"Not long after she was born, he left again. There was war in the north, and he always preferred that to being home—to inactivity. He was getting older and must have felt it. He did not return. Not then; not when he should have. Rosa grew up, and mother died. Without father's iron control, the guards, and the local nobles, such as they were, squabbled, and fought. Rosa remained in the castle. She managed to get the captain of the guard to fall in love with her, and used him to maintain a level of control, but there was nothing left but a shell of what had once been.

"Then my father returned. He came in the night, riding into the courtyard, leaving his horse at the bottom of the stairs and casting any who stood before him aside like children. He did not appear a day older than he had when he left. His eyes were dark, and his anger—while not *gone* exactly—had changed into a deep, gnawing hunger."

"He was a vampire," Copper said.

Adela nodded.

"He killed them all. The guards, the servants, but he could not bring himself to kill Rosa. He turned her, and he left her in the ruins of our home, alone but for the corpses of the fallen, his final gift a fear planted so deeply in the hearts of the villagers below that none would come after her. None would come near that dark, crumbling palace.

"That is when I fled. I knew of the passages, the place you call the Labyrinth. I entered and sped away, not caring where or when I ended up, as long as Estrella was far away, and as long as I did not have to see what had become of my family."

"And somehow," Edgar said softly, "Either you, or Grimm, found me."

She nodded again. "When we left the palace, our form was that of a raven, as you see him now. When we found you, he changed, and we became a crow. Darker, somehow more powerful for your presence. I felt safe."

"Until I drew you," Eleanor said. "Until I freed you from that spell, and drew that evil, evil woman to you, and she took you away again."

"She was not that cruel, not when we were alone," Adela said. "She never would have let me go, but for you, lady. You set me free, and you knew what might happen. That tree, that awful trap, so many years…"

Eleanor rose and moved to sit beside the girl She wrapped her arms around Adela's shoulders and pulled her close.

"I would do it again," she said. "It's my nature. It's what I do. I cannot bear to see another trapped, or helpless. It was a willing sacrifice, and, in the end, we are all free."

"More so than before, in some ways," Edgar said. "I came to the Dismal Swamp in search of something that could cure my wife, my cousin, Virginia. It was a very complicated love, but she refused any and all help I could have offered, turned from anything not born of her own world or the religion of her father's. I could have saved her, but instead, I simply disappeared."

"But, you didn't," Copper said. "They found your body in the park."

Edgar smiled.

"In all the stories I have experienced, and shared, I have found one single element that was always the same. I have met some aspect of myself, another man, another me. Not all of them fared well in those stories. Not all of them lived. Since I have chosen to walk the many trails of my imagination, I thought it might be best if I brought one of them here. I left that body that long-ago night, used it to purchase my own freedom."

"From the Masquerade," Donovan said. "Or, should I say, "The Masque of the Red Death.""

"So," Copper said thoughtfully. "Those words I keep repeating, words that have felt so compelling, and so real, are truer than ever I imagined. I—who have run the night as a wolf and known the touch of beauty, and of madness—have learned that there is so much more, so many layers and levels to this reality, and others. Truly, everything we see, or seem…"

"Is but a dream within a dream," Edgar finished. He raised his glass and drained it.

Having sat quietly through the telling of the tales, Gunter Krieg spoke up. "I wonder," he said, "how one can explain the juxtaposition of matter involved in two beings, one human, and one avian, inhabiting only the space required for the one—without proportionate gains in mass or weight? This is all so fascinating. I do believe, though, that Mr. Poe has solidified my beliefs on the multiverse, while throwing other wrenches into the gears, as it were. Simply fascinating."

"While you, my friend," Donovan said with a chuckle, "have perfectly illustrated my long-believed and often belittled theory that science, mathematics, computers, and physics are all facets of the same, brilliant gem. I will not soon forget how you turned Estrella's spell back on her, merely by paying attention."

Gunter blinked, as if he had not really considered how remarkable that was until the moment Donovan mentioned it.

"It may be years before we all know the length and breadth of this particular tale," Bullfinch said. He rose and refilled their glasses. "I recommend we share a toast, and then get some rest. We will fly out tomorrow. I have reports to make, and I believe some of you have unfinished business in North Carolina."

"Indeed," Donovan said. "We owe Cletus and Nettie a story, and, if you will accompany us, Princess, I believe they may have something for you, as well."

"Please," she said. "Calle me Adela. I am no longer the princess of anything, nor do I wish to be."

"Adela, then," Donovan said.

"If no one objects," Alicia said, standing, "I will propose that toast then."

They raised their glasses, and she smiled.

"To a cloak that renders you invisible, may it always protect you. To a horse that can take you wherever you need to go. To a key that can open any lock. To stories, and poetry, and music and light, and to science." She winked at Gunter when she said this, and he smiled in return.

"And to the children of the night," Edgar added.

They all turned to him, Copper and Donovan both laughing, and everyone drank.

"What?" Edgar said, his smile enigmatic. "Did you believe I'd sat in that library all these years without reading?"

"I assure you," Alicia said laughing. "I *do* drink—wine."

There was more laughter, and then, slowly, they all slipped out of the basement chamber and up to their rooms in the Inn, leaving the two vampires alone. Once they were gone, Copper grabbed a book and sat on one of the long couches.

"What do you have tonight?" Alicia asked.

He turned it so she could see the cover. It was a copy of the Complete Works of Edgar Allan Poe. "Edgar gave it to me," he said. "It's not a first edition, but it's signed."

She laughed. Very apropos.

As he opened the old book and began, silently, to read, she slipped into the next room and picked a lute from the wall. She carried it back, sat at the far end of the couch, and began to play. Copper glanced up at once, recognizing the song. That song that had drawn men to their death, that had drawn a young musician to his doom, that had belonged to Rosa, so long ago. As she played, and began, very softly, to sing, he returned to the book. Before he could continue, he noticed a flap of paper sticking out in the back. Curious, he flipped the back cover open, and a small sheaf of folded papers fell into his lap.

"What's this?" he said.

Alicia stopped playing, set the lute aside, and slid close. Copper unfolded the pages and stared. It was a hand-written manuscript, the letters carefully and artfully formed. At the top of the first page were the words, "The Cat," but Cat was lined out and beside it, the correction it read, "The Black Cat."

On the final page, when he flipped through, were the words "The End," and a bold signature.

Copper stared for a moment then turned to meet Alicia's gaze. Without speaking a word, he leaned closer so she could see over his shoulder, and they began to read.

The next morning, they all said their goodbyes, gathered once more in the underground room. The sun wasn't quite up, but it was safer for Alicia and Copper.

"Are you certain you don't want to fly back, old boy?" Bullfinch asked Donovan. "We make pretty good time, and the bar is well stocked."

"Any other time, I'd be with you," Donovan said. "Eleanor had a pretty intense experience with some faces in the clouds, and I don't want to put her through that again so soon. Also, it might be a bit much for Adela. With Grimm, Asmodeus, Cleo—and now Pluto along—we'll find our way back through the Labyrinth pretty quickly. We may be in Old Mill before you reach the airfield. It's always difficult to anticipate."

Copper took Edgar's hand, and shook it.

"You have given me a special gift, my friend," he said.

"Something I never expected to see—a new story from Edgar Alan Poe."

"It is an older story," Poe replied, "and well-gifted, I think. I don't know if you travel the roads below, but if you do, you are welcome in my home. Perhaps Donovan might escort you one day. I assure you, there are many stories you have not read. Or, at least versions of stories that would be new. I would be proud to share them."

"We are off on a journey of our own," Alicia said, "But when that is done, we have nothing but time. I am sure you will see us again, Edgar. I look forward to it."

Eleanor took Alicia's hands. "As do I. Perhaps, when you visit, you will allow me to draw you? I am uncertain that I can do it justice, but I will try."

"I would love that," Alicia assured her. We have issues with mirrors. Perhaps you can be my mirror one day."

They exchanged a few more words and promises, and then Alicia and Copper climbed into the sun-blocked limousine for the drive to the airport. Bullfinch stopped by the door and called out to Donovan.

"You will owe me a story, Magic Man," he said.

Gunter slid in beside Copper in the back of the limo. The dazed look had left his eyes. He had a writing pad in his lap and a pen.

"I have been looking forward to continuing our discussions," he said, as if nothing had happened. I have revised my theory slightly, after listening to Mr. Poe's stories, and meeting that evil woman. I admit, I am quite excited."

Everyone stared at him. Then, in unison, they burst into laughter.

"This," Bullfinch said sliding into the driver's seat, "Is going to be a very interesting flight."

Moments later, they pulled away, and the others, led by Donovan and Edgar, started off back up the mountain. They needed to reach an entrance to the Labyrinth, and the cats seemed intent on leading them upward to find it. It was a beautiful morning, with the sun rising over the mountain in brilliant colors.

Father Adolph, who had taken his leave the night before, arrived just in time to see them disappearing into the trees. He stood for a long time, watching the spot where they had been, then glanced up over the trees toward the castle.

Shaking his head, he turned and started slowly off down the trail to the chapel. He thought it was just about time for a cup of tea, and a good book.

Chapter Thirty-One

When Donovan stepped out into the North Carolina morning sunlight, he was surprised to find he was not alone. Nettie was there, and Cletus as well, leaning on the tailgate of his old Bronco. The stag, and the younger girl, were nowhere to be seen, but he sensed they were nearby, as well.

The others climbed the ruined stairs behind him, one after another, and as Eleanor stepped free, Nettie stepped forward and embraced her tightly. It was not like a meeting of two strangers, more a reunion of family.

"I will never forget what you did for me and mine, girl," Nettie said, pulling back. "Anything you need of me, or my swamp..."

Eleanor blushed, but was smiling.

"It is over," she said. "Or, more truthfully, it is just beginning. The journey I set out on so long ago, I mean. And I will not be alone."

"Never," Edgar said, "though you may regret travelling with me as we pass through some of those doors. I have yet to walk into a sweet romance."

Next, Nettie stepped up to Adela and took her hands gently.

"I have not seen you for a very long time, young one," she said. "We tried to protect you."

"I know," Adela said. "I was never truly free to be protected. "I have never truly been free in my entire life. I was born a princess, but I grew to adulthood in the mind of a very wise old bird. I have never had a life to be taken, nor do I fully understand what I should do with it now that it's mine."

"We were hoping," Nettie said, "That you might stay here a

while, with me, and the girl. There are things I can teach you, and, if he behaves himself, Cletus over there can help to explain the craziness out beyond the trees and the roads. If you work in gradually, you will find that life very intriguing."

"You have friends," Donovan said. "You can call on us, and visit, whenever you please. It's a very odd family that we share, but one should never deny the power of such bonds."

"It goes without saying," Eleanor added, "that you are welcome to visit, and travel with us, when you feel the urge. I admit that I share some of your trepidation. This is not the world I left behind, and I suspect that none of those realms Edgar will show me will be. The last time we both stood here," she glanced around the half-cleared, half-overgrown ruin of the hotel, "there were people, and boats—lives and loves—that have now gone to dust.

"Still, I feel very much alive, and ready for new adventures. I also believe, having spent some time in the company of Grimm myself, that you could scarcely have learned from a wiser, fiercer, more powerful teacher than the ones Estrella randomly chose for you. She might have picked any raven, but he found you. It would not surprise me to find that, rather than ourselves, it is these creatures—these familiars who watch over us so diligently—who orchestrated this entire multi-century rescue."

"It's an interesting thought," Amethyst said. "I would have laughed only a few days back, even after seeing Donovan with Cleo and Moe." She glanced up and waved at Asmodeus, who glared back. "Now that I've met Pluto, I am a lot less certain who is in charge."

"Moe?" Donovan said with a chuckle.

"Sorry, but I just can't bring myself to say 'Asmodeus' every time I mention him. Cleo is Kleopatra, yes? The Medieval alchemist?"

"She knew such a person, I believe," Donovan said. "Whether she *is* that person is an entirely different matter, but point taken. 'Moe' it is."

The raven squawked and launched from his branch to land on Donovan's shoulder with a light thud.

"If you folks don't mind," Cletus said, pushing off of his

truck and stepping forward, "I think we should all take a walk back to the lake, and get one last look at that tree. Then I have to be off. Seems I have a date with a gal named Willow, something I've put off for far too long."

Amethyst glanced over at him, ready to speak, but he held up his hand.

"I know. I *know*," he said. "I will tell her. Not Jasper. I'll be double-D goddamned if I'd have let her name him that anyway. I'd never hear the end of it from Jaz, and he talks too much as it is."

The group turned and headed in through the trees. They were entering the park at a point where it was not allowed, but with Nettie along, no one was worried about that. Before the fences and gates and walkways had been placed on the outskirts of the swamp, she'd been there, and when they all crumbled to rust and dust, she would remain. The world might have moved on, but Nettie endured.

It was a short walk to the clearing opening onto the banks of Lake Drummond, and for the most part, they walked it in silence. Each had their own memories of this place, and their own nightmares. Edgar held Eleanor's hand, and, as they drew near to the twisted old tree, still in the shape of a woman, her hand outstretched to the lapping waves, Eleanor had to lean close and whisper to him that he was gripping too tightly and hurting her fingers.

They stood in a semi-circle around the tree and simply watched it.

"I sense her," Adela said.

"We all do, dear," Nettie said. "She has touched every one of us in some way. But it's very distant. I find no weakness in her trap—she built it well. She does not have even the ability that you had," the old woman turned to Lenore, "to reach out."

"My gift is release," Eleanor said. "Perhaps I was harder to hold than others might have been. If so, I am grateful for it. Without the times you were here, talking to me, or your companions—or Edgar reading to me by moonlight—I would certainly be mad by now. I was a prisoner, but I never felt alone.

"Sorta makes your brain bounce from a chainsaw to a

bonfire, though, don't it?" Cletus muttered. "I used to come here to fish. Now, well, there's plenty of other places in the swamp, and I believe I'll stick to those."

They turned away then, all except Eleanor and Edgar, who stood, hand in hand, not looking at the tree any longer, but out over the expanse of the lake.

Edgar began to speak, slowly, and haltingly:

Ah, mended is that golden bowl! Her spirit free, forever!

Let the bell toll!—a saintly soul, this day has been delivered.

And, Edgar Poe shall shed no tear, shall mourn her nevermore!

He stands with her, and holds the heart of the lovely Eleanor.

"It needs work, I fear," he said. The original was far too dreary, and I am afraid Guy deVere, born of my despair, must now be forgotten. I need no other seeking to compete for your heart."

"It is yours, sweet man," Eleanor said with a laugh. "It was yours the moment we met, so long ago, when our love was doomed. And the poem, as you first wrote it, speaks to me of ascending to a better world, which I certainly have done. Let us not linger over the works or stories already told. I think it's time we two moved on. We have a lot to say, and do, and to catch up on. And then, one day," she turned back and watched Donovan, who was slowly wandering back toward the ruins and the road, "we must return to one of their flying machines and see what can be done for the faces in those clouds."

Edgar laughed.

"Ride! Boldly Ride, the shade replied, if you seek for El Dorado!"

When they were all gathered back by Cletus' truck, they made yet another round of farewells. Donovan, who had been off to one side with his ear pressed to his phone, slipped it back into his jacket pocket and smiled.

"It seems that Geoffrey wasted no time," he said. "Bullfinch has dispatched a team to gather the texts, documents, instruments, and artifacts from Rosa's hideaway beneath the castle. We are invited, of course, to study and share in them at any time. I may have to give them a once-over to be certain there is nothing dangerous among them. Much as I trust Bullfinch, I distrust teams and bureaucracy."

"I believe I will hang onto the book with the Grimm Brother's notes," Edgar said. "I should like to study them, and I wonder—since they were such a help in sorting this affair—if there might not be others among their tales with secrets to divulge."

"I have no doubt that they will," Donovan said, "nor do I doubt you will find them. Once the two of you have spent some time together, and are feeling adventurous, you know where to find me. Who knows where our dual paths may lead over time? We will walk with you as far as your library, but Amethyst and I will continue on to home, where I would very much like to stay for some time to come."

"Yes," Amethyst said with a grin. "It seems I'm going to have to shop for a litter box."

Pluto looked up at her and let out a slow growl.

"Kidding," she said, laughing. "Just kidding."

Grimm and Asmodeus dropped from the trees to plant on Edgar and Donovan's shoulders, and Cleo rubbed up against Eleanor's leg.

"You come back and see me, Magic Man," Nettie called after them. "Still plenty to learn and see in my swamp. Don't forget the whiskey."

Donovan laughed. "You can count on it. I think you'll have your hands full for a while, though."

Adela stood beside the old woman, looking nervous, but happy.

Cletus watched her for a moment, and then shook his head. "A double-D goddamn princess, talking birds, Edgar Allan-freakin' Poe. I need a beer. I'll be seein' all of you. Nettie, you need anything for your new charge, you let me know."

Nettie nodded. Cletus turned to climb into his truck, and when he glanced into the rearview mirror, all of them were gone. He sat there for a few moments, enjoying the silence, then he reached for his phone and dialed Willow's number.

"What is it, Cletus?" she said. "You backing out on our first date?"

"Not a chance," he said. "I was just wondering. How do you feel about the name Earl?"

.

About the Author

David Niall Wilson has been writing and publishing horror, dark fantasy, and science fiction since the mid-eighties. An ordained minister, once President of the Horror Writers Association and multiple recipient of the Bram Stoker Award, his novels include Maelstrom, *The Mote in Andrea's Eye, Deep Blue, the Grails Covenant Trilogy, Star Trek Voyager: Chrysalis, Except You Go Through Shadow, This is My Blood, Ancient Eyes, On the Third Day, The Orffyreus Wheel*, The DeChance Chronicles, including *Heart of a Dragon, Vintage Soul, My Soul to Keep, Kali's Tale* and the stand-alone spinoff *Nevermore – A Novel of Love, Loss & Edgar Allan Poe*. His novels in the O.C.L.T. series include *The Parting, Crockatiel*, and the novella *The Temple of Camazotz* .He is also the author of the memoir / cookbook *American Pies: Baking with Dave the Pie Guy*. David can be found at: www.davidniallwilson.com and can be reached by e-mail at david@davidniallwilson.com .

Curious about other Crossroad Press books?
Stop by our site:
http://store.crossroadpress.com
We offer quality writing
in digital, audio, and print formats.

Enter the code FIRSTBOOK
to get 20% off your first order from our store!
Stop by today!